Jem

and

Coral

C.A. HEAVEN

ISBN: 1466272163
ISBN-13: 9781466272163

This book is dedicated to the following special people…

Elspeth, your artistic flair and zest for life have been an inspiration to me. But please check that your parachute is attached the next time you go sky-diving. It's hard being the mother of a dare-devil.

Gabriel, your ruthless candour and ethereal sixth-sense have given me constant food for thought. And thank you for the music - it speaks in ways that cannot be quantified.

Paul - my long suffering husband - I would have starved a long time ago if it weren't for your economic and emotional support.

To Claudia & Karolyn & all the children at the Merlin Theatre whose love and passion for the performing arts continues to fuel my soul and tend my heart to this day.

To all the 'individual students' I have taught over the years. I am sure that I have learnt far more from you!

Lastly, this book is dedicated to all those people with a passion for the natural world and who are committed to preserving our planet's fragile eco-systems for generations to come.

Chantal
August 31st 2011

"We do not inherit the earth from our ancestors,
we borrow it from our children."

Antoine de Saint Exupery.
1900 - 1944.
(Aviator, poet & writer)

A loving heart can heal the wounds of this world.

Author's Note

C. A. Heaven was born in Rochford, England, to a French mother and English father. Her childhood years were spent by the coast in England and France, hunting for cockles and evading jelly-fish. Oil slicks and seaside rubbish-dumps featured highly in her earliest memories, together with happier times spent on the London river barges. After a short spell spent as a campaigner for Keep Britain Tidy, Chantal began her career as an Abstractor at Reuters News Agency, writing international news 'abstracts' for Reuters Text-Line, an on-line news service. She started writing short stories and plays in her spare time and decided to quit journalism and train to be a Drama and History teacher at Bath University. She currently works as a theatre practitioner at the Merlin Theatre, Frome, and has written and directed eighteen shows to date for the Children's Drama Group in addition to working as a private Drama and History tutor.

Contents

CHAPTER ONE

Old Man's Elbow

The sea rose and fell in little eddies at the base of Old Man's Elbow. The black column of rock shimmered in the dazzling sunlight, its serrated edges sharp enough to draw blood.

Jem jogged down to the water's edge and knelt down on the shingle, a small wind-up radio cradled protectively in his arms. He caressed the radio tenderly as if it were a living thing. Perhaps in Jem's old-fashioned mind it was?

He cranked the handle, pressed his ear against the speaker and eagerly waited for the mechanism to spring into life. The radio crackled and fizzed. Then silence.

Jem stared at the radio, dumbfounded. Why wouldst it not work? He frantically turned the tuning-dial desperate to hear the sound of voices - friendly voices - but the radio gave one last splutter and died leaving him all alone in the tiny Atlantic cove with nothing but the roaring waves as company.

Tears formed in Jem's eyes. He blinked them away savagely. Crying was a self-indulgence he couldst not afford.

Jem abandoned the radio on the foreshore and marched back up the beach towards the Liberty, his fourteen-foot fishing-boat. The burnished wood of the upturned boat sparkled in the midday sun. The wood flashed the colour of topaz - the same colour as Jem's luminescent eyes - lonely eyes that could look back two hundred years to a time long forgotten.

The minutes ticked past. Jem rooted about under the boat for his father's old fishing-net and dragged it out into the open. Bulbous tentacles of seaweed coiled themselves about the rope like a living parasite.

Frowning, he sat down on the shingle and started to untangle the net. His dextrous fingers unravelled the knots with consummate grace. He hummed as he worked - a Sarabande by Bach - and little by little, he began to relax. His mind travelled back in time to the year 1800 when Hartland Quay was still a thriving fishing port and scores of young boys like him used to sit on the shore weaving nets and making canvas sails. He hadst plenty of mates back then!

At the age of nine he was apprenticed as a sail-maker. The hours were long but he knew that if he worked hard after seven years he would be able to call himself a Master Sail-Maker. Every evening Mother dressed and bound his blistered hands only for the wounds to open up again the next day. But nothing could beat the pride and joy he felt when the ships of His Majesty's Royal Navy returned to drop anchor at Portsmouth Harbour.

Jem's cheeks flushed a deep pomegranate red. He remembered the lines of sailors, eyes bright, lips taut, standing to attention before the roaring crowds as the City of Portsmouth welcomed home the victorious British fleet. Napoleon ne'er stood a chance against those hand-made Hartland sails!

The sound of laughter interrupted Jem's thoughts. He looked up sharply. The light pop of a coke can being crushed beneath heavy-duty Doc Martens - candyfloss pink Doc Martens with a fancy daisy motif. Their owner was a green-eyed brunette with a razor-sharp fringe and a razor-sharp heart to match. Antonia Lockheart, who else?

Jem watched in gathering alarm as Antonia stalked along the shingle ridge towards him. Her thick brown ponytail swayed from side to side giving her the air of a very superior race-horse. Antonia was a thorough-bred in every sense of the word.

In addition to the daisy tread of her designer boots, Antonia's calling-card consisted of two empty crisp packets, a packet of gum and a half-eaten take-away food carton, the latter coated with a liberal sprinkling of ash, saliva, and on this occasion, vomit. Jem screwed up his face in disgust. He was always clearing up after Antonia and her gang: Tom, James and kid sister Kim.

"Race you to the shore!" James shouted as he emerged from the wood that bordered the pretty horse-shoe cove.

"You're on!" Tom replied, letting go of Kim's waist and surging forwards with tremendous speed.

The two youths struck out across the beach. They made an incongruous sight: Tom with his skinny albino frame and James with his tanned muscular body, his biceps bulging from his flying arms like two hard brown toffee apples.

Both lads reached the shoreline at the same time.

"A dead heat!" Antonia cheered, clapping wildly.

"Rubbish. Tom won," Kim said grumpily.

Antonia curled her top lip into a lynx-like sneer. Then without warning she struck out with her red lacquered nails.

Blood oozed from Kim's exposed belly-button and trickled down her dainty tummy to collect in the elasticated rim of her silver bikini bottom.

"Ouch! What did you do that for?" Kim exclaimed tearfully, dabbing the delicate skin around her belly-button with her stubby finger-nails.

"It was a dead heat," Antonia repeated, eyes like granite.

"That's no reason to hurt me!" Kim blubbered, fumbling in her handbag for a tissue to stem the flow of blood.

Antonia's lips elongated into a serpentine smile…

"Don't be such a wimp Kim. I only gave you a little tap across the tummy. Besides, I told you not to get your belly-button pierced. You should have got a diamond nose-stud like me."

"My Mum wouldn't let me."

"Neither would mine," Antonia snorted disdainfully. "But that didn't stop me."

"At least I can wear my belly-bar whenever I want to. I don't have to take it out the moment my Dad walks through the door like you do!"

Antonia pretended not to have heard Kim's last remark. Instead she turned and gazed out to sea, her high cheekbones puncturing the sky with grim disapproval.

A black cormorant dived below the bobbing waves. Antonia watched the expanse of water intently, waiting for the bird to re-surface. After exactly eighty-five seconds, the cormorant re-emerged, a fish held fast in its rapier-beak. Antonia smiled in approval. Then she spun round and stamped down hard on Kim's flimsy flip-flops with her heavy-duty Doc Martens.

"Ouch!" Kim cried out in pain. She stared at Antonia aghast.

A smile slithered across Antonia's moist lips. Then she slowly lifted up her boot to reveal a delicate daisy-petal motif engraved on Kim's three middle toes.

"Oh look - a daisy. How pretty," Antonia intoned breathlessly. "I knew we both shared the same taste. We really shouldn't fight Kim. After all, we're on the same side." Antonia reached forwards and delicately plucked a speck of mascara from Kim's lower eyelid with the tip of her index finger. "Let's be friends. You know it makes good sense."

Kim swallowed. She glanced up the beach towards Tom and James. They were leaping up and down in the white breakers totally unaware of what was going on. There was no point in her saying anything to Tom about Antonia's aggressive behaviour because he simply wouldn't believe her.

"Friends," Kim whispered hoarsely, her voice like shredded bark.

Antonia nodded. Then her dark-brown eyes settled sympathetically on Kim's puppy-dog face. She felt sorry for the kid. Kim didn't amount to much with her shapeless chewing-gum nose and mouse-coloured hair. Not to mention the rash of brown freckles that splattered her cheeks like some obscure skin disease. However Kim was James's younger sister so it paid to be nice to her occasionally.

"Come on Kim. Let's go and check up on the guys. It's not wise to leave them alone for too long."

Then Antonia laughed a deep garrulous laugh that reminded Jem of a brook that had just burst its banks.

Jem watched engrossed as the teenage girls struck out across the ridge of shingle. Kim followed at Antonia's heels like a loyal gundog. Jem frowned. Would Kim ever break free from Antonia's control? As much as he loathed Antonia's cruelty, he had to admit that Antonia had a spirit and passion for life that he secretly admired. Kim, by contrast, was like an empty vessel with the misfortune of being able to soak up whatever was poured into her, both good and bad.

The girls neared the shoreline. Jem's heart missed a beat as he realised that he had left his precious radio by the water's edge. He watched as the teenagers drew nearer and nearer to it. He swallowed hard. It was not safe to try and rescue it. He could not endure another witch-hunt!

Jem's hands began to tremble. Saliva flooded the back of his throat. He winced as he remembered the chase up the beach last summer. A mob of angry villagers had hurled pebbles at his beach-hut whilst a pair of snarling black Dobermans had lunged at his ankles repeatedly. It was a miracle he wasn't now an invalid.

The villagers had finally given up and called the dogs off. No-one ever did find out why the Dobermans had behaved in such a frenzied manner but thankfully dogs can't speak and Jem wasn't about to reveal his two hundred year old secret. He had had a lucky escape but he could not be guaranteed another one. He wisely retreated to the Liberty, resigned to a life on the side-lines.

"Fancy a swim?" Antonia called across to James.

"What did you say?" James shouted back, the sound of the surf muffling Antonia's words.

The ocean sprayed James's cheeks. He scooped up a heavy boulder and gripped it tightly, probing the dimpled limestone surface with his finger-tips, interested in the little hollows and indentations in the stone.

"I said do you fancy a swim?" Antonia repeated, walking towards him, her hips swaying from side to side provocatively.

James shook his head.

"I don't have my board-shorts with me."

"Neither do I…" Antonia purred, her pretty fingers coquettishly plucking at her fringe as if she were playing her grandmother's harp at Sudbury Court.

"I'll pretend I didn't hear that," James replied, turning away.

"The water's gorgeously warm James. It's a shame to waste it," Antonia persisted, tilting her head like a turtle-dove.

James's jaw hardened. Kim was only thirteen. His kid-sister might be a pain in the arse but it was his job to look after her and there was no way they were all going skinny-dipping in Hartland Cove this evening or any other evening. There were limits.

"We're not going swimming Toni and that's final," James said firmly, his brown eyes ablaze.

"OK James, I was only kidding," Antonia replied, quickly backtracking. Then she stooped forwards and sprinkled a handful of white shale into the sea as if she were dusting a cake with icing sugar. "Honestly James, you've got to learn how to take a joke sometimes."

"Whatever," James growled, flexing his muscles and cannoning the heavy boulder into oblivion.

Jem let out a sigh of relief. There was a time and a place for skinny-dipping and now was not the time. He enjoyed the bracing feel of salt water against his bare body but that was late at night when the sky was an ink-black, the stars sparse and the coastline deserted.

"Modesty becometh the Man," Mother used to say to him as she thrust a cotton towel into his palms and sent him outside to the wash-house.

Jem smiled ruefully. The world had changed much since his youth but there was always a place for modesty and manners. They were never out-of-date.

"Hey, what's that over there on the sand?" Tom said suddenly, his hawk-eyes locked onto a square wooden object on the foreshore.

In seconds Tom had sprinted across and was holding Jem's wind-up radio in his ghost-white hands. He cranked the handle impatiently, curiosity writ large in his intelligent face. The radio emitted a low whirring sound as the coil inside tightened. Seconds later an indecipherable fizz reached his eardrums.

"It's just a clapped-out old radio," Tom said dismissively, hurling it head-long into the bobbing waves.

"No!" Jem shouted soundlessly.

Salt-tears coursed down Jem's cheeks. It had taken him months to get the radio working and now that insolent boy had tossed it into the sea without a moment's thought.

Jem had discovered the radio perched high on a ledge in Lion's Lair. The secret underwater cavern was one of his favourite haunts. Filled with ink-blue mussel beds and fire-red anemones, the cavern was a jewellery box of living organisms. The radio had been quite dry, protected from the sea-spray by a wedge of shiny black schist rock that protruded from the roof of the cavern.

Initially he had struggled to understand how the radio worked. But after a couple of trips to the public library in Bude he had managed to get it working with the aid of a mechanical engineering manual and hours of trial and error.

The joy the radio had given him went far beyond mere words. It was like having Mother, Father and eight year old Flossie back home with him again. He had ceased to be alone in the world. In fact he had grown quite fond of the local DJs with their West Country humour and quirky accents.

And now that ragamuffin of a boy had lobbed the reeds of his heart back into the sea without so much as a second's thought!

The crunch of black converses on shingle as Tom walked briskly along the beach towards the upturned boat, his pale eyes embracing another object of interest: a hand-woven fishing-net.

Jem lay flat on his stomach, determined to avoid a confrontation. The last time he had intervened to protect his possessions from an inquisitive member of the public, someone had called the 'authorities' and the beach had been crawling with sniffer dogs and uniformed police officers for a week. He had escaped a second man-hunt but it had been a close-shave.

Tom knelt down on the golden sand and draped the lightweight rope over the bridge of his palm as if he were weighing gold.

"Interesting," Tom murmured, running the edge of his sepulchre white thumb over one of Jem's carefully tied knots.

Then Tom cocked his head on one side and considered the rope long and hard.

Tom had lean features, a pointed fox-like jaw, white eyelashes and short sandy-white hair. Indeed Tom seemed very fox-like to Jem right now as he inspected the beautifully crafted net. His pearlescent eyes narrowed into slits as he pondered the source of the net. Most of the fishermen kept their trawlers berthed at Bideford. No-one fished out of Hartland Cove any more. Hartland Quay still had a handful of working boats but fish stocks were low and it was only a matter of time before the Old Guard hung up their hooks for good. Hartland village was now a tourist haven for the Beige Brigade who arrived by the coach-load, did a snail's tour of Hartland Abbey and then tottered down to Hartland Cove to snap a few photographs before retiring for a cream tea in the Abbey Tea Rooms.

The salt-spray doused Tom's face. He chewed the inside of his gums in contemplation. The more he thought about it, the more convinced he became that the well-kept fishing-net had not been abandoned on the beach. The net was clearly on the beach because it was currently being used. The question was: by whom?

A breathless Kim appeared at Tom's side. She was nursing a cut belly-button and sore feet. Tom chose not to ask about the injury to her belly-button and Kim chose not to mention it. Instead both found comfort in a tender kiss.

"What are you up to Tom?" Kim asked, squeezing his forearm, wishing that she hadn't run out of chewing-gum. She needed something to steady her nerves.

"Thinking," Tom replied, his inquisitive mind sifting through all the possible explanations behind the net's abandonment.

"What about?"

"Who this net belongs to…"

Kim's lips exploded into a starburst smile.

"That's easy! It belongs in that old beach-hut," she said brightly, delighted to be of use for a change. She pointed excitedly at Jem's ramshackle wooden shack, her face a picture of innocence.

"You might be right," Tom conceded, mulling over the pieces of information.

But who did the beach-hut belong to? Was it owned by Hartland Abbey or the National Trust? The beach-hut was a bit of an enigma and as a consequence had been of interest to him for as long as he could remember. Some people said an old tramp lived there. Others said it wasn't a tramp at all but Sir Aubrey, the Abbey Ghost.

He had tried to break into the hut on numerous occasions but he had always failed, waking up with a sore head and without any memory of how he had come to be unconscious. He had not told Kim or the others about his failed break-in attempts. His pride wouldn't allow it.

However the fact remained that there was something distinctly odd about the beach-hut, just as there was something peculiar about the fishing-net in his hand. Indeed, if he didn't know any better, he would say he could actually feel the net's owner breathing down his neck at this every moment.

Tom shivered, remembering the time he tried to cut through the padlocked chain on the front door of the hut with a pair of bolt-cutters. Someone had crept up behind him and knocked him out with a clean blow to the back of the head. When he came round, the bolt-cutters had gone. He had been grounded for a week on account of his dad's missing bolt-cutters but the injury to his pride had hurt far more than the punishment.

"Tom! Kim! Stop gassing and come and play softball," James shouted up the beach, juggling with three empty coke cans in an attempt to keep Antonia amused.

Tom did not move.

"What's the matter?" Kim asked, tenderly placing her hand on Tom's shoulder.

"I don't know," he replied truthfully.

Tom squeezed Kim's hand and stared out to sea, his eyes locked in grim concentration. But the undulating waves refused to yield the secret of the mysterious fishing-net.

"Come on, let's go. They're waiting for us," Kim urged, placing her right hand delicately on his shoulder and looking into his troubled eyes. She ran her hand nervously through his sandy hair wishing that she were brave enough to confide in him properly. "Please Tom, let's go. Antonia's getting impatient. I don't want her to get angry with me."

Tom bit into his lower lip, undecided. He wanted to play softball but he also wanted to get even with the person who had stolen the bolt-cutters. He was certain that the owner of the fishing-net and the person who had taken the bolt-cutters were one and the same person. Suddenly an idea came to him. He gasped at the simplicity of the idea.

"Stand back Kim."

"What Tom?"

"I said stand back or you'll get hurt."

Kim did as she was told. The next minute Tom seized the net with both hands and began to spin round and round on the spot. The net sliced through the air with a whipping sound. Tom spun faster and faster like a whirlwind.

"One, two, three!" Tom shouted, letting go of the net on the count of three.

Kim held her breath as the net shot a massive twenty feet into the air then landed in the rippling blue waves. The rope floated briefly on the surface then sank without a trace.

"No!" Jem roared.

Jem sprinted down the beach, temples pounding, his eyes locked onto the exact spot in the ocean where his father's precious fishing-net had disappeared. Then he let out another almighty roar and dived into the sea fully clothed. He struck out furiously towards his beloved fishing-net in a vigorous front-crawl.

No mean-minded ruffian would destroy his father's net! No knuckle-headed youth would succeed in burying the handiwork of all the forgotten sail-makers and net-makers of Hartland Quay.

"What is that?" Antonia said slowly, squinting at the ripples of white froth whipped up by Jem's vigorous front-crawl.

"Maybe it's a pod of dolphins?" Kim said excitedly, springing up and down excitedly. "Mum says that dolphins can often be seen on the south side of Lundy Island in the summer months. The warm currents of the North Atlantic Drift bring them this way."

"If they were dolphins Kim we'd be able to see them leaping out of the water," Antonia sneered contemptuously.

James laughed. Kim looked down, embarrassed. But Tom was in no mood for idle banter. Ashen-faced, he stood rooted to the spot like a condemned man.

"Tom? Tom, are you OK?" Kim asked nervously, catching hold of his thin, reed-like arm.

He did not answer.

"What is that?" Antonia said slowly, her eyes locked onto the rippling water.

The bubbles multiplied. Suddenly the net burst forth and hovered above the waves suspended in mid-air. Then more bubbles rapidly appeared as the net surged towards them, dragging the waves with it.

"The net's alive! It's alive and it's coming to get us!" Kim screamed, turning hard on her heels and crashing headlong into Tom. Her neck collided with his ribcage and the pair of them tumbled backwards onto the wet sand in a Grim-Reaper embrace.

"Run Kim! Head for Hartland Wood. You'll be safe there," Tom instructed, helping the terrified girl to her feet and propelling her up the beach with the flat of his palms.

Kim did not stop to ask questions. The order given, she sprinted up the beach, vaulted over the stone-stile into Hartland Wood and did not stop running until she was surrounded by the dense leafy cloak of oak, ash and birch.

Meanwhile Jem reached the shallows, his body invisible to the naked eye. He planted his feet firmly on the wet sand and slowly lifted the net high above him. Then he walked up the shore towards the shingle ridge, the net held fast above his head like a crown of thorns.

"But that's not poss-i-ble," Antonia said slowly, her eyes widening in astonishment.

"Let's get the hell out of here!" James shouted, backing away fearfully. "Run Toni. Now!"

"Run? I'm not running anywhere," Antonia replied bullishly, pressing the heels of her pink boots deep into the sand, determined to stand her ground.

Then a loud whooshing sound echoed through the air as the net changed direction and spiralled towards them like a whirling rope-tornado. The next moment the net reared up above the heads of Tom and James and plunged down on top of them in one swift movement.

Tom floundered like a fish out of water, gasping for breath, winded and disorientated. He fell to his knees and curled up with his face in his hands, deciding that there was no point in resisting the net's violent embrace.

James, by contrast, fought madly, twisting his head from left to right, trying to free himself from the net's fibrous grip. But the harder James fought, the tighter the rope coiled itself about his arms and torso. Finally the rope pressed down hard on his windpipe and he began to gag. His vision blurred. His face began to turn blue.

Suddenly a wild-cat snarl rent the air as Antonia hurled herself at the marauding net.

Her red lacquered nails tore into the rope. She raised her knees and lashed out with her Doc Martens again and again, aiming for the shins of the unseen assailant. The coarse fibres dug into her palms but she refused to give in, redoubling her efforts to free James and Tom. Then she opened her mouth wide and sank her teeth into the rope like a Jack Russell, pulling hard with her jaw for all she was worth.

However Antonia's heroic efforts were in vain. Try as she might, she was no match for the net. First Tom, then James, succumbed to the net's ferocious attack. The lads slumped to the ground inert. Antonia abruptly let go of the net and drew back. Knees grazed and bleeding, she watched in silence as the net placidly bound the boys together. They emerged back to back, trussed up like a joint of meat.

All was still. A smudge-like gloam enveloped the foreshore. The faint outline of Old Man's Elbow shimmered in the thinning light. Then the plaintive call of a harp seal pup calling to its mother echoed across the bay. Antonia stared numbly at the bound bodies, wondering why the rope had spared her.

Then she turned and stared across the water, her ears heightened to every sound. She could hear the sound of the waves breaking on the base of the giant stack and the splash of a lone seal as it turned for Lundy Island and home. She could hear the shrill cries of the seagulls calling to each other on the wing and the high-pitched call of a peregrine falcon as it floated on the warm thermals above Docton Moor. But the loudest and most distinct sound of all was the sound of her own heart-beat as it pounded against her ribcage, demanding answers to the event that she had just witnessed.

The crunch of bare feet on shingle; Antonia froze as still as a pearl in its shell. Then she turned slowly, her eyes trained on the smooth indentations in the sand where she knew two invisible feet must surely be…

Solemnly Jem stared at Antonia's blood-stained cheeks and tangled coal-dust hair, at her diamond nose-stud and the determined glint in her eye. Then he turned and walked slowly away, tears of shame piercing his ruby cheeks.

Jem did not stop walking until he reached the base of Hartland Cliff. Then he sank to the ground and let out a deep, piercing cry, furious with himself for having allowed his temper to get the better of him.

Tears erupted from Jem's topaz eyes. He hung his head in shame.

Grace, humility and kindness… Kindness was the one virtue that his mother had valued above all the others. He had failed Mother! He had failed Father! But above all, he had failed himself.

Father would ne'er hath raised a hand to a blind man and those boys had been like blind men before him, powerless to protect themselves.

Jem abruptly stopped crying and started to laugh. What did it matter what Father thought? Father had been dead for two centuries. All his kith and kin were dead! What did it matter whether his radio worked or not? The presenters were not his real family but make-believe family members.

Then from deep within him came the crashing of Jem's heart against his ribcage, pleading for no more emptiness…

Warm memories settled in the torn corners of his mind. His sadness and despair gave way to wonder at the natural world and of life itself. Humility flooded his heart as he considered how the sea had borne silent witness to so many incredible exploits: all those shipwrecks, all those great military sea battles and on-going struggles between smugglers, pirates and the British Navy. His problems and worries were nothing compared to all the combined endeavours and sufferings of mankind. He was but a grain of sand amongst billions.

Then Jem's lips creased into a crescent-moon smile as he thought of Flossie hiding behind Mother's wood-burner, triangles of hot caramel thrust deep inside her calico apron pockets. Flossie would never forgive him for being so down in the dumps. On the contrary Flossie would scold him for being so sentimental.

"Pull thyself together Jem. Life is far better than thou dost think!"

Then a burst of joy as Flossie's spinning-top laughter spiralled through the centuries towards him and it seemed as if it were only yesterday that he was holding her podgy palm in his.

"Stop blubbering Tom," Antonia snapped irritably, removing the mangled fishing-net from his battered body. "I've seen more fighting spirit in a dead jellyfish."

"But the bloody thing attacked us!" Tom retorted, his mind struggling to come to terms with what had just happened.

"The net did not attack you," Antonia said calmly, eyes like stone.

"Yes it did," James glowered, removing a sinew of rope from his bleeding left cheek.

It was bad enough being attacked. The last thing he needed was Antonia rubbing salt into his wounds by pretending that nothing had happened.

"The net did no such thing," Antonia repeated, voice like ice. "It was a mirage."

"But you saw, we all saw!" Tom exclaimed hoarsely.

Antonia's pupils hardened.

"We saw nothing," she repeated.

"What's got into you Toni? Have you gone soft in the head?" James remonstrated.

Antonia glowered at him, too angry to speak.

Slowly a shadow of understanding crossed Tom's brow.

"Antonia's right," Tom said quietly. "We didn't hear anything. It was all a figment of our imaginations."

"What the hell? Have you both gone mad?" James shouted furiously, slamming his fists down hard on the wet sand.

"On the contrary, we're both one hundred per cent sane. But our priority James is to get off this beach in one piece," Antonia hissed between gritted teeth.

"What? Why? I still don't get it!" James exclaimed, flinging his hands in the air in despair.

"I don't either James. But the moment I do understand what we're up against, we act," Antonia replied. "But right now it's time to get off this beach whilst we can because whatever is out there might come back any minute. And I for one, have no intention whatsoever of being around when it does."

Then Antonia stepped forwards, grabbed both lads by the elbow and hauled them manfully from the beach.

CHAPTER TWO

Shell Cottage

Shell Cottage is situated in a small dip in the land known locally as Pancake Hollow. In summer it can get so hot that you can fry an egg on the tarmac drive if you have the know-how. Hazel has the know-how.

Light filtered through the calico curtains into Coral's bedroom. Hazel stole quietly into the room and planted a kiss on her daughter's left cheek. Coral had such huge, moon-shaped cheeks. They were the very antithesis of her pinched cheeks, tarnished by sun spots and possessing the leathery bookworm veneer that comes with middle-age. Hazel sighed as she remembered her age – forty-five – she found it hard to believe that she was that old. It seemed like only yesterday that she was eighteen riding pillion on the back of John's black Triumph Thunderbird across the Yorkshire Moors to Sheffield.

Coral coughed then turned over in her sleep, dreaming of inkpot ponies and long meadow grass. She smiled, listening to the mellifluous drone of the bumblebees as they gathered nectar from the honey-suckle outside her bedroom window.

Then without warning Coral's arms lashed out in self-defence as Antonia jarred her in the ribs with a well aimed elbow. Coral grabbed the edge of the duvet and braced herself for the next blow.

The blow never came.

Instead Hazel's cool palm stroked Coral's brow, making everything alright again.

"Hush sweetheart. It's OK darling. It's only a nightmare. There's nothing to worry about."

Coral relaxed. The inkpot ponies were back with her, nuzzling her ribcage and licking her forehead with their furry tongues, sniffing out her jacket pockets for the odd carrot or two.

Jem woke early the next day. He felt exhausted. Visions of Antonia's sharp nails and his broken radio had combined to make sleep impossible. He felt horribly guilty. He shouldn't have punched those lads so hard. It had been like juggling with feathers!

Significantly the only mark on his body was a one-inch cut made by Antonia when her thumb-nail connected with the soft underside of his chin. How much Antonia knew about him or understood, he did not know. *But there was little he couldst do about it.*

Brushing his worries aside, Jem threw on some clothes, downed a pint glass of milk, grabbed a couple of English Russets from the fruit bowl and set off for St Merriam's Churchyard. *Nay, Mother would tell him what to do.*

After an hour spent at Mother's graveside, he always felt stronger. The act of tending her grave fed his soul. With every till of the earth each worry was plucked from his mind and released like a dandelion puff on the wind.

Jem reached Docton Moor and paused. He took an apple out of his pocket. The skin was a glorious golden brown. He raised it to his lips and took a bite. The sugary juices exploded in his mouth. Then he hurried on, his eyes fixed on the rose-tinted horizon.

After ten minutes of solid walking Jem arrived at Two-Tree Junction, the site of two twisted oak trees, their trunks fused together as one. He paused and looked out to sea, mesmerised by the deep cobalt blue.

The whistle-like call of the kittiwake chicks nesting on the cliffs echoed across the bay. Then a flurry of swooping wings as the parent birds returned to their nests with food for their young.

One hundred and fifty years ago a very different scene would have met his eyes. Back then hunters lowered themselves down the cliff on ropes and raided the nests. They cut off the kittiwakes' wings and flung the seabirds back into the sea to drown, still alive; and all because the Duchess of Devonshire and fashionable young ladies liked to wear kittiwake feathers in their hats! Jem grimaced at the memory, outraged. *Father and the sailmakers of Hartland Quay wouldst never have done such a cruel-hearted thing! Father and his friends knew better than the generation of men that came after! History went round in circles - it was not linear and logical - that's what too few people understood.*

But with the passage of time, comes change. Now the hunting of kittiwakes was illegal. Conservation was the new fashion. The Royal Society for the Protection of Birds protected the kittiwake breeding grounds throughout the British Isles. The hunters of yore had been replaced by marine biologists in hoodies and middle-aged volunteers with binoculars and bushy beards. The eagle-eyed public now patrolled the nesting sites, ensuring that the young chicks hatched safely.

Jem glanced one last time at the nesting kittiwakes and turned inland. He could just make out the rickety chimney-top of Shell Cottage, its tall chimney piercing the blue sky like a witch's broom. He smiled, wondering who lived there.

Once or twice he thought that he had seen a girl with long golden hair peering out of the topmost window. The girl had reminded him of Rapunzel because her hair was so long. Jem blushed, embarrassed at the thought. Rapunzel was only a Romantic character from one of Flossie's picture books and as every sensible adult knows there is no truth in fables.

Or is there? Is there a greater truth and magic waiting to be discovered in traditional children's stories than is commonly understood? - Truths that only the young at heart can discover?

Jem froze, deep in magical thought.

The minutes slid past like sand through an hour-glass. A kittiwake chick called to its parents for more food. Then Jem snapped out of his day-dreaming and marched back across the moor, headed for St Merriam's Churchyard and his appointment with Mother.

Inside Shell Cottage Hazel continued to stroke Coral's forehead, trying hard not to worry about her. Although not quite sixteen years of age, a thin horizontal line ran through the middle of Coral's forehead like the spine of a leaf. The line had first appeared when Coral was eight years old. It was the year her father had died. Over the years the line had developed into a deep furrow.

Hazel sighed. Perhaps they should have stayed in Sheffield after John's death? There were plenty of things for teenagers to do in the city: cinemas, skate-parks, street theatre, carnivals, the list was endless.

But Hazel had not wanted Coral to grow cement gills and tarmac lungs like her father had. Coral was too much like her namesake - a fragile coral reef - to be beaten into shape on the blacksmith's blunt and heavy anvil.

Of course they **could** have stayed in Sheffield and Coral would have adapted to competitive city life. But Hazel had not wanted her delicate daughter to make those subtle Darwinian adjustments in order to survive.

Hazel stooped forward and extracted a thread of golden hair that was coiled about Coral's right thumb. Coral always sucked her thumb whilst she slept. John had hated the habit. But if the rhythmic ductile motion aided sleep, where was the crime? Sucking ones thumb was certainly a lot better than getting hooked on sleeping tablets which Hazel knew to her own cost. She had taken enough sleeping tablets since John's death to build the Empire State Building twice over - a state of affairs that she would caution against! The irony of a health food practitioner keeping the pharmaceutical families in business never failed to amuse Hazel. But it is one thing believing in something. It is all together harder to live out ones beliefs. Compromise is all too often the human lot.

Hazel leant forwards and gave Coral one last homespun kiss. Then she slotted a paper note under Coral's pillow and slipped seamlessly from the room.

Iridescent stars coursed through the bevelled glass of the landing window. Hazel descended the stairs, her fingers curled over the wooden banisters like the crinkled leaves of two well-read books. In the hallway she paused to coax a sun-hat from beneath a pile of tangled coats. Then she hoisted her leather bag onto her shoulder and stepped boldly out into the brilliant August sunshine.

The crunch of thin espadrilles on pea-gravel followed by the low slur of the sea lapping against the northerly shore; Hazel breathed in deeply, tasting the salt-air.

A light breeze skimmed over the tops of the hedgerows and rippled the hem of her cheese-cloth skirt. She caught hold of the hem and laughed. The good thing about living in the middle of nowhere was that there was no-one around to pass comment, except for the resident song-thrush. But what was a flash of petticoats between old friends?

At the garden gate Hazel blew a final, quicksilver kiss up to Coral's bedroom window. Then she turned and set off down the country lane looking forward to another hard day's work at the Good Earth Café.

Sunlight filtered through Coral's buttercup curtains. Her long fingers tweaked the edge of her cotton duvet as she dreamt about taking the bus to the seaside. She dreamt that she was hanging out by a row of a multi-coloured camper vans, chatting away to the surfer dudes. In real life she wouldn't in a million years dare approach a group of surfers but in her dreams she could do anything.

Hazel's kiss lingered in the room. Coral woke with a start, read Hazel's note and leapt out of bed. She hurried to the window and drew back the curtains hoping to catch sight of Hazel climbing the brow of the hill out of Pancake Hollow. But all she could see was a sea of purple bell-heather and the crooked oak trees at Two-Tree Junction.

Disappointed, Coral quickly got dressed in a pair of denim shorts and a white halter-neck top. Then she bounded down the stairs two treads at a time. In the kitchen she bolted down a breakfast of fresh pineapple and yoghurt. Then she split open a half baguette and stuffed it with white goat's cheese and fresh watercress. She filled two battered-looking plastic bottles with tap-water and rammed the whole lot into the bottom of her ruck-sack along with a handful of apples, her sketch-pad, some kitchen-roll and a blistered paint-box.

It was the first week of the summer holidays and Coral meant to make the most of her new-found freedom. No more stupid school rules, snide asides and cowardly jibes; instead she was free to roam wherever she wanted, answerable to no-one and no-body!

All packed and ready to go, Coral grabbed a white cap from the sideboard and pulled it down low over her forehead. Then she exited via the back-door without bothering to lock it. There was no need.

She scrambled up the garden wall and skirted along the top, her papyrus-thin ankles navigating their way through the 'cocks' and 'hens' of the dry-stone wall. At the lip of Pancake Hollow she stared out across the Hartland Peninsular. The wildness and raw beauty of the moor never failed to move her. She shut her eyes and tilted her head back, revelling in the sheer sensation of the summer breeze tickling her neck and shoulders.

Then she opened her eyes and leapt down from the wall onto the moor, mindful not to dislodge the red campion that sprouted from the cracks.

Her mind set on adventure, she set off through the bell-heather, determined to follow her nose wherever it might lead her. This was **her country**. You could blind-fold her and she would still be able to find her way home.

Indeed, two summers ago Coral had been forced to do just that when an innocent game of Blind Man's Bluff had stopped being fun and developed into something other. The party held to celebrate the end of the year exams had quickly got out of hand. The festivities spilled out of the school grounds onto the beach. Scratched and bruised, Coral had finally managed to free herself from Antonia's stubborn knot. Then she had let go of the bad memory as easily as she had let go of her father's wintry smile. Some things are best kept buried deep beneath the cold earth.

A high-pitched bark ricocheted across the moor. Coral stopped dead in her tracks and listened. Otters! There must be otters in the beck! She sprinted across the moor, leapt over the stone-stile into the adjacent fields and raced towards Speke's Mouth, gathering buttercups between her toes as she went.

Another playful yelp rent the air. Coral reached the little beck and scrambled up onto the wooden foot-bridge that straddled the beck. Four young otter pups tumbled heads-over-heels towards her. Sunlight glanced off their ruffled backs, their sequined fur sparkling with all the colours of the rainbow.

Suddenly the alpha male – ears flat, eyes bright – launched himself at its nearest sibling, only to be jumped on in turn by the rest of the litter. The rough and tumble continued for some ten minutes. Then their energy spent, the young pups flopped down on the mossy bank and lay panting on their stomachs.

White clouds scudded low over the blue-bell sky. The pups' mother emerged from the beck, a silver fish shimmering in her jaws. Ravenous, the female otter dragged the fish onto the far bank and tore into the flesh with her needle-sharp teeth, ignoring the probing snouts of her hungry offspring.

The pups soon tired of being ignored and decamped to a grassy knoll and curled up tight into a knot of bodies. A row of ponderous green gunneras stood guard, their parasol-shaped leaves the perfect foil to passing predators.

Coral watched the scene keenly, marvelling at nature's versatility and resourcefulness. Then she sat down on the foot-bridge, got out her water-colours and sketch-pad and started to paint the scene before her.

The sun edged further west. Globules of sweat shimmered on Coral's forehead like silverfish. After two hours of solid painting, she completed her composition and signed her name in the bottom right-hand corner. Then she sauntered down to the water's edge, cupped her hands and drank freely from the little beck.

Her thirst quenched, she wiped her checks dry with the back of her hands and lay down on the bank and dozed in the sun for an hour or so. Then she returned to the foot-bridge, checked the colours had set and methodically packed up her artwork. She glanced one last time at the sleeping pups and smiled.

"Thank you little ones for allowing me to paint you. And don't stray too far from the safety of the little beck."

Coral now set off along the main foot-path, walking parallel with the beck. The iridescent water gathered momentum and gradually widened into a fully-fledged stream. Then a low roar as the stream leapt off the cliff-edge transformed into a full-blown waterfall.

Coral darted swiftly forwards, mirroring the action of the suicidal stream. Her toes curled over the edge of the cliff-top. She laughed, seized by an unspoken desire to leap into the unknown. The greater the danger, the more alive she felt!

Then the muscles in the backs of her legs tightened like tent-rods. An oak-apple formed in her heart and she withdrew from the edge of the cliff, berating herself for being so selfish. One death in the family was enough. It was foolish of her to put her life at risk. Hazel would never recover from a second death.

Still chastising herself, Coral continued along the coastal path. Gradually her temper eased and her pulse slowed. Carpets of rose-pink thrift rubbed against her ankles. She paused to pick one of the tough little flowers and slotted it through the strap of her ruck-sack. Then she quickened her pace, impatient to get down onto the sandy beach.

The only way down to Speke's Mouth Beach was via an eighteen-foot rope that was suspended from a metal bracket nailed into the cliff-face. The brackets and nails stuck out from the wall of rock like the fixed jaw of an angler-fish.

Coral carefully began to lower herself down the rope. Then two-thirds of the way down she got bored and let go…

Adrenaline coursed through her. She twisted in mid-air like a cat and landed safely on the level sand. Moss and tiny granules of rock confetti showered her head and shoulders. Exhilarated, she shook the fragments of moss and debris from her hair and turned to face the sea.

The tide was out. The exposed wet sand glistened like white marble. Each shell and pebble looked magnified.

Life itself seemed magnified.

She wiggled her toes playfully, enjoying the sensation of running water tickling the underside of her feet. Then she thought of her father John, a no-nonsense Yorkshire man.

John had been such a warm hearted guy - always laughing - a roll-up lodged permanently in the side of his mouth. Sometimes John laughed so hard that the roll-up fell out and landed on the workshop floor along with the nails and bolts from the motorbike that he happened to be working on at the time. Then he'd pick up the nails and pop them between his teeth for a joke and laugh a great monster's laugh until water seeped out of his pale blue eyes and Hazel told him to stop fooling around and get on with fixing the bike so they could all go out for a picnic on the moor.

But one day John's number came up. A car pulled out in front of him at a junction at Grindleford. John was knocked off his bike and left for dead. The car-driver did not bother to stop. Death was like that: sudden and brutal.

However Coral had accepted John's death as easily as she accepted the fact that her ankles and toes were now covered in wet sand. She felt no enmity or anger towards the car-driver who had killed her father. It was not her place to challenge the passage of time. Instead she accepted her place in the world and her father's absence from it with total equanimity and an open mind.

Jem appeared at the top of the cliff-path just above Hartland Cove and paused to gaze out to sea. He had spent the whole morning at Saint Merriam's churchyard chatting with Mother, Flossie and Father. He had a laid a bunch of white meadowsweet on Mother's and Father's grave and draped wild pink shrub roses about Flossie's headstone. The rest of his brothers and sisters had had to make do with bunches of yellow king-cups picked from the meadow.

Now as Jem headed home along the coastal path, he felt his usual happy self. He thanked the Good Lord for having been born into such a wonderful family and vowed to continue humbly in Mother's unerring foot-steps.

Coral walked the length of Speke's Mouth Beach. At the far corner of the beach rose the pillar of rock known locally as Old Man's Elbow. She reached the foot of the giant stack and was seized by a sudden urge to climb it. The razor-sharp block of rock was all that remained between her and Hartland Cove.

She took off her sandals and placed them neatly at the foot of the stack. Then she began to free-climb, curling the tips of her toes into the rock so that she could secure a firm foot-hold.

Her progress was slow but accurate. Little by little she inched closer to the top of the fifteen metre high monolith. Then her pale hands curled about the top of the stack and she peered over. A collection of ink-black rock-pools met her adventurous eyes. All she had to do now was to climb down the other side to find out what lived inside them. Coral squinted into the sun - climbing down was not going to be easy. But it would be fun! And you can't have fun in life without sometimes taking risks.

Jem sat down on the shingle, his back resting against the Liberty, a mug of mint tea cupped in his weather-beaten hands. Wisps of hot steam curled up towards his sore chin. Twists of fresh mint bobbed on the surface of the tea. He pursed his lips together and blew lightly. Then he drew the mug to his lips and drank. Warm liquid coated the back of his throat. He shifted sideways on the shingle and looked out to sea. The tide was turning. The water looked deceptively still and serene.

But it wouldst not be long before the shallow channels swelled into dangerous snake-currents that couldst drag a man out to his death in seconds.

He twisted round and scanned the far perimeter of the cove, checking that everything was in order. The pair of resident black cormorants looked happy enough installed in their crevice-nest. Cormorants mated for life and this particular pair had built a nest on the exact same spot these past three years. Their long black necks weaved in and out as their bills kissed. A ring of seaweed decorated the edge of the nest. The male bird had an eye for detail and the female for good house-keeping. Their young would be in safe hands once they hatched.

Above the cormorants, scores of kittiwake chicks sunned themselves on their cliff ledge perches. It was a sight to dazzle the eyes.

Jem drew his mug to his lips and drank some more tea. Then his eyes alighted on the base of Old Man's Elbow. His topaz eyes slowly travelled up the massive rock. When his gaze reached the top of the stack, he started with surprise.

A pair of pale hands was moving sideways along the topmost section of the giant rock! What was the numbskull of a climber trying to do?

A matchstick leg suddenly appeared, quickly followed by another as the climber rounded the side of the stack and began his descent. The climber had a ruck-sack strapped to his back. How the boy was managing to free-climb with that load on his back was little short of miraculous.

Half-way down, the climber ran into difficulty.

Jem caught his breath, urging the foolhardy lad to turn back. There was no way through the barrier of razor-sharp rocks and craggy rock-pools below. The only sensible course of action was to retreat.

Then to Jem's uttermost horror, the climber twisted round and launched himself sideways into the air!

By rights Coral ought to have fallen to her death. But instead she landed on a thin spine of rock some three metres below her. The only damage she accrued was the loss of her base-ball hat. Her long hair flopped into her eyes, making it harder for her to see. She edged forwards along the narrow spit of rock, pausing every now and then to test the rock's strength with her toes, forced to navigate by touch alone.

Jem stared at the climber in disbelief. The climber was a girl! A mere scrap of a girl! He stood up and sprinted along the top-shore, determined to get to her before she fell to her death on the unforgiving rock-pools below. *A rock-pool doth not as easily forgive a man's mistakes as the Good Lord!*

He reached the base of Old Man's Elbow and stopped dead in his tracks. *Where was she?* The girl had totally disappeared.

After several anxious minutes, Jem spotted the girl crawling out from behind a rock-pool, a magnificent Queen Scallop held fast in her hand. The girl popped the pale-cream shell into her ruck-sack and darted forwards in search of another specimen to add to her collection.

Coral was in her element. There was such an incredible range of rocks and shells on the beach, ranging from sparkling white and yellow crystals buried in the chunks of limestone to smooth slabs of slate. She stood a really good chance of finding a fossil - the cove was an absolute treasure trove of geological wonders - and if she were really lucky she might even find an ammonite or a trilobite.

Jem watched as if in a trance. *Was he dreaming?* The girl's hair rippled as she moved like an underwater kelp forest. When she paused her limbs took on the stillness and permanence of granite. The speed with which she darted from rock-pool to rock-pool reminded him of a shoal of fish constantly changing direction in order to keep one step ahead of potential predators. *But what colour were her eyes? He hadst to know the colour of her eyes!* He crept closer still…

Suddenly Coral halted before a large rock-pool, its outer rim decorated with ink-blue mussels. Five minutes elapsed. Coral remained motionless, her eyes locked onto the still water. Then without warning she thrust her arms deep into the watery depths and pulled out a gigantic King Crab.

The mighty crustacean boxed the air with its front pincers. Coral held on tightly to its body-plate. Then she tilted the crab backwards so that it was permanently off-balance. Immobilised, the crab strummed the air with its six hind-legs whilst stabbing the sky with its front pincers.

Jem watched, captivated by both the girl **and** the crab. The crab reminded him of a bare-knuckle fighter being gradually worn down by a more agile and nimble opponent.

Soon the crustacean began to tire. Jem frowned. It was high-time the girl put the creature out of its misery. But how was she going to kill it? He felt sure that the girl would do the right thing and kill it kindly. What she needed was his filleting knife. One sharp stab through the bony shell into the crab's jelly-brain would despatch it swiftly with minimum pain. He fumbled in his back trouser pocket for his penknife. Then he gasped with surprise as the girl did something altogether unthinkable. She began to talk to the crab!

"You're lucky I'm a vegetarian or I'd have taken you home as a present for Hazel. Hazel loves dressed crab on a bed of gem-lettuce," Coral said good-naturedly. "You have a wonderful exoskeleton. One of the best I've ever seen. In fact I could look at you for hours. And I'd love to paint you. But I guess I better put you back where you belong. Thanks for allowing me to examine you."

Then Coral plunged the crab back into the rock-pool and quickly let go.

"No!" Jem cried out, appalled at the loss of a perfectly good meal; a crab that size could provide him both lunch **and** dinner.

Coral tensed.

"Who's there?" she demanded, spinning round on the balls of her feet.

Jem froze, too shocked to say anything. *The girl couldst hear him!* Not only could she hear him, she was actually looking straight at him with dagger-eyes.

"What do you want?" Coral demanded fiercely, her hands tightened into walnut-shaped fists.

Jem stared at the girl speechless. **Nobody** could see him. He was invisible: a **non-person.** Nobody had seen him for over two hundred years.

"What do you want?" Coral repeated. "If Antonia has sent you to spy on me, you can tell her I'm not interested in her pathetic little games!"

Jem tried to reply but his voice refused to obey his command. He punched the side of his thighs in frustration. *He hadst been alone for too long! He hadst forgotten how to hold a conversation.* He stared at the girl's electric blue eyes at a total loss.

"Stop staring at me," Coral said fiercely, mastering her nerves.

Then she unclenched her fists as a gesture of goodwill. Her fingers travelled sideways in search of the straps of her rucksack. If she could just keep him talking then maybe she could make a run for it when he least expected?

Jem noticed how the girl's fingers surreptitiously clasped the straps of her ruck-sack. Suddenly he understood. *The girl was as scared of him as he was of her!* He raised his hands in a placatory gesture.

"I'm sorry I startled thee. Antonia and James are no friends of mine."

Coral gazed at Jem long and hard, trying to divine the truth.

"I mean thee no harm. I swear it on the King James Bible," Jem continued in earnest, his voice tremulous.

"You speak funnily!" Coral exclaimed, her lips curling into a moonbeam smile.

"Which means you **can't** be friends with Antonia. She wouldn't dream of having you as a member of her gang with an accent like yours." Coral held out her hand. "I'm Coral. Pleased to meet you."

"Jem. Pleased to meet thee likewise," Jem replied, wondering just what sort of an accent Coral thought he had.

Jem blushed. Coral's hand was as soft as thistle-down. He subconsciously tightened his grip, not wanting to let go.

"Ouch. You're hurting me!" Coral cried out sharply.

"Sorry. I didst not mean to hurt thee!" Jem exclaimed, abruptly letting go of Coral's hand. "Nay, I wouldst never hurt thee. But for a moment I mistook thee for my little sister Flossie with a square of hot caramel hidden in her apron pocket. Thou hast the same blue eyes as Flossie and the same hair!" Jem exclaimed. He fell silent, his thoughts jumbled. "I held thee tight because I didst not want thee to run away. Mother wouldst not want Flossie to run away with hot caramel in her pocket," Jem garbled, all flustered.

"I'm sure your mother wouldn't. Hot caramel can burn," Coral replied, smiling at Jem uncertainly.

Could she trust Jem? Or should she stick to Plan A and make a run for it at the earliest opportunity? She glanced past the rock-pools trying to gauge the distance to Hartland Wood. She decided to stick to Plan A.

"Do you come here often Jem?"

"All the time."

"I've never been here before. I thought it was a private beach," Coral confessed guiltily. "But I couldn't resist climbing Old Man's Elbow. I've always wanted to climb it and today I did," she added shyly.

"Aye, that you did," Jem replied, nodding thoughtfully. "But if I may be so bold as to say, there is no such thing as a private beach in England. A millionaire can buy a plot of land o'er-looking the sea but he cannot buy the beach. All the beaches between low and high tide belong to Her Majesty and in her good wisdom Her Majesty allows all her subjects constant access to the seaside. Thou canst walk the length of the country from John O'Groats to Land's End and thou wouldst be walking on Crown Land - **our land** - 'tis the great wonder of the British and our way of doing things. No other country in the world has such a liberal core!" Jem said proudly, puffing up his chest. "That's why we British make such good smugglers - we canst outwit a custom's clerk in a bat of an eye! We've had thousands of years of practice!"

"Wow, you sound just like my father when he was on a roll!" Coral exclaimed. "And he was no lover of the monarchy. In fact he was a keen republican." Then Coral's jaw tightened and she caressed John's memory with her mind. "Well it's been nice chatting to you Jem, but I really must be getting on my way. I've got all the shells and specimens I need. It would be greedy to take more. And Hazel is expecting me home for lunch."

"Hazel? Is she thy sister? I have six sisters, Flossie, Catherine, Hannah, Jane, Emmie and Lizzie," Jem rattled on, desperate to prolong the conversation. "Then there's Jacob and Edward. There's twelve of us all-told, plus Father and Mother." He bit his lip, sensing that he had said more than he ought.

Coral smiled, relaxing a little.

"Hazel is my mother. Only I never call her that, she'd be horrified. Hazel believes in calling everyone by their first names. Hazel's a bit of a rebel if you get my drift."

Jem stared back, dumbfounded. Then he watched, transfixed, as Coral stooped down and gathered the shells at her feet and slotted them into her ruck-sack for safe-keeping.

"Good-bye Jem. It was nice meeting you. Give my regards to your mother and the rest of the family - especially little Flossie."

Coral stepped forward confidently. Jem drew back and allowed Coral free passage through the labyrinth of rock-pools. As she stalked warily past, he breathed in the sweet scent of bell-heather permeating her hair.

Then in a flash Coral was halfway up the shore en route for Hartland Wood. Jem frowned, knowing that he had frightened her despite his best efforts to the contrary. He pummelled his thighs with his fists, furious with himself for being so awkward and tongue-tied.

Then he watched in awe as Coral darted across the pebble ridge and leapt over the stone-stile that marked the boundary into Hartland Wood. He caught his breath as Coral melted into the leaf canopy, her long hair assuming the form of corkscrew hazel. Was she animal, vegetable or mineral? Whatever she was, Jem knew one thing for certain: he was determined to see her again.

CHAPTER THREE

Skin and Bone

Antonia and James lay side by side beneath the silver-birch trees on the southerly slopes of Hartland Wood, their heads heavy with a combination of heatstroke and wine, smudges of melted chocolate delineating their lips.

A knot of cellophane was wedged inside the fork of the silver-birch tree directly behind them both. Antonia's pink Doc Martens hung from the lowest bough, the laces knotted together in a pretty bow. A bottle of Sunday Bay Sauvignon Blanc was propped up against the silvery base of the trunk. A half empty box of Belgian chocolates nestled in the soft folds of the tartan rug.

James opened his eyes and blinked.

"I don't know why you bought these chocolates Toni. They were bound to melt," he grumbled, propping himself up on his elbows and trying to separate a glutinous chocolate from its gold foil wrapping.

"There's no pleasing some people," Antonia snapped, her top lip curled in warning.

Then Antonia tilted her head back and drained the remainder of the wine in one gulp. James watched her neck muscles ripple as the liquid trickled down the back of her throat en route for her stomach. Then his brows knotted in concentration as he contemplated the fragility of the female neck.

One snap was all that it would take…

Antonia cast the wine bottle lazily aside. The dark green bottle rolled down the hill until it came to rest against an old tree stump covered in grey lichen. It landed face-upwards and immediately provoked an enquiry from a magpie attracted to the brightly coloured label depicting the turquoise blue shore-line of Sunday Bay.

Antonia yawned. Then she reached up and removed a strip of silver bark from the trunk of the birch tree behind her. She carefully wrapped the filament of bark about her wrist and tied a clumsy bow. Then she held out her wrist to show James. The fragile bracelet fell apart as she extended her arm. Disappointed, she tossed the fragments aside and raked the trunk with her long lacquered nails.

Curls of bark floated into her lap like shredded Barber-Shop hair. She impatiently brushed them away and carved a heart on the denuded trunk with the sharp edge of her nail. Inside the heart she inscribed the words: "James and Antonia Forever."

James recoiled at the prospect of being with Antonia forever but he had the common sense to keep his thoughts to himself. Instead he leant forward and carved a heart next to hers.

The snapping of twigs closeby… James looked up and x-rayed the trees with his hard brown irises. Then his lips quivered with delight as he spied Coral weaving her way in and out of the undergrowth. A rush of notes echoed through the air as Coral sang to herself Shadows and Light by seventies folk singer Joni Mitchell.

Antonia stood up and scanned the woodland. She caught sight of Coral and let out a snort of disgust. It was that stupid girl again - the hippy freak with the starfish earrings and baby blue eyes muttering to herself like some New Age lunatic.

Incensed that Coral might disturb her intimate moment with James, Antonia glowered in Coral's direction, her face a knot of fury.

"Chill out Toni," James murmured, flattered by Antonia's jealousy.

"What's the eco-freak up to now?" Antonia demanded, unhooking her heavy pink boots from the branch and hastily putting them on.

"What does it matter to you?" James remarked languidly.

"It doesn't matter to me one bit!" Antonia retorted, loping off to take a closer look.

"Don't be gone too long Toni. I want that shoulder massage you promised," James drawled languidly, rolling over to lie on his stomach. Then he shut his dulcet brown eyes and stretched out his arms like a teenage rock God.

Coral moved swiftly through the trees, her ruck-sack bouncing lightly against her ribcage. Pools of sweat collected in the humped bridge of her back-bone. She paused and loosened the straps of her ruck-sack feeling a good deal less worried now that she had put a safe distance between herself and Jem.

The more she thought about Jem, the more he freaked her out! She couldn't put her finger on what exactly was wrong with him but he had a kind of otherworldly quality that she couldn't explain and certainly didn't trust.

She pressed on, delighted to be in Hartland Wood. Wild rhododendron combined with hazel, birch and ash to create a living tapestry of bark and leaf. All being well, she planned to picnic somewhere in the shade, then spend the cool of the afternoon sketching the wild ponies up on the heath.

Suddenly three young fallow deer broke for cover a few yards in front of her. She stopped and watched in awe as their vertical white tails bobbed up and down like white arrows. The way ahead clear, she continued up the narrow hill path.

Her silver filigree necklace bounced lightly up and down against her collar-bone as she climbed. She fingered the filigree metalwork protectively. The necklace was a family heirloom that she had inherited from her Russian Great-Grandmother Alexandrine. She lowered her neck and drew the orb-like pendant to her lips and kissed it. *Thank you Alexandrine for leaving it to me; I shall treasure it always.*

Alexandrine had met Coral's Great-Grandfather, John Pearson, in Moscow in 1880. Quite why John Pearson had travelled all the way from Sheffield to Moscow by stage-coach, ship and train, nobody in her family could tell her but Coral thought that there must be a great secret waiting to be discovered. One day she planned to travel to Moscow and find out. All she had as a guide was a collection of love stories by Chekhov that had belonged to her Great-Grandfather, but who could undo Chekhov? He was guide enough.

Cracks appeared in the ground in front of her. She carefully avoided the fissures and tangle of sharp tree roots, wishing that she hadn't left her sandals at Speke's Mouth Beach. But it was far too late to retrieve them now. The sea would have long since claimed them.

At length she happened upon the main woodland path. A thin layer of coarse gravel had been spread over the path by the countryside wardens in order to combat soil erosion. Coral dutifully picked her way forward, ignoring the pain in the soles of her feet. It never once occurred to her to walk parallel to the path.

The sun beat down inexorably on the roof of the woodland canopy. Coral wiped her brow, exhausted by the all pervasive heat. The trees shimmered before her eyes in a haze of white and silver light. The leaves hung from their stalks panting, desperate for rain.

One flick of a match was all it would take to set the whole area ablaze.

"Hey, what do you know, here comes the Stick-Insect," Antonia shouted cruelly, her voice ricocheting from tree-trunk to tree-trunk.

Coral stopped dead in her tracks and looked from left to right. Suddenly she spotted James sprawled out on the tartan blanket beneath a copse of silver-birch trees. She sighed with relief. James wouldn't let things get out of hand. He knew how to keep Antonia in check.

"Can't your Mum afford to feed you?" Antonia jeered, her voice spiked with wine-coloured invective.

Then silence as the magpie alighted on an oak stump a few feet from James. The bird cocked its head on one side and hopped onto the tartan blanket, its beady eyes locked onto the gold necklace that dangled temptingly about James's neck.

One peck in the eyes was all that it would take.

"I said Bone-Bags! Can't your Mum afford to feed you?" Antonia shouted from her hiding place deep in the rhododendron bushes. "Or don't Eco-warriors need food like the rest of us? Do you just smoke pot instead?"

"Hazel doesn't take drugs!" Coral shouted back angrily.

"Of course she doesn't Flower," Antonia mocked malevolently.

Coral narrowed her eyes and peered into the dense foliage, trying to distinguish light from dark and sunlight from shadow. But the glossy green shrubs with their mauve fist-sized flowers provided an impenetrable shield behind which Antonia skulked.

Then a burst of purple petals blasted Coral's eyeballs, challenging her to step forward and fight.

"What's the matter Baby-Doll? Can't you see anything?" Antonia jeered. "You need to save up and buy yourself a decent pair of sunglasses," Antonia laughed sarcastically.

Then Antonia emerged from behind a rhododendron bush, a decapitated purple flower-head stuck behind her left ear. She planted her feet either side of the gravel path barring Coral's way.

"Hi Antonia," Coral said calmly, ignoring the jibe about the sunglasses. "I see you've been having a picnic in the wood. Good idea. It's far too hot out in the open."

"It's never too hot for me," Antonia purred, stroking the underside of her chin with her little finger. "So what are you up to Baby-Doll?"

"Nothing in particular," Coral replied casually.

"What's happened to your shoes?" Antonia asked, noticing with delight that Coral was barefoot. "Come and take a look at this James! The Stick-Insect has taken to walking barefoot!"

But James had no intention whatsoever of jumping to attention just because Antonia demanded it. Instead he twisted sideways on the rug and eyed both girls thoughtfully, contemplating how to play them. There were two jokers in every pack and Antonia contained enough vanity and arrogance to constitute two jokers all on her own. But she was also loyal and brave which made her less of the Knave and more of a Queen to his Kingship. Coral, by contrast, would not know how to play a game of poker if her life depended on it. She was innocent and naïve and therefore of no interest to him. He pressed his shoulder-blades into the soft tartan material and shut his eyes, deciding to play dead.

Coral waited on tenter-hooks, hoping that James would defuse the situation. But James did not come to her aid. He remained on the tartan blanket, pretending to sleep.

Then Coral let out a gasp of surprise as she noticed a brown love-bite on the side of his beautiful sinewy neck.

"What are you gawping at Baby-Doll? Haven't you ever seen a love-bite before?" Antonia sneered. "Not that a boy with any brains would kiss you," Antonia goaded, her hard brown eyes contemptuously roving up and down Coral's lean androgynous frame.

James opened one eye, curious to know what Antonia was getting all emotional about. Coral wasn't **that** interesting. His languid eyes roamed lazily across Coral's tumbledown hair, then on down her swan-neck towards her narrow breast-plate and pronounced collar-bone.

Then a curious thing happened. A mixture of desire and loathing rose simultaneously within him. Desire for Coral's slender shoulders and delicious swan-neck combined with shame for feeling anything for such a weak, pathetic creature.

"James. Get your butt over here!" Antonia shouted imperiously.

James refused to move. Furious, Antonia started back up the hill, her patience at breaking point.

"What the hell do you think you're playing at James?" Antonia barked angrily as James rolled over and ignored her.

"Not now Toni. I don't want to get involved," James mumbled sleepily.

Coral did not wait to see what would happen next. Sensing an opportunity, she turned and sprinted diagonally down the hill towards Hartland Cove. The woodland floor spiked her bare feet as she ran but she blanked out the pain as best she could. If she could just get to the rock-pools before Antonia, she would be alright. There was no way Antonia would be agile enough to climb through the rock-pool labyrinth to Old Man's Elbow.

Then John's no-nonsense Yorkshire vowels resounded in her ears, commanding her to slow down and stand her ground.

"Don't run Coral! Walk. Don't let 'em know you're scared."

Coral slowed down.

"Come back Stick-Insect! I haven't given you permission to leave!" Antonia shouted, turning her back on James and giving chase.

Antonia surged forwards, her heavy pink boots crushing the life out of everything green that lay in her path.

James jumped to his feet and watched keenly. Then he threw back his head and laughed. Antonia looked ridiculous in her pearl-white swimsuit and pink Doc Martens sprinting through the trees like a cartoon Tank Girl.

He settled back down on his blanket, resolved not to help either girl. Antonia was plenty capable of fighting her own battles and Coral was a law unto herself. Instead he helped himself to another chocolate and greedily sank his teeth into the soft fondant filling. Then he leant back against the tree-trunk and awaited the outcome of the impending confrontation with cruel delight.

The sound of bubble-gum popping as Tom appeared on the coastal path. Then a girlish, rice-crispy laugh as Kim appeared alongside him sporting plaits and a brand-new puff-ball skirt.

Coral jogged to a halt. She was trapped.

"Hi Antonia, sorry we're late!" Tom called out as he leapfrogged the wooden stile into Hartland Wood from the cliff-top path. "The bus broke down five miles out of Bude and we've had to hike the rest of the way."

Then Tom spun round and gallantly helped Kim over the stile. He smiled at Kim indulgently. It was a careworn smile that bore testimony to a fractious morning spent shopping in Bude plus another two miles hike on the coastal path negotiating Kim's up-and-down moods. The poor girl was still freaked out about the fishing-net incident and it had taken him all his charm to coax her along the coastal path for a picnic with the others.

"You're not late. You're bang on time," Antonia replied, striding forward to greet them. Then she drew level with Coral and clamped two hard clammy hands on Coral's narrow shoulder-blades. "Look what I've just found: a piece of stray coral. I know it looks a bit scrawny at the moment but it'll look great in the display cabinet at Sudbury Court once I've polished it up."

Coral ignored the cruel jibe about her appearance and smiled at the newcomers.

"Hi guys. I haven't seen you in a while. I love your blue-bell flip-flops Kim. Are they new?"

"Yes! Tom got them for me this morning in Animal," Kim trilled, delighted that someone other than Tom was actually taking an interest in her. "They're got a massive sale on. Eighty per cent off all beach-wear! You ought to go there."

"But what Kim chose wasn't in the sale," Tom said wistfully, patting his back-pocket containing his wallet. His bank balance was now some thirty pounds lighter.

"It's always the way," Coral replied, trying to ignore the fact that Antonia was still pinching her shoulders with her invasive hands.

"Primark? What a surprise!" Antonia said sarcastically as she examined the faded label in Coral's halter-neck top. "If you start saving now Coral you might be able to afford a decent bikini by next Christmas."

"Yeah well, we can't all be as fortunate as you," Coral replied, twisting free from Antonia's grip. "Nice seeing you Tom, Kim. See you around."

Coral started to walk briskly away, headed for the stone-stile and Hartland Beach.

"Not so fast!" Antonia shouted, darting after Coral and grabbing her right arm. She jerked Coral backwards into an arm-lock. "Don't imagine you can get away from me so easily!"

"Stop it! Let go of me!" Coral shouted, struggling to free herself.

"Not on your life sweet-heart," Antonia retorted, her vulpine lips curled into an arc.

Coral stopped struggling, knowing when she was beaten. She slowly raised her head and appealed with her eyes to both Kim and Tom for their help.

Kim looked away, terrified. Tom thrust his hands into the pockets of his board-shorts, ill-at-ease. He rolled his feet sideways so that the rubber soles of each shoe faced each other. Coral glanced from Kim to Tom fearfully. The situation wasn't looking good.

"Just where are you in such a hurry to get to Coral?" Antonia demanded, thrusting her head into Coral's face. Her hot breath probed Coral's neck, delighting in her discomfort.

"I'm not going anywhere in particular," Coral replied.

"Cut the crap! You just ran downhill for a reason Coral. Why?"

"It's easier to run downhill than up?"

"Not good enough!" Antonia growled, twisting Coral's elbow higher up against the small of her back.

An arrow of pain coursed down Coral's arm from her shoulder to her elbow. Then the pain stalled and began to spread outwards in eddying curves across her forearm and wrist in the same way that waves spread sideways and upwards on the pebble shore-line.

Kim winced in empathy with Coral, familiar with Antonia's well honed capacity to inflict pain at random. Tom shut his eyes, sickened by his own cowardice.

"Can't we just drop it and move on?" Coral asked, twisting her neck round so that she could make eye contact with Antonia.

Soft pale blue eyes met fiery molten brown ones. The brown eyes won.

"No we cannot just drop it and move on! You **were** climbing up the hill! You were heading for Hartland Abbey and the moor. Then you turned round. What made you change your mind? What made you think that you'd be safer on the beach rather than at the Abbey?" Antonia shouted, the muscles in her neck pronounced.

"Nothing made me. You're looking for reasons Antonia where there aren't any," Coral replied calmly, digging her bare heels into the red clay, trying to keep her footing.

She could not afford to fall over. Balance was everything. She had to maintain her physical and her mental balance. Everything hinged on it.

"What are you thinking Coral? I can tell you're thinking something. Or are you thinking of someone? Is there someone on the beach you'd like to tell me about?" Antonia asked, tightening her hold on Coral's wrist.

One twist was all that it would take to break it…

Coral coloured.

"I don't know what you're talking about Antonia."

"Oh yes you do!" Antonia shouted, spitting into Coral's face.

Globules of Antonia's spittle landed on Coral's cheeks and the underside of her chin.

"Stop hurting me Antonia! I've got nothing to tell you!"

"I'll stop hurting you when you tell me about the person on the beach that you're so keen to meet!" Antonia broke off and added slyly: "Does your friend live in the beach-hut by any chance?"

"My friends are none of your business!" Coral retorted angrily.

"I disagree. All your friends are my business, not that you have many, unless you count those pathetic ponies."

"They're not pathetic! They're far tougher than you are! You wouldn't last one night out on the moor," Coral said angrily, blood rushing to her face.

Antonia tightened her grip on Coral's arm. Her long lacquered nails dug deep into Coral's flesh.

"I'd be careful what I say if I were you. Coral reefs are fragile habitats, you know. It doesn't take much to make them wither and die."

One stamp of the boot was all that it would take…

Tom looked away, disgusted. He was not in the mood for any more of Antonia's cruel games. Besides, if Coral's friend was the mystery man he thought, then Hartland Cove was the last place on earth he wanted to be right now…

Coral feigned a smile. Flight and fight were not an option. Dialogue was the only way forward.

"Look Antonia, I don't know what the problem is but there really is no point in any of this. Really there isn't. So why not just let me go?"

"The problem is **you** Baby-Doll!" Antonia shrieked, letting go of Coral's arm and propelling her sideways with an angular flash of the hands.

Coral stumbled forwards, not expecting to be let go. She quickly recovered her balance and seizing the opportunity, broke into a run…

Antonia watched as Coral leapt over the stone-stile. She smiled a brooding, blood-red smile. Then with a flick of the ponytail, Antonia lowered her head and began to jog leisurely after Coral. She reached the stile and climbed over slowly. Her brown eyes x-rayed the shingle shore with surgical accuracy. There was no hurry. The horse-shoe beach was a dead-end.

There was no way past the rock-pools. She could afford to take her time.

Tom turned away, unable to witness the long drawn-out chase. Kim glanced down at the fresh scab on her tummy and flinched.

The long jagged shadow of James appeared on the top-shore. Coral stopped. She had not factored in James taking a short-cut. Now what?

James smiled at Coral benignly. He was dressed in a pair of blue jeans and white converses. Flying ants clustered about his bare torso. He seemed quite unperturbed by the ants' presence. A couple of the insects flew directly at his face and got tangled up in his long black eyelashes. He wiped the ants away with his thumb then blinked several more times to remove the residue of broken wings. A fly landed on his sealed mouth, he swiped it away with the side of his hand. He studied the squashed corpse with detached disdain. Then he smiled savagely, knowing that he held Coral's future in the palm of his hand.

Antonia was right. Coral **was** as fragile as a coral reef. But she was also beautiful in a tragic, victim-like way… Her pale lips glistened at him with a lustre born of fear and anticipation. Arms that he had once dismissed as skinny, he now perceived as having a lithesome quality of their own. Her large blue eyes ebbed and flowed with an intensity to rival the ocean-depths. And her deceptively flat silhouette presented him with all manner of possibilities. He knew what a woman with breast implants looked like, but what did Coral look like in the flesh? He found himself thinking of the silver-birch trees with their delicate catkin-like buds in an altogether different way.

Then shame overwhelmed James as he remembered the scrawny kid with whom he used to body-board, whose hippy mother drove a tatty pink Citroen ZX, the bonnet of which was so thin that if you leant on it with your elbow it buckled.

Coral and her mother were light-weights: eco-freaks that were out of date and not fit for purpose.

His pupils hardened. The glimmer of desire in them dissolved. He looked afresh at Coral's sea-blue eyes and instead of seeing the limitless possibilities of the ocean depths he saw stagnant ditch-water. How could he have been attracted to such a simple cellular structure? Coral had more in common with an amoeba than Antonia.

Antonia arrived on the scene with a reluctant Tom and a bewildered-looking Kim. James smiled at them both in greeting.

Coral tensed. James only smiled like that when he was spoiling for a fight.

"I agree with Toni," James said softly, wrapping his arms about Antonia's generous waist. "Coral forms part of a fragile eco-system. However, the question we have to ask ourselves is this: is the species of coral we have in front of us indigenous to the British Isles? Or it is foreign?" James paused. "What do you think Tom? Does Coral **belong** here or is she too **exotic** for our native shores?"

"Too exotic," Tom replied, his voice dull, like flat beer.

Tom looked down, acutely ashamed of his betrayal. But he was in no position to challenge James right now. He had tried to go against James's wishes once before and had acquired a black eye for his efforts.

"What do you think Kim? Is Coral **native** or **foreign**?" James asked again, his voice sweeter than honey.

"Native," Kim replied truthfully, thinking of the rich coral reef that surrounded Lundy Island. Then she exclaimed in pain as Tom pinched her hand. "I mean foreign," Kim corrected, shooting bewildered looks at Tom.

"And what do you think Toni?" James asked, running his hand tenderly through his girlfriend's tinder-dry hair. His hand located her fulsome hips and he squeezed her flank appreciatively.

"Foreign," Antonia intoned imperiously, her voice like granite. "Coral does not belong here."

"My thoughts entirely," James replied, his eyes glazed. "So, let me see, we have established that Coral is exotic and not native to the British Isles. Now we have to decide what to do with her. Do we allow her to remain in Hartland or should we deport her back to where she belongs?"

"Stop it James! This is ridiculous! This is not a court of law!" Coral interrupted. "And even if it were a court of law, Kim is right, coral **is** a native species. Coral grows all around the southwest coast. You know it does! We used to snorkel around the coral reef at Lundy Island every summer when we were kids. Or don't you remember watching the sea-horses with me? Have you forgotten the cuttle-fish and the fire anemones? Or was that all a dream James?" Coral asked, her blue eyes shimmering like a dragonfly's diaphanous wings.

"Shut up!" Antonia barked. "Contempt of court!"

"No I will not shut-up!" Coral replied shrilly, her voice like the North Wind as it rushes across the North York moors. She thought of her father astride his black Thunderbird racing across the moors with Hazel riding pillion behind him and she refused to back down. "I'm going! I've had enough of this lunacy!"

Coral strode past Tom and Kim, every inch her father's daughter. Tom and Kim instinctively drew aside, stung by the latent criticism etched in her ice-blue eyes.

Free once more, Coral sprinted across the pristine white sand towards the base of Old Man's Elbow. There were just fifty more metres to go and then she'd be at the rock-pools and safety. Even James could not compete with her when it came to free-climbing. She was the best and he knew it.

But Coral did not get near enough to Old Man's Elbow to test her climbing skills. James caught up with her just before the rock-pools. His right arm shot out and he caught hold of her beautiful long blonde hair.

Coral screamed in pain as James slowly began to reel in his catch. Then she fell backwards into his braced torso. James smiled then relaxed his hold. He ran his fingers through Coral's straw hair like a basket weaver. Then he lowered his head and ingested the sweet scent of her scalp.

Bell-heather mixed with apple-blossom. Just as he remembered!

Coral froze, immobilised by a mixture of fear and indecision. She scanned the coastline, praying that Jem would appear and put an end to this lunacy. But all she could see was the vast expanse of blue where the sky meets the ocean.

James continued to examine Coral's Rapunzel hair, surprised by how smooth and silky it was compared with Antonia's coarse wiry mane. Then he ran his wedge-like thumb down the side of Coral's slender neck and checked her pulse. He pressed lightly on her jugular vein and counted her heart-beats. Sixty-four, sixty-five, sixty-six... Only sixty-nine beats per minute! Coral was nowhere near scared enough! What did it mean? Did Coral secretly desire him? James mulled over this tantalising new bit of information.

"James, what in the hell do you think you're doing?" Antonia snapped angrily, bursting onto the scene.

She caught her breath. This was not part of her game plan.

"I haven't decided yet," James replied, his voice like satin-silk.

"Well I have! We need to teach Coral a lesson," Antonia rasped, her eyes like acid.

"Steady on Toni. You've had your fun. Let's leave it there," James replied, beginning to feel uneasy about the whole business.

"No we can't leave it there James! We've come this far. There's no going back now," Antonia replied, her eyes roving over Coral's lean androgynous frame. Then her gaze fixed on Coral's long Rapunzel hair and a sly smile danced across her red lips. "I know, let's stick her head in a rock-pool."

"Don't be crazy Toni. You've had your little joke. Let's just quit now whilst we're ahead," James said calmly, trying to defuse the situation.

"No way!" Antonia shouted angrily, eaten up with jealousy.

James leant forwards and whispered in Coral's ear…

"Just tell Toni you're sorry Coral and she'll calm down."

"I've done nothing wrong to say sorry for," Coral protested.

"Just because you haven't done anything wrong **yet** doesn't mean that you won't in the future," Antonia said viciously.

"This is crazy! James, tell Antonia to back off," Coral pleaded. Why was this happening? It shouldn't be happening. On every logical level it made no sense. There was no reason for any of this. She had no desire to come between James and Antonia.

"Say you're sorry Coral and Antonia will back off," James whispered again.

"I'm not saying sorry for something I haven't done!" Coral replied stubbornly.

Principles weren't principles if you caved in at the first test.

"Then I can't help you Coral. My hands are tied," James replied, gently letting go of her hair.

"But why James? Why are you doing this? I don't understand…" Coral repeated, her velvet eyes boring into his.

"Ask you mother," James replied, his voice as cold as steel.

Visions of his wrecked black Vespa flashed before his eyes. Coral's mother had accidentally knocked over his brand-new scooter whilst trying to park her Citroen ZX. Pathetic! They were both pathetic. Both mother and daughter deserved all they got.

"Please James - show some mercy - doesn't our past mean anything to you?" Coral asked, speaking plainly. *Let the truth be out. The truth couldn't hurt her.*

"We're ancient history. The past is dead Coral. **Dead.** Do you understand me? Your sweetness can't save you now."

"Please James. I don't deserve this!"

"I know you don't," James murmured, succumbing once more to those fraught blue eyes.

Then a battle roar as Antonia lost her patience with the pair of them and charged forwards, daisy-tread boots at the ready.

"Get out of my way James, she's all mine!"

"Toni no!"

The soles of boots are never gentle…

Antonia's metal toe-caps pressed down hard on Coral's face. Angular muscles moved in for the kill. Then a volley of machine-gun voices peppered the air as Kim and then Tom joined in the mob violence. More kicks - a pair of black converses - brand-new blue flip-flops - then one last kick from those candyfloss pink boots.

Warm blood trickled down the back of Coral's throat.

The soles of boots are absolute.

As Coral lay flat on her back in the sand, dazed, she knew that James was right and that she had been fighting a losing battle since her birth. The battle lines had been drawn the moment her parents had named her after the Australian Barrier Reef and proceeded to teach her the difference between a vertebrate and an invertebrate whilst all the other kids at Nursery School were posting plastic shapes through colour-coded slots. She never went to Nursery School. As for triangles and octagons, she had had to figure them out for herself.

But Hazel had taught her about stigmas and stamens, about sharp serrated edges and delicate pinnatifid edges, about truncate forms and tripartite forms, about porous limestone and impermeable millstone grit. And John had taken her to Arkwright's Mill in Derbyshire and narrated to her the history of the Industrial Revolution. Together they took a ride on a one hundred year old barge along the River Thames and saw London from a seafaring man's perspective, in the same way that Mark Twain experienced nineteenth century America via the conduit of the Mississippi.

Coral had learnt a huge amount about her industrial and natural heritage from both her parents. But the school playground with its secret rules had remained a mystery to her.

A volley of pebbles rent the air. James was flung backwards. His back hit the stone-stile with an ear-splitting crack. He dropped to the ground and lay on the sand beside Coral, knocked out cold.

Antonia screamed and charged forwards to protect James. The next moment she was hoisted into the air by invisible arms. She crashed down beside James. Blood spilled from her lower lip.

"Let go of me!" Kim screamed hysterically as delicate thumbs now pressed into the soft insides of her elbows and lifted her up, up, into the air before depositing her gently on the forest floor.

Kim slumped back against an oak tree in a state of shock. She stared numbly at the woodland floor, her new blue flip-flops stained a dirty brown. Seconds later Tom sprinted up to her side, his face ashen.

"Get up Kim! You've got to get out of here! It's not safe!" Tom shouted hoarsely, pulling her roughly to her feet. "Go! Make straight for Hartland Abbey. You'll be safe there. I'm going back to help the others."

"No. I'm not leaving you like I did last time! I'm not making the same mistake twice," Kim replied stubbornly, her plain features suddenly dancing with energy and life.

Tom sighed. He removed a speck of moss from the tip of Kim's freckled nose and smiled at her lovingly.

"OK Kim. Wait by the silver-birch trees. But be ready to run. I don't want you getting hurt unnecessarily. Promise?"

"I promise."

Tom nodded and turned back towards the beach.

"Be careful!" Kim called after him, watching as his slim albino frame leapt over the stone stile to merge with the white sand.

But Tom did not get a chance to be careful. The moment his feet landed on the soft sand, invisible hands seized his right arm and bent it behind his back in an arm-lock. Pain coursed through his shoulder like an electric current. He clamped his jaws shut, refusing to cry out in pain. Then he took a deep breath and addressed his invisible assailant.

"I won't fight you. I came here to help the others, not to fight."

The invisible hand let go. Tom spun round on the balls of his feet and stared at the thin air. Then he turned in terror and fled back up into Hartland Wood. James and Antonia would have to fend for themselves.

Ten minutes later Tom and Kim flung themselves down by the duck pond in the private grounds of Hartland Abbey. Waves of nausea washed over Tom. He thrust his injured arm into the ice-cold water of the pond and waited for numbness to take hold. Why hadn't they stayed in Bude all day shopping? If they had stayed in Bude, none of this would have happened. He withdrew his arm then rolled onto his back.

Kim smiled weakly and knelt down beside him. Then her eyes alighted upon a patch of daisies growing by the water's edge. She stooped forwards and plucked a handful of the dainty white flowers with their pale-pink rims, deciding to make Tom a daisy-chain to cheer him up.

Meanwhile on Hartland Beach Antonia bent over James desperately trying to revive him. His pulse was weak. She prised open his mouth and blew several times into his mouth. *Why didn't they teach First Aid in school?* She stopped blowing and clamped his jaw shut. She felt both his temples. Did he have a blood-clot? She didn't have a clue what to do!

"Wake up James!" Antonia shouted, slapping him across both cheeks.

"Ouch, stop that! What are you trying to do woman, kill me?" James muttered thickly, opening his eyes and glaring at Antonia, the brown iris of his left eye ringed with red from a burst blood-vessel.

"You're conscious! Why didn't you tell me you were conscious?"

"Because I wasn't until just now," James replied, rolling onto his side to ease the pain in his back and neck. Then he noticed Antonia's bleeding bottom lip and leant forward to take a closer look. "Give me your tissue," he said brusquely.

"What for?"

"I said give me your tissue!"

He snatched the pink tissue from Antonia's hand and pressed it against her cut lip. Then he removed the tissue and examined the amount of blood that was soaked into the paper. He screwed the tissue up into a ball and tossed it aside.

"You'll live," he said dully.

"Are you OK?" Antonia asked softly, her thick brows furrowed in concern.

"No, I'm not bloody OK Toni! Do I look OK? I've just had the crap kicked out of me."

"You ought to go to hospital James. You might have internal bleeding."

"Stop exaggerating."

"I'm not exaggerating. I heard your back go crack."

"Whatever. I'm not going to hospital."

"But you **need** an x-ray."

"No I don't need an x-ray! I just need to be left in peace!"

"But…"

"Drop it Toni. I can't go to hospital because I would have to tell them that I've just been in a fight and they'd want to know who with."

"Not necessarily."

"The police would."

"Then tell them the truth."

"What tell them I've been in a fight with an invisible man? Are you serious? They'll think I'm mad."

"No they won't. They'll just think you're suffering from concussion."

James glowered. Antonia glowered back at him, too angry to speak. Then she turned her back on him and began to check her arms and legs for more cuts. Apart from the cut on her bottom lip and some grit in her hair, she appeared to have got off pretty lightly. Then she noticed the splodge of red clay on her white bikini and let out a scream.

"My bikini! It's ruined!"

"Buy another one."

"I don't want to buy another one. It's from Joe Brown's, Limited Edition. Do you think it would be OK if I bleach it white again? Or will the bleach stain the bikini a horrible off-white?"

"How should I know? Forget the bikini. It's your hair that needs seeing to. It needs conditioning. It's tough as old boots, unlike Coral's."

Antonia's cheeks flushed crimson. Then she remembered the fact that James had just received a blow to the head and persuaded herself that it was just the concussion talking and that James did not really mean what he had just said.

"What do you think happened just now?" Antonia asked cautiously.

"The same thing that happened yesterday! We were attacked by some kind of ghost," James replied grimly.

Then he suddenly remembered Coral and stood up. He scanned the beach and drew a blank.

"Where's Coral?" he asked, lips taut.

"Coral? Why do you care where she is?" Antonia said jealously.

"I don't **care** about her! At least not in the way you think I do. But I do **care** where she is right now. She **ought** to be lying somewhere unconscious on the beach only I can't see her body anywhere."

"Rubbish. Of course Coral is on the beach. Like I said, you need to go hospital, you're not thinking straight," Antonia replied, scanning the beach, fully expecting to see Coral.

Antonia's eyes travelled along the smooth white sand-bank up to the pebble ridge, then on to the patchwork of pine, birch and ash that marked the perimeter of Hartland Wood. She started with surprise. There was no trace of Coral. James was right. Coral was nowhere in sight! Her body had totally disappeared!

A ray of sunlight glanced upon Coral's silver filigree pendant lying in the sand a few feet away from them at the tide-line. Antonia scooped up the necklace and spun the filigree orb round and round in the palm of her hand.

"He must have taken Coral with him," Antonia said slowly, closing her palm over the precious necklace.

"Taken her where?" James asked, standing up and roughly prising open Antonia's hand.

Ah yes! Coral's antique filigree necklace! He hadn't seen that in a while. It had a lot more class than Antonia's cheap costume jewellery.

"To the beach-hut of course," Antonia replied, opening the clasp of the silver necklace intending to wear it herself.

"I'll have that Toni. It doesn't belong to you," James said, snatching the necklace out of her hands.

"It doesn't belong to you either!"

"I have plans for it."

"What kind of plans?"

"I haven't decided yet. But I'll tell you when I have," he replied, popping the pendant into the back pocket of his jeans.

Then James walked slowly up the beach towards the Liberty. He walked stiffly, his body bruised and raw. He paused and slowly bent down to inspect the interior of the boat. Just as he suspected: one hand-made fishing-net plus tiny fragments of clay-pipe. He picked up the clay pieces and slipped them into his back pocket. Then a new thought crossed his mind; a sly smile stole across his sandblasted lips. He retreated quietly, a smug look on his face.

"What is it James?" Antonia asked suspiciously.

"Nothing a flick of a match can't handle…"

"You can't be serious James! You can't set fire to the beach-hut!" Antonia exclaimed, appalled. "That's arson. You could kill some-one."

"You can't kill a man twice," James replied.

"But what about Coral?" Antonia demanded, horrified.

"What about her? I thought you hated her guts."

"I do. But I don't want her dead!"

Antonia's jaw dropped open, lost for words. It must be that bump to the head. James definitely wasn't thinking straight.

"You wanted her dead a moment ago."

"No I didn't! I was just jealous, that's all!"

James leant forwards and kissed her full on the lips. Antonia pushed him away, repelled by his black thoughts.

"James, promise me that you won't set fire to the beach-hut!"

He drew out the silver necklace from his back pocket and fingered the filigree orb pensively.

"James? Are you listening to me? James, say something!"

But James had no intention of saying anything. Instead he gazed at Antonia with dull expressionless eyes. Then he leant forwards and kissed her violently.

Reluctantly Antonia returned his greedy kiss - anything to distract herself from his repellent thoughts - anything to make-belief that none of this was really happening.

CHAPTER FOUR

Picking Up The Pieces

Jem carried Coral over the threshold into his modest home and gently deposited her on his metal bed. The cowardice of the attack angered him more than the actual injuries Coral had sustained.

What hadst the young hooligans been thinking of? Hadst they been thinking at all? T'was worse than the Axbridge bull-baiting!

Coral let out a low moan. Jem rushed over to her bedside.

"Coral, canst thou hear me?"

She did not reply. Her eyelashes flickered momentarily then she rolled over onto her side and lay quite still, her eyes shut, her face masked by the ornate tubular bed-frame.

Jem glanced down at her blood-stained clothing and sprang into action. *He had to clean her wounds.* He cupped the back of her neck and rolled her gently onto her back. Then he lowered her head into the centre of the soft goose-down pillow. He delicately removed his trapped fingers out from beneath her hair. Her eyelids flickered momentarily, a pocket of air caught in the back of her throat and her lips parted as if she were about to say something… Then her lips closed and her breathing returned to a gentle even rhythm.

Jem grabbed a china pitcher from the sideboard and hurried outside to fetch some fresh water. The water-butt was located in the narrow gap between the cliff-face and the back of the beach-hut, well out of view from the public eye but in a good position to collect rainwater. It consisted of a tin-drum onto which Jem had soldered a metal drinking-spout and tap.

He quickly filled the pitcher then hastened back inside. He emptied the water into a porcelain bowl on the free-standing marble wash-stand then hurried back outside to fetch more water. Once the bowl in the wash-stand was three-quarters full, he added four drops of liquid soapwort and whipped the whole lot up into a pale pink froth with his fanned fingers. He frowned, his tulip-shaped brows knotted in concentration.

Hadst he added too much soapwort? If the mixture were too strong it would inflame Coral's cheeks further. But if the mixture were too weak infection would take hold. He had made the soapwort strictly according to Mother's Recipe: "Mix one bushel of freshly picked soapwort flowers and half a pint of boiled water. Allow to steep for two weeks. Add a teaspoonful of rosemary tincture and use sparingly."

The tiny soapwort plant grew in the local hedgerows. It flowered in early July and carried a pungent raspberry scent. Every summer Jem picked the flowers and judiciously followed Mother's recipe. The latter dated from the thirteenth century.

According to Mother, spice merchants from the Mediterranean used to stop off at Hartland Point before making their way overland first to Hartland Abbey and thereafter to

Glastonbury Abbey. The English medieval monks were famous for their remedies. They also had a reputation for driving a hard bargain! The foreign merchants had to be on their toes!

A whole panoply of goods were bought and sold with much hand gesticulation and long pauses. The English monks sold herbs from the Abbey gardens, including wild ransom, soapwort, bloodwort and chamomile flowers. The Mediterranean merchants in turn traded Egyptian sea-salt from the Marmluks of the Upper Nile, silk from the Levant, spices from Constantinople and bottles of ink extracted from the 'Purpura' sea-mollusc.

Purpura ink was much sought-after in England and used in the dyeing of cloth. The newly upwardly-mobile knights liked their wives to be seen in the new colour purple: the colour announced that they had made it! It was also a lot safer to wear than black cloth which was achieved via a mixture of various plant dyes, with the addition of mercury, the fumes of which made a man permanently light-headed!

Jem dipped a sea-sponge into the basin of pale pink soapwort and carefully cleansed Coral's face with the lotion. There was no way of telling if the liquid stung Coral's cheeks but he had faith in the ancient herbal remedy.

Then he took a deep breath and studied Coral's face critically. Sand and grit was embedded in the roots of her hair. Traces of grit had spilled out onto her cheeks. He drew her hair back from her forehead so that he could get a closer look at her eyes. The left eyelid looked very sore and puffy. There was a deep gash beneath her left eye. He steadied his hand and delicately removed all the grit and dirt from the pitted daisy-tread wound. The gash looked ominously deep and continued to seep blood. He quickly hurried over to his medicine chest and took out a small glass vial containing home-made bloodwort tincture. He pulled out the cork stopper and added a few drops of precious bloodwort to some wadding. Then he applied the wadding directly to the deep cut under her left eye. He pressed down firmly and counted to fifty. Then he let go of the wadding.

The material remained adhered to her skin as he had hoped. He relaxed a little, comforted by the knowledge that the ancient cure had treated Richard the Lionheart's Christian Crusaders and Saladin's Islamic warriors alike.

He now turned his attention to the rest of Coral's battered body. Her knees were cut in several places and her fore-arms were a bright red from being trampled upon repeatedly. Soon the red patches on her arms and legs wouldst turn into angry blue bruises!

However her face was the part of her body most badly affected. The bridge of flesh connecting her lower left eyelid and cheekbone wouldst soon swell up into a mountainous ridge but provided he hadst succeeded in getting all the dirt out, the swelling would go down in time and the wounds heal. To this end, Jem placed two fresh squares of cotton-wool soaked in witch-hazel on top of Coral's eyelids.

He decided to leave the rest of her face to air dry. Then he sank back into his father's wing-back chair and shut his eyes, exhausted both physically and mentally by the whole ordeal.

The carriage clock ticked away on the mantelpiece, reminding Jem that his work was not over yet. He had one last difficult job to do, one that he wanted to avoid but which he knew he must not shirk from doing. He hadst to remove Coral's white cotton top. He recoiled at the thought but he knew that if he did not remove Coral's top and swab her stomach wounds, she might die from blood-poisoning.

The clock chimed the quarter-hour. Jem reluctantly opened his eyes and squinted at the strange item of clothing that Coral was wearing, trying to figure out how best to remove it.

Fashion was impossible. Women seemed to conspire to make life as difficult for men as possible. The whale-bone corsets that Mother used to wear hadst always been a mystery to him and Emmie's light-weight girdles hadst taken her half an hour to get in and out of. But at least it was obvious where to tie and untie a corset whereas this strange top of Coral's had no obvious signs of buttons, zips or any other fastenings.

He stared blankly at the scrap of white cotton stained with red daisy-tread marks. *Didst the top do up at the back like one of Flossie's cotton smocks?*

The more he searched for clues, the more the red petals seemed to jeer at him, rejoicing in Coral's injuries.

Suddenly an arrow of anger shot through Jem and he whipped out his penknife and cut a slit across the centre of the blood-stained top. He removed the cotton material, exposing Coral's torso. She was not wearing a bra. Shocked, Jem shut his eyes. Then with his eyes averted, he carefully ran a clean sea-sponge across her stomach.

He examined the sponge for fresh blood and was relieved to find that it was stained with sand and grit. The blood that had soaked into the white top must belong to one of the other teenagers but not Coral.

Encouraged by this discovery, Jem sneaked a look at Coral's stomach. The skin was a smooth yellowy-white. He screwed up his eyes again, still deeply embarrassed. Then he counted to five in his head and forced himself to look at the rest of her torso. There was an open wound in the inside of her arm-pit where she had been kicked repeatedly.

Annoyed with himself for not having noticed the wound earlier, he quickly jumped up and got some more cotton-wool and some bandages from the sideboard. He packed Coral's arm-pit with cotton-wool soaked in bloodwort. Then he bound her shoulder and the topmost part of her arm in plaster-strip, winding the plaster round and round until she looked like an Egyptian Mummy. He took a step back and assessed his handiwork. *He couldst do no more on the surgical front. Now he hadst to find her some clothes to wear!*

After much rummaging inside his mother's old laundry trunk, Jem dug out a white dress-shirt that he used to wear to church on the Sabbath. The garment was nearly two hundred years old but was still in good condition even if it did smell a bit musty.

He approached Coral's bedside, the dress-shirt held fast in his heavy hands. He screwed up his eyes and by touch alone succeeded in passing Coral's arms through the rolled up aperture of each sleeve. He quickly drew the shirt flaps loosely across her stomach. Then with his eyelashes parted a few millimetres, he carefully slotted the fragile bone-buttons in place. He had to pause every few minutes to stop his hands from shaking. Finally he collapsed back into the armchair and emitted a great sigh of relief. *Thank Goodness that was all over with!*

He mopped his brow, drenched in sweat. His whole body ached. The wear and tear of two centuries spent pounding the beaches in all weathers had left its mark. Not to mention the exertions of the past two days. He shut his eyes and allowed sleep to envelope him.

The carriage-clock sounded seven in the evening. Jem woke with a start, starving. His stomach rumbled. He had not eaten anything since breakfast. He hauled his aching limbs out of Father's chair and plodded into the kitchen to get some food.

He unhooked some mackerel from the smoking-rack and flung the fish onto a china plate along with a wedge of bread. He grabbed a couple of carrots and expertly scraped the outer skin off with his pocket-knife. Then he sat back down in front of the wood-burner and bit into a stick of raw carrot. The sweet taste of fresh carrot immediately revived him. The natural sugars gave him an instant boost of much needed energy. Then he took several bites of bread and shovelled a huge lump of mackerel into his mouth, not caring if he swallowed any bones. That was the one benefit of being immortal. *He didst not risk choking to death on a fish-bone!*

He smiled fondly, remembering Mother's puddings. *How he missed Mother's cooking!* Especially Mother's fresh egg custard! But his all-time favourite was Summer Pudding - a pyramid of white bread soaked in a rich berry sauce and filled with strawberries, redcurrants, black-currants and any other berry that Mother couldst get her hands on.

Nowadays his diet consisted mostly of seasonal vegetables and fish. However it was getting increasingly hard to catch the fish with a line anymore. Massive scallop dredgers guzzled up everything that lay in their path, including the delicate coral and tube beds around Lundy Island, home to seahorses, lobsters and young fry. He used to love watching the sea-otters dive amongst the tube beds but nowadays they remained inland, rarely venturing out to sea.

Jem tore off another chunk of white bread, enjoying the gooey uncooked texture. Every Saturday he sneaked into Hartland Bakery and took a loaf straight out of Mrs Mac. Mahon's bread-oven, ten minutes before it was due to come out. He would have liked to have paid Mrs Mac. Mahon for her efforts but he simply did not have the money. There weren't any jobs going for **his kind**.

However he always left some freshly caught mackerel or Atlantic cod on the front doorstep as payment. Mrs Mac. Mahon seemed happy enough with her mysterious fishy gifts. Indeed, Jem had the distinct impression that she always baked an extra large loaf on Saturday especially for him.

Jem finished his meal and reflected on all that had happened. He could not help but think that if Antonia and her friends spent more time with their families and did regular jobs about the house, then they might not feel the urge to go looking for innocent victims like Coral to pick on in order to relieve their boredom.

He glanced across to the bookshelf where he kept Father's set of clay pipes. Now the skill in making a clay pipe would keep a clever lad like Tom out of mischief for hours. Then there were Mother's embroidery squares. He couldst not picture Antonia with a needle and thread but he could see her polishing her pink boots the old-fashioned way with spit and shine!

He glanced across at his side table with its spindle legs. Wood-turning! Now there another art. How many people these days knew how to make a wheel? Jem knew that civilisation was in trouble when grown-men had forgotten how to make a simple wooden wheel. Get fourteen and fifteen year old lads learning the wheelwright's art and then there would be something for everyone to cheer about! All that young people needed was the chance to master an interesting and useful skill and the world couldst easily be set to rights! And with wood-turning the sky was the limit. The lads couldst learn to make their own transportation and amusement - beach buggies, go-carts, snooker tables, canoes, rowing boats, bows - there was no limit to the scope of the imagination.

Jem's gaze alighted on the clay bowl in the centre of the low coffee table containing some dried honesty-seeds.

Honesty: now that was another ingredient that was thin on the ground these days. The black and white silvery seed-pods reminded him of Emmie's sharp black eyes, always urging him to be truthful: "Always tell the truth Jem. It's the only way to be happy. Mother says so."

A leather-bound bible lay on the edge of the table. A stem of pink thrift peaked out from between its well-thumbed covers. Flossie had picked the summer sea-flower two centuries ago. *Thrift truly did last forever!*

Jem smiled, remembering his childhood. The highlight of the week used to be the family bath. It was the one day of the week that could be guaranteed to end in laughter. Father went first, then elder brothers Edward, Zackary, Jacob, Tom and Charlie. Then it was **his** turn. Then came the girls in strict order of age: eldest sister Emmie, then Catherine, Lizzie, Hannah, Jane, and last but by no means least, Flossie, the baby of the family. By the time Flossie had finished her bath, the whole building was a hot house of steam and the sound of everyone laughing couldst be heard all the way to Hartland light-house and back. *Those were happy days! If only they couldst have gone on forever. But time does not stand still.*

A wave of sadness overcame him. He bit his bottom lip as he remembered the day of his death. It had been just another ordinary October day. *But the day had turned out all wrong. Everything had been wrong ever since. He had made just one tiny mistake and now he was paying for that mistake a hundred times over!*

Jem sprang to his feet seized by a sudden fear that everything might go wrong with Coral too. He drew back her sleeve and pressed his thumb on the veins of her wrist. He began to count her heart-beats. Her pulse was a stable sixty-seven beats per minute. He relaxed. *Coral was going to be alright. He must not let his morbid imagination get the better of him. It was unmanly.* Then he looked down at Coral and delicately stroked her moon-shaped cheeks. *Everything was going to be alright.*

A week passed. There was no discernible change in Coral's condition. Jem spent hour after hour at her bedside trickling water from a teaspoon into the corner of her mouth in order to keep her hydrated. She was able to swallow and she could open her lips of her own accord. But she had not yet spoken. Her body was able to function in a mechanical way but her mind was some place else.

Physically, she still looked dreadful. Her eyelids remained swollen like two inflated puffer-fish. An angry daisy-shaped bruise glowered at him from beneath her left eye. But the swelling was gradually going down. She was getting better gradually.

Time was the answer. Time alone couldst heal her.

A second week passed. Coral continued to slip in and out of consciousness. Sometimes her ribbon-like fingers would clutch the edge of the cotton sheets and she would tug at them fretfully. At other times she would kick the metal foot-board with the soles of her feet as if fighting off an imaginary assailant. Jem remained at her bedside keeping constant vigil. Fortunately he was of a patient disposition and had a wealth of experience to draw upon. Flossie had been in bed for nine weeks with scarlet fever one winter. But pugnacious Flossie had fought back famously, shouting through her delirium, her brows puckered and her fists screwed like a mad march hare! Jem felt certain that Coral, like Flossie, would fight her way back to a full recovery. The only thing that troubled him was the fact that Coral's family did not know what had happened to her.

But how couldst he contact the police? He couldst not risk anyone finding out that he lived in Hartland Cove. The isolated beach-hut was his **home** and he meant to stay there as long as he could, even if that did mean temporarily keeping Coral's family in the dark as to her whereabouts.

Of course had Jem known about the wild speculation in the newspapers and its adverse effect on Hazel, he might have acted differently. But Jem did not know about the spurious press reports for the simple reason that he did not read the tabloid newspapers. And having been born in a century when large families were the norm, Jem did not suspect for one moment that Coral was an only child and Hazel a single-mother. Instead Jem persuaded himself that Coral's large extended family was plenty capable of riding out the storm of separation and that everything would come good in the end.

The truth was the polar opposite. After a week of sleepless nights, Hazel sank into a deep malaise unable to comprehend Coral's decision to leave home without warning.

Hazel stubbornly refused to consider foul play or an accident. As far as she was concerned Coral was far too strong a swimmer to have come to grief swimming in the bay and far too agile to have fallen whilst rock-climbing.

And as Coral was the sweetest, gentlest creature alive, how could anyone possibly have harmed her?

The idea of abduction was simply too painful a scenario for Hazel to consider.

She rejected the idea, burying it deep in the frosted ground along with all the other unpleasant aspects of modern life that she disliked. In many ways Hazel was not so very different from Jem.

Finally Hazel's spirit snapped like the brittle branch of a young plum tree that has been burdened by too heavy a crop of plums. Hazel concluded that if Coral had left home, she had done so out of choice. The fault must therefore rest squarely on her own failings as a mother!

Hazel berated herself again and again for having uprooted Coral. If they had only remained in Sheffield things might have turned out differently. Coral would have developed a network of friends her own age instead of having to make do with the Exmoor ponies as her main companions.

The fact that not one school-friend had come to Shell Cottage to enquire about Coral, struck Hazel as distinctly odd.

Coral really had been an island unto herself. She had evolved to suit her environment. *But now, in a totally new environment, how would Coral cope? How would she deal with the unfamiliar and the unknown?*

CHAPTER FIVE

Storm Clouds

The hunt for 'the Runaway Devon School Girl' gathered momentum. Every time Hazel stepped outside the front door of Shell Cottage, she was blinded by flash bulbs and questioned by journalists, hungry for the latest sound-bite. Hazel pursed her lips and said nothing.

Her walk to work became a nightmare of sharp elbows and intrusive zoom lenses. Twice she stumbled and fell. Twice she recovered herself and escaped across the bell-heather to The Good Earth Café, sneaking in through the back-door to seek comfort in a plate of chocolate brownies.

At home in the evenings, the world stood still. Hazel sat motionless on the edge of Coral's bed, staring at the brightly coloured walls with their complex collage of posters, paintings and magazine cuttings. The coloured patchwork pictures became the only meaningful things in Hazel's life.

A photograph of a young woman with a bec-hive bun, blowing bubbles, greeted Hazel every time she entered Coral's bedroom. The model was wearing a short pink dress with a stiff hoop hem. In the adjacent picture, a model with her hair twisted up into the shape of the words 'Miss Dior Cherie' gazed directly at the lens. On closer inspection the hair turned out to be made of twirls of twisted paper.

A large magazine poster of the Lacoste crocodile with its tail upturned jauntily had the caption: "un peu de air sur terre" - "a little air on the ground." The crocodile was hemmed in on all four sides by surfing postcards featuring the latest board design. Tickets from numerous surfing events had been stuck to the edge of the skirting-board making a paper border. One ticket read: Surf Village, Rip Curl Board Masters, Fistral Beach, 2008. But the postcard that intrigued Hazel the most and best summed up Coral was a photograph of a wall of water with a surfer riding his board inside the curled wave. Like the surfer, Coral was a day-devil through and through. The question was this: where had her adventurous nature taken her?

After a fortnight of machine-gun questions, the press battalions tired of the Missing Devon School Girl story and headed east to report on the MPs' Expenses Scandal at Westminster. Alone at last, Hazel ventured out onto the verandah and sat down in John's old wicker chair. She drew a moth-eaten woollen blanket over her knees and kept watch, hoping against hope that Coral would return across the dusky heath.

Her solemn grey eyes tracked the horse-shoe bats as they wheeled across the hedgerows catching midges on the wing. At each downwards swoop she caught her breath, imagining that Coral was seated next to her, sharing the nocturnal spectacle.

Come midnight Hazel tiptoed back indoors. The floorboards creaked as she picked her way past the flotsam of abandoned coffee cups, old newspapers and plates of half-eaten biscuits. Food turned to ash in her mouth. She ceased to eat.

Then as the fourth week of Coral's disappearance commenced, Hazel withdrew from the world entirely. She took one last early morning walk across the heath to Hartland Village and stuck a sign up in the window of The Good Earth saying "Closed until Further Notice." She walked back home, unplugged her PC and let the battery of her mobile phone wind down. Then she lay down on Coral's bed and curled up tight in a ball, seeking refuge in her memories.

Over at Montcliffe Manor, the news of Coral's continued disappearance threw Tom, Kim, James and Antonia into total disarray. What on earth had happened to Coral?

Had her unconscious body been washed out to sea by the high tide? Or was James correct in thinking that the mysterious occupant of the beach-hut had abducted her and was currently holding her captive before planning his revenge against them all? The thought made their blood run cold.

Not one of them dared go to the police. How could they? The last thing they wanted was to end up in court charged with grievous bodily harm even if Antonia's father was a successful London barrister.

Sick of the wild speculation, Antonia called a Council of War. They needed an alibi. It was unanimously agreed that they had all spent the day of Coral's disappearance at Sudbury Court attending a swimming pool 'gathering.' Sudbury Court was owned by Antonia's grandmother, Lady Hortensia. The latter was currently holidaying in Portugal. No-one except Sudbury Court's resident Siamese cats could challenge the group's alibi, an unlikely outcome given that cats can't talk. Antonia was currently charged with feeding both felines twice a day whilst Lady Hortensia pursued the serious business of acquiring a full-body tan. The swimming-pool party idea was fool-proof.

However, the boys did not get off so lightly. Tom's mother, furious with him for having got involved in a brawl resulting in two black eyes, soon packed him off to his aunt's in Cirencester where he was forced to spend every day lugging her croquet equipment from match to match, between shifts of pouring tea and serving watercress sandwiches to women with Botox-eyes and jaws like piranhas. His aunt was President of the Cheltenham Ladies Croquet Guild and did not take 'no' for an answer.

James got off more lightly than Tom. He was grounded for a month and forced to have a private Maths tutor. His parents had been wondering how they were going to force him to study in view of his lousy GCSE results. His 'fight' with Tom had given them all the ammunition they needed to lay down the law. Meanwhile Antonia arrived at his house every afternoon and followed him about like an irritating horsefly. Antonia had not forgotten his threat to burn the beach-hut to the ground.

Kim, by contrast, needed no injunction to self-correct. She stayed upstairs in her bedroom for week after week sobbing her heart out, unable to get the memory of Coral's punch-drunk body out of her mind.

Then just when Kim thought she had no more tears left inside her, the enormity of what she had done overwhelmed her all over again. It didn't matter how hard she cried or how tightly she cuddled her thirteen year old teddy-bear Dunlop to her chest, she simply could not get the memory of that dreadful beating out of her mind. Every time she shut her eyes, she saw Coral's face, blood streaming from her crushed nostrils, her hair a tangled mess of sand, stones, grit and spit. And to think it had all started off so innocently with a trip to Bude to go shopping with Tom! How could things go so badly wrong?

CHAPTER SIX

Lavender Fields

September arrived. The schools went back and the weather improved. The blackberries swelled on their stalks, ready for picking. The ripe elderberries glistened on their fragile stalks like black diamonds. Huge garlands of delicate Old Man's Beard draped themselves over the hedgerows, their fluffy white seed-heads creating a snowy spectacle. On Docton Moor, the purple heather faded and the bilberry bushes died back. A sombre palette of dull beiges and browns delineated the bleak, bone-dry heath.

The swallows began to gather in communal clusters on the telegraph cables, getting ready for their great flight south. The young birds still chased each other energetically round and round the eaves of the pretty thatched cottages. The countryside held its breath, waiting for the leaves to change from modest green to golden-brown and finally a vivid red.

Meanwhile Coral underwent a spectacular transformation of her own. The angry bruises on her arms and legs gave way to smudges of pale ochre and warm honey-browns. She remained totally dependent on Jem for all her daily needs but she ate and drank as instructed, responding to Jem's simple commands whilst still half-asleep. She used his china chamber-pot as directed but without murmuring a word. She sensed her way forward like a blind desert mole-rat.

Jem now felt able to leave her bedside to attend to his daily chores. But come sunset, he returned to her beside and sat patiently beside her every evening. He did not talk. He did not feel the need to talk. As he stroked her hair, he was reminded of the faint smudge on the horizon that the old village folk used to call the will-o'-the-wisp. Coral seemed to him to be trapped inside an ethereal world of her imagination, close to him but not with him, like ignis fatuus, the flickering bluish flame seen over the Braunton marshes.

Then early one Tuesday morning, exactly five weeks after the attack, Jem got up early and got dressed in a white collarless Grandad shirt and braces, a pair of brown worsted trousers and his best check waistcoat. Then he set off through the woods for the Walled Garden at Hartland Abbey. He returned several hours later, his ruby cheeks aglow, cradling bunches of late flowering Dutch lavender.

Bursting with energy, he immediately set to work twisting the lavender sprigs about the tubular metal poles of Coral's head-board. His mother used to place a handkerchief sprinkled in lavender-water beneath Flossie's pillow every night to help her sleep. Jem secretly wished to prolong Coral's slumbers. He was terrified of having to explain to her why he had kept her hidden in Hartland Cove for such a long time. *But he couldst not bear the thought of her leaving him to go back to live with Hazel in Shell Cottage.* He draped one last sprig of lavender about Coral's goose-down pillow and retreated to the kitchen area.

Long garlands of pale pink hops were looped about the wooden rafters. A basket of loose pine-cones stood in pride of place in the middle of the kitchen table. A stack of dried logs in the corner gave off a musty woodland scent. Jem took a deep breath and inhaled the pungent aroma of pine-cone, lavender and wood. Then he lowered his head and set about polishing his black leather walking-boots.

Coral's nostrils flared. She smiled in her sleep, her head heavy with the scent of lavender perfume. Mile upon mile of lavender fields stretched out before her. The tapered flower-heads billowed in the breeze whilst Hazel and John sipped iced tea on the verandah of La Boheme, their dilapidated French farmhouse in the rolling lavender fields of Saint Etienne-les-Orgues in Haute Provence.

A curl of saliva dribbled out of the corner of Coral's mouth as she tasted once more those zingy lemon slices! Then the sharp crush of ice-crystals between her teeth as iced water flooded her palate.

Coral's eyes snapped open, expecting to see John's sunburnt cheeks and Hazel's sunbeam smile. But there was no Mum or Dad. Instead everything was an impenetrable black.

A spasm of fear shot through her. *Where was she?* She rapidly set about trying to make sense of her predicament. There **had** to be a logical reason why she couldn't see anything. There was **always** a logical explanation to explain everything. She prodded her eyes with her finger-tips and connected with cold wet fabric.

The bandage was soft and springy like wet moss but the skin underneath felt as tight as a kettle-drum. *Was she in hospital? It did not feel like an ordinary bandage…*

Coral lowered both hands and began to explore the bed-covers. The blanket was coarse to the touch, not soft and cosy like her familiar duvet. A stiff cotton sheet held her torso in place like a strait-jacket. The sheet smelt of French lavender - fields and fields of the stuff! Confused, she tentatively peeled back the edges of her bandage, trying to figure out what had happened to her. She couldn't remember a single thing.

"Don't fiddle with thine wadding," Jem remarked casually as he scrubbed away with a blacking brush, bringing his walking-boots to a brilliant shine.

Jem was used to the sight of Coral fiddling with her bandages in her sleep. He did not realise that she had regained full consciousness.

"Am I badly injured?" Coral asked.

Jem froze in the act of threading a boot-lace. Then he bounded across to her bedside, terrified and exhilarated at the same time.

"Thou hast woken up!" he exclaimed, his eyes lit like moonstones.

He placed his hand on the top sheet in his excitement. Then he withdrew his arm abruptly, realising that he had shoe-polish all over his hands. Black finger-marks criss-crossed the white sheet like a cat's dirty paw-prints.

"Don't move. I shalt get thee a cloth!" Jem exclaimed again, dashing over to the marble wash-stand.

"What's up?" Coral asked, wondering what all the fuss was about.

"I've got shoe-polish all over the sheet. Do not move or thou shalt get covered in blacking-polish."

Coral suppressed a laugh, more curious than ever. It was a strange sort of hospital that allowed its staff to polish their shoes whilst on duty. And this particular member of staff had a very peculiar way of speaking.

"Am I in hospital?" Coral asked, checking that she had interpreted her current situation properly.

"Er...no," Jem replied uncertainly.

"I knew it! The sheets don't smell right! They smell of lavender not of hospital antiseptic."

Coral hated hospitals. They reminded her of death.

"But if I'm **not** in hospital, then where am I?" Coral asked abruptly as the reality dawned on her that she was alone, injured, and at the mercy of a total stranger whom she knew absolutely nothing about.

"At home - my home," Jem replied hesitantly. "It's me - Jem. We met on the beach near Old Man's Elbow," he said softly, hurt that Coral had not recognised his voice.

A pang of guilt flared across Coral's chest. She racked her brains for clues. The name Jem meant nothing to her. There was a girl called Gemma in the Lower Sixth but she definitely didn't know any guys by the name of Jem.

"Sorry. I don't remember a thing. I must be suffering from amnesia. What's happened to me? Have I been in an accident?"

"Yes," Jem replied, his voice as soft as rush-grass. "I found thee unconscious on the beach so I took thee home and dressed thy wounds."

"You found me on the beach?" Coral repeated slowly. "What was I doing on the beach? Oh this is so infuriating! Why can't

I remember?" she exclaimed, thumping her mattress with her tight walnut fist.

"Careful, thou might hurt thyself!"

"Never mind that, I'm hurt already. Let me think. I must be able to remember something… One thing I do remember is eating fresh pineapple. **And** I remember walking across the moor and stopping to feed the inkpot ponies…"

Jem smiled at the expression inkpot ponies, already a little in love with Coral.

"Then what did I do? What happened after I fed the ponies? Damn! What's happened to my memory?"

"Don't fret, thy memory will return in time."

Coral frowned.

"Perhaps if you tell me a bit about yourself it will help jog my memory. You said something about Old Man's Elbow?"

A lump formed in the back of Jem's throat. He was not sure that he wanted to go back to their first meeting at Old Man's Elbow. That first meeting had gone awry. Coral had been suspicious of his motives and he had not helped his cause by staring at her gormlessly like a village idiot.

"We met close to the rock-pools. Thoust caught a crab."

"A crab?" Coral repeated, totally unable to recall the incident but interested all the same. "What kind of a crab?"

"A magnificent King Crab!" Jem said brightly, his eyes lighting up like stars.

Despite his outward seriousness, Jem's youthful exuberance bubbled away just beneath the surface, waiting to be tapped. And he never looked more boyish nor sounded more joyful than when talking about crabs, especially magnificent King Crabs with a girth the size of a dinner plate.

The old fisher-folk called the brick-red crustaceans King Crabs on account of their giant size. Jem grinned at Coral excitedly. *Nothing could beat wading about knee-deep in mud looking for King Crabs at low-tide!*

"A King Crab?" Coral queried. "Are you sure you mean a King Crab? *Paralithodes Camtschaticus*? Only they don't live in British waters. The water isn't cold enough for them. They live further north in the Bering Straits and in the Arctic Ocean. Perhaps you mean a Spiny Spider Crab? They're not dissimilar to King Crabs and can be found in British waters all summer long. Their legs are long, thin and knobbly, hence the name Spider Crab - *Maya Squinado* in Latin."

"I don't speak Latin. I left school at eight. But it was a huge crab, the biggest I've ever seen. In fact I was so shocked by its size that I exclaimed out-loud." Jem paused and looked down momentarily. He pressed his right thumb into his left palm. The criss-cross lines stared up at him, intimating all the paths that the conversation could take. He gulped nervously. "I'm afraid I startled thee, Coral. Thou were not well pleased with me," he confessed, his cheeks colouring.

Coral concentrated hard on visualising the scene. The dark water of the rock-pool slowly came back to her, its surface smooth and matt like a slab of unpolished slate.

"I remember now!" Coral exclaimed suddenly. "The crab was a real whopper - far bigger than I expected - its pincers were big enough to do a lot of damage."

"That's true enough," Jem agreed, nodding.

"And then what did I do?" Coral demanded eagerly.

Jem hesitated before replying, not wanting to embarrass Coral by mentioning the fact that he had overheard her talking to the crab.

Coral caught her breath, suddenly anxious.

"I didn't hurt the crab, did I? I did put the crab back into the rock-pool Jem? Jem, why aren't you saying anything?" Coral asked anxiously, her voice spiked with fear.

"Oh no thou didst not hurt the crab," Jem replied softly, seeking to reassure her. "On the contrary, thou thanked the crab for allowing thee to examine it. Then thou didst return it to the rock-pool."

"Thank goodness! I thought for a moment that I may have harmed it unintentionally. Promise me Jem that you won't hide anything from me. There's nothing I hate more than duplicity, especially little white lies designed to protect me."

"I promise," Jem solemnly replied, in total awe of her.

"Now tell me everything Jem," Coral said eagerly, shuffling forward on her mattress. "Tell me why you have bandaged my face up like an Egyptian Mummy."

Jem fell silent, not knowing how much he could or should tell her. Deep down he felt that it would be far better for Coral **not** to know the full details of the brutal beating. It would only give her nightmares and might give her reason to be bitter. Indeed the more he thought about it, the more he came to the conclusion that it was a good thing that she could not remember the attack.

Coral sensed his hesitation.

"Tell me the truth Jem. And don't tell me a gentler version of the truth just because it is easier to do so. I want to know the whole truth."

"I'm not sure that I can tell thee more than thou dost know already. Thou fed the inkpot ponies. Then I found thee on the beach," Jem replied, deciding to compromise and tell a half-lie.

Coral thought back to her walk across Docton Moor. She recalled the slight prickling sensation of the bell-heather scratching her ankles. She remembered racing through the field of golden king-cups towards the inkpot ponies. But she could not remember the beach.

Then a loud splash as the otter pups tumbled back into view. How could she have forgotten the four young otter pups in the beck, their white whiskers beaded with foam?

Time fast-forwarded. She was back standing at the top of Speke's Mouth Waterfall staring into the abyss. Then her hands alighted on the rope that led down to Speke's Mouth Cove. She lowered herself down, crab-like, then let go!

Now she was on the beach staring up Old Man's Elbow, taking off her sandals determined to climb it… And there was Jem, standing by the rock-pools, his broad shoulders set at perfect right-angles to the crystal blue sky. And there was the magnificent Spider Crab, its shell as hard as a policeman's helmet!

Then a splash of water and a burst of bright pink daisies.

Daisies?

Why could she remember daisies? Daisies don't grow on the beach.

Then Coral's hands began to tremble and her chest tightened as she remembered far more than she wanted to remember.

A line of silver-birches and lilac rhododendron flowers flickered into view. Antonia's daisy-tread boots appeared either side of the woodland path barring her way. A wall of pink daisies towered above them both, their delicate white petals dipped in blood.

Her blood.

Then the daisies grew and grew in size until they became one large conjoined flower. But instead of a single yellow centre there was one hard, diamond-studded fist.

Antonia's fist.

Then with an almighty effort Coral expelled the diamond-fist from her mind and embraced the lavender fields instead. The low mellifluous murmur of the honey bees came to her rescue, followed by the clink of her parents' glasses as they sipped iced tea on the verandah. Then the taste of zingy lemon flooded her gums and she vowed to think of lavender fields forever.

"It's OK Jem. You don't have to tell me what happened. I remember everything," Coral said faintly. "Thank you for finding me and for bringing me here. I don't know what I would have done without your help. You saved my life."

"It was the least that I could do," Jem replied, thankful that he would not have to relate to her all the grim details of the violent attack.

"How long have I been here?" Coral asked, trying to dispel the vision of the blood-rimmed daisy from her mind.

Jem swallowed. *This was the one question that he had feared above all else.*

"Five weeks and six days," he replied, bracing himself for a torrent of angry words.

"Six weeks?" Coral exclaimed incredulous. "Does Hazel know where I am?"

Jem nervously ran his hand through his burnished brown hair.

"I didst not know what to do Coral. I didst not know who to contact, I…"

"You mean Hazel doesn't know I'm here? Why in the hell didn't you telephone her?" Coral thundered angrily. "Hazel must be sick with worry, all on her own, wondering what's happened to me."

"I apologise. I didst not know that Hazel lives alone. And I do not have one of those newfangled telephones. So I did nothing. I didst not mean any harm, I didst not know Hazel lives alone," Jem repeated, distraught. "I didst not know what to do."

"Take these bandages off immediately. I'm going home now!" Coral said angrily, flinging back the bed-covers.

She swung her legs forwards, then froze, remembering that she couldn't see anything. She perched on the edge of the bed, her hands gripped tightly on the edge of the mattress as she deliberated what to do next.

"Please Coral, it's not as it seems. I couldst not tell anyone. It was impossible for me to tell anyone because I'm invisible," Jem blurted out unintentionally.

"Invisible? Now I've heard everything," Coral said sarcastically, starting to peel away the bandages from her face.

"But it's true. You're the only person that has ever been able to see me! No one else can."

"A likely story," Coral replied, her voice hard like burnished steel. Then she angrily began to tear away the top layer of gauze that covered her face.

"Careful! Thy skin is tender."

"Never mind my skin! I want to go home. You've no right to hold me here against my will. Damn it! Why don't these bandages come off? They're stuck to my eyes!"

"Please don't go Coral! Not until thou hast heard **my** story," Jem pleaded, grabbing hold of her forearms. "Careful, don't fight me! Thine eyesight is fragile!"

Coral's forehead collided with Jem's braced chest. She pushed upwards with her head, ramming the edge of her forehead into his solar plexus. Partially winded, he tensed his stomach muscles. Then he gritted his teeth and pushed her back down onto the mattress, his hands clamped round her wrists.

"Let go of me! You've no right to keep me here! I'm not interested in your ridiculous story!" Coral shouted, kicking with her legs.

But Jem pinned Coral to the mattress as surely as Coral herself had held the King Crab at her mercy.

"Please Coral, hear me out. I rescued thee from great danger! If thou didst but know what happened to thee!"

Coral froze, immediately suspicious.

"Rescued me? What from?" she demanded. "I thought you said you found me on the beach."

Jem tensed, Antonia's boot carved into the back of his mind. He grimaced as he saw Antonia raise her pink boot again and again, unrelenting in its monotony and its mechanical purpose. Then he loosened his hold on Coral's wrists, not wanting to hurt her.

"I'm sorry," Jem said softly.

"I said what did you rescue me from Jem?" Coral demanded, pushing upwards with all her strength.

"From the sea," Jem lied, reeling at the pinprick to his conscience. "Thou wouldst have been washed out to sea had I not found thee on the shore and brought thee here."

Then his jaw locked as he re-lived the attack. He watched again as Coral was kicked senseless, her attackers engaged in a collective act of frenzy that denied individual responsibility. Then he travelled back in time to Clevedon Pier and watched as Punchinello slammed Judy's carved head onto the wooden floor of the puppeteer's stage whilst the other children looked on, their eyes round.

Something in Jem's strained breathing and taut muscles struck home. Coral sensed that he had spoken from the heart. He may not have told her everything but he had told her enough for her to trust him.

"It's OK Jem. I won't fight you any more. And I won't take off my bandages until you tell me it's safe to do so. You don't need to tell me all that happened. I know enough."

"Dost thou really mean that?"

"Yes."

He gently let go of her wrists.

"Jem…"

"Yes Coral? What is it?"

Coral hesitated. There was a yearning in Jem's voice that reminded her of the harp seal pups calling to their mothers at dusk. It was a call that she could not ignore a moment longer.

"Tell me your story Jem. I promise to believe you, however far-fetched it may sound."

CHAPTER SEVEN

Jem's Story

Jem gathered his thoughts. How could he put into words what it was like to have been born in the eighteenth century? The world had changed so much since his youth. With every passing year he felt more and more adrift. Indeed sometimes he found himself sitting on the rocks at sunset wondering whether the human species had evolved beyond all recognition.

In 1800 the Hartland fishermen used to rise at dawn and return home at noon. The fish was gutted and filleted on the beach then sold as soon as it was landed. On Fridays a few enterprising fishermen took their catch as far afield as Twerton or Barnstaple fish markets where housewives paid for it 'on the nail.'

In times past, the people of Barnstaple were mighty proud of their nail. It was in fact not a nail at all but a wrought-iron plinth fashioned in the shape of an inverted cone, some three feet high and with a flat table-like top. It stood permanently in the market-place, the base of the cone embedded in the cobblestones. After a deal was struck, money was placed on the nail and the sale would be binding.

The Barnstaple nail was still there in the High Street sandwiched in between a Starbuck's Coffee-house and a Boston Tea-house. A Farmer's Market was still held in the square every Saturday but there was no longer a Fish Market on a Friday.

Nowadays most people walked past the nail without giving it a moment's glance. A few children tried to leapfrog over it, carrying on a childhood tradition that his mates would have been proud of.

Jem smiled proudly. *Children will be children whatever the century. And a mighty good thing that was too! It's the grown-ups that caused all the problems.*

And now the grown-ups had taken to going to sea in giant ships instead of small fishing-boats. The giant ships caught as many fish in one day as the entire Hartland fishing fleet of small boats used to catch in one year. But instead of the freshly caught fish going straight to market, the fish ended up in huge warehouses where it was frozen, packaged, and shipped abroad. The upshot of this topsy-turvy way of doing things was that local Hartland river-salmon ended up being sold in Canada whilst Canadian salmon was sold in Hartland. *It was a very odd way of doing things that would have confused Mother and Father no end.*

And the same topsy-turvy change had happened to farming! Where once the local hedgerows had echoed to the sound of men swinging scythes, there was now a lone tractor doing the job that ten men used to do. There was still a Summer Fayre with an Annual Sheep Run through the village but hardly anybody at the Fayre could be spotted wearing a jumper made from local

Exmoor sheep's wool. Instead people wore jumpers made out of Lycra and Rayon, man-made fibres derived from petroleum extracted from the Arabian Desert.

How could he explain so much change to Coral? It was impossible. And yet he wanted to tell Coral about his childhood, he really did.

"What's on your mind?" Coral said softly, sensing that something was wrong.

"Nothing and everything," Jem replied quietly.

"Try telling me about it."

"I don't know how to. It's so hard to know where to begin!"

"Begin at the beginning."

"That is easier said than done," Jem replied, images of children with pockets full of thistle-down looming before his eyes. "It's so hard to find the right words," he murmured, his voice taking on a dreamlike quality as he turned the luminous pages of his memory.

"Use the first words that spring to mind," Coral replied, her voice as soft as mulberry silk.

Time slipped seamlessly through the hour-glass of life. The grey gulls swooped low over the waves, hunting for fish. Jem smiled shyly at Coral. Then he took a deep breath, leant forwards in his chair and began.

"My name is James Franklin Havelock. I was born on August 10th, 1795, into a family of fisher-folk. I was nick-named Jem by my eldest sister Emmie."

Jem paused, expecting Coral to exclaim out-loud in disbelief, or at the very least to say something. But instead she was silent.

Encouraged, Jem leant back in his chair and listened to the sound of the sea lapping against the foreshore.

"Canst thou hear the sea Coral?"

"Yes," she replied softly.

"I have been listening to the sea for over two centuries Coral! Canst thou imagine how it feels to have been listening to the same song for so long?"

"I can't begin to imagine how you must feel," Coral replied truthfully.

Jem nodded. Then he rummaged in his pocket and pulled out a smooth round pebble. He caressed it tenderly with the underside of his thumb. The pebble was smooth and black, the size of a Victorian penny piece.

"I was born by the sea, Coral. I have lived by the sea all my life. I could ne'er be parted from it."

He looked down at the pebble and stared at it pensively. Then he drew the pebble to his mouth and kissed it as if he were trying to extract life itself from it.

"It's so hard Coral. I want to forget yet I cannot! I want to break free from the past but it is always within me! I want... I want too much Coral! I am selfish."

"No you're not selfish, Jem," Coral replied, her voice strong and resonant like a ship's bell. "You're just lonely."

Jem nodded. Then he continued with his story, his voice deep and sonorous, in tune with the sea.

"When I was eight years old I would sit on the foreshore with the other boys from the village making fishing-nets. We would make nets by day and skim pebbles at dusk. It was the closest thing to the divine I ever knew!"

Jem paused. Salt tears coursed down his sun-burnished cheeks.

"After work we would swim out to Old Man's Elbow and practice diving. The rock was wider and far easier to climb in those days."

Coral nodded, picturing the scene.

"Sometimes we went to Hartland Quay and didst climb up the light-house ladder when no-one was looking!"

Jem laughed; a deep garrulous laugh that spoke of forbidden pleasures and secret adventures.

"I once put out the light-house keeper's oil-lamp for a dare. The keeper – Old Tom was his name – caught me by the scruff of the neck. Old Tom let me know the full weight of his hand! I had to sleep on my side for a fortnight my ribs hurt so! But Old Tom never breathed a word to Mother so I didst not complain."

Coral leant back on the metal headboard, captivated, twirls of lavender encasing her shoulders. With each fresh word Jem spoke, she felt a bond tightening between them that was tougher than the stoutest sailor's knot and sweeter than the lavender perfume that enveloped them both.

"In the summer months I didst get up to no end of mischief with my friends Jared and Luke. Mother scolded us rotten! But we minded not. Then one day we removed Mother's petticoats from the washing-line and exchanged them for Old Master Dimwick's bloomers! Thou shouldst have seen Mother's face when she discovered what we had done!" Jem exclaimed animatedly, his eyes shimmering like dew-drops. "I did feel so alive back then! With a brace of pals for company, life could not have been better."

Jem laughed again, a light quicksilver laugh. Then he shut his eyes and heard afresh Emmie's girlish giggles, Luke's guffaws and Flossie's hooplas. His nostrils flared and he inhaled the acrid smoke of Father's pungent tobacco as between puffs on his clay-pipe the dark-eyed man in the corner narrated another Icelandic yarn.

Coral listened to Jem's laughter, emboldened by the change that had come over him. She marvelled at the light-heartedness of his voice. She imagined that she could reach out and pluck his vocal chords with her fingers and play a tune with them.

"Father didst so love to tell us children stories," Jem reminisced, his topaz eyes gazing down in wonder at Coral's corn blonde hair. Despite her bandages, Coral was the very epitome of an Icelandic Goddess!

"What sort of stories?" Coral prompted.

"Every kind of story thou canst imagine. Father told us how the God Thor got his hammer and how the Viking Kingdom of Midgarde was surrounded by a vast blue ocean. The waves of the ocean were buckled to the land by the tight grip of a giant snake."

"And where did your father learn these incredible stories?"

"Father joined a Sealing Fleet at the age of fourteen and travelled north into the Arctic Circle. After a hard day's work skinning seals, the sailors would sit about a brazier and tell each other stories, competing with each other to tell the most thrilling and the most blood-curdling yarn."

Coral stifled a gasp at the mention of seals being skinned.

"Thou hast reason to exclaim Coral. Slaughter is an ugly scene. It fair turned Father's stomach the first time he saw the men of a sealing fleet at work, their wrists dripping in blood. But Father soon learnt how to kill and skin seals like the best of them. It was a job of work - a man's job - a grim job. But a job that taught Father the value of life."

106

Coral listened grimly.

"Father didst what he had to do," Jem continued. "But that dost not mean he enjoyed the killing bit of it! Then after eight years Father hadst made enough money to marry Mother and start a family. And on a cold winter's evening Father loved nothing better than to sit down with us children round the fire and tell us stories from his days in the frozen north. Father was a fine orator. He wouldst have made a fine actor or parliamentarian had he been born a man of means!"

Coral smiled warmly, imagining Jem seated at his father's knee, listening to swashbuckling tales of adventure whilst the fire crackled away in the grate before them. She ran her fingers along the edge of the metal tubes of the headboard. Then she sighed longingly, wishing that she could remember similar scenes with her own father but John had never read to her.

On the contrary, John had been of the opinion that in the real world there were no Fairy Godmothers or Albus Dumbledores with magic wands at hand, ready to help. Children had to stand on their own two feet and fend for themselves.

"Are you alright Coral?" Jem asked sharply, sensing that a change had come over her.

"I was just thinking of my own father. He never told me any children's stories."

"Did your mother read to you?" Jem asked gently, sensing her answer.

"Not exactly," Coral said defensively. "Hazel gave me a sketch book and artist's pencils and showed me how to draw. I copied lots of plant and animal specimens from the natural history books in the house. But no-one actually read to me. Then again, I never asked anyone to so I can't really complain. After John died,

I visited the local library and read loads of children's books." She paused. Her eye-brows puckered. "But it was too late by then."

"What dost thou mean by **too late**?" Jem asked gently.

"I'd grown too old. I'd learnt to look at the world in a different way from the other children."

"In what kind of way?"

"A different way. I can't explain."

"Try."

"Do you know the story of Peter Pan by J.M. Barrie?"

"No Coral, I'm afraid that I don't know the story."

"Never mind, I'll tell you. Peter Pan is a boy who never grows up. He's a bit like you Jem. Only **you're** wise, whereas Peter is ignorant and selfish and obsessed with having fun at everybody else's cost. Peter teaches Wendy and her brothers how to fly. Then he lures them out of their bedroom in London and leads them to Neverland. The children's parents are left alone, distraught, not knowing what has happened to their children."

Coral paused.

"I guess there's a parallel between their story and mine! But that's where the parallel ends. In Neverland the children meet Captain Hook, the villain of the piece. It's at that point in the plot that the book stops working for me. The trouble is that instead of disliking Hook, I feel sorry for him trapped in Neverland with only a group of dim-witted pirates as company. I'm not saying that Hook is a good man but he's not all bad either. All Hook needs is a little intellectual stimulation and the genuine companionship of true friends to set him on the right track. By contrast, no amount of kindness from Wendy could ever make vain, egotistical Peter any less selfish! So when Hook and Pan start fighting, I end up rooting for Hook!"

Jem smiled.

"Perhaps J.M. Barrie is challenging his readers to consider what constitutes a hero and a villain? Perhaps he would agree with you? Have you ever thought of that Coral?"

"Perhaps," Coral conceded. "But the book still irritates me big time! And I can't stand Peter!"

"Don't take it so seriously Coral!" Jem replied, chuckling good-naturedly. "It's only a book. You shouldn't read too much into it."

"There is no such thing as **only a book**! All good writing has multiple meanings and hidden story-lines. But the problem that I have with many children's books is that the authors don't seem to be on my wave-length. I mean, isn't the tiger Shere Khan in the Jungle Book just following his instinct, killing in order to eat? And why does J.K. Rowling hate snakes so much? I feel sorry for the deadly basilisk trapped inside the bowels of Hogwarts. Snakes need sunshine! Adders love nothing better than to lie on the moor all day long and bask in the summer's sun."

Jem smiled, amused by Coral's indignation.

"And one other thing, Jem, why do snakes always have to be the bad-guys? Why did a snake have to give Eve an apple in the Garden of Eden? Why couldn't it have been some other creature? It's so facile and predictable!"

"Enough! What thou art saying is blasphemous!" Jem exclaimed, shocked.

Coral fell silent.

"Sorry. I didn't mean to offend you."

Jem glowered at the lavender wrapped about the tubular headboard. Then he counted quietly to five in his head.

Meanwhile Coral kneaded the edge of her heavy blanket with her hot palms, wishing that she could see Jem's face. *It was so difficult trying to have a conversation with some-one she couldn't see.* She needed to be able to read Jem's facial expressions in order to gauge what she should and should not say.

"I'm sorry Jem," Coral repeated, genuinely contrite.

The muscles of Jem's jaw relaxed. It was not Coral's fault that she thought the way that she did. She was a product of her time, just as he was a product of his. It was not his role to judge to what degree her thoughts were blasphemous. He shouldst tend his own garden, rather than cast aspersions on hers.

"Apology accepted," Jem said gruffly.

"Thank you Jem," Coral replied, much relieved.

Silence. Then a cacophony of discordant cries as the grey gulls called to each other on the wing. Several gulls alighted on Jem's boat and watched hungrily as the tide retreated and the shoreline crabs hastily buried themselves in the sand, seeking refuge from the birds' rapacious beaks.

"Carry on with your story Jem," Coral prompted.

"As you wish," he replied, his voice like crushed velvet.

Jem smiled a half-moon smile. His eyes shimmered like liquid-gold. Then he crossed his arms and continued with his narrative.

"Flossie used to love listening to Father's Icelandic tales. She would sit on Father's knee and listen to him talk for hour after hour! But sometimes Father went too far and Mother would jump up and scold him for frightening us children with such heathen tales! Then her anger would subside and Mother would stand up and sing us all a sweet lullaby."

Jem smiled, picturing Mother standing in the middle of the room, her russet hair twisted into a tight plait, her apple-pink cheeks glowing with warmth as she sang about Spencer's Faerie Queen.

"It sounds like you were a very tight-knit family," Coral remarked, wishing that she had been born into such a large and happy household rather than being born an only child.

"We were," Jem replied, his voice wistful. Then suddenly his face contorted with pain. "We were happy until one afternoon I recklessly went diving in Lion's Lair! It was a foolhardy thing to do but I **didst so want** to get Flossie a Queen Scallop for her birthday! I was young and didst not believe that any harm could come to me. I found the Queen Scallop easily enough but the rip-current caught me on my way back to shore. I was ten yards from the beach and slowed my pace, thinking that I was safe." Jem's voice broke off. Then his eyes darkened and he thundered angrily: "I shouldst not have gone diving on the Sabbath! It was divine judgment for breaking the Good Lord's ways."

"Don't be so hard on yourself!" Coral exclaimed, appalled. "It was an accident Jem. Anyone could have made the same mistake."

"No it was divine judgment," Jem replied fiercely. "Why else didst I wake up half-way through my own funeral?"

"You did that?"

"May the Lord forgive me but I did!"

Jem began to tremble. Sweat shimmered on his forehead like silver sequins. He grasped hold of Coral's right hand and held it tightly, his whole upper body shaking with fear as he re-lived the traumatic event.

"Nobody couldst hear me. I banged and banged on the coffin-lid until my knuckles were raw but no-one came. They didst not hear me! The Reverend Symonds rambled on with his sermon, talking about the After-Life and how I hadst gone to sit down with the Lamb of God. I screamed at the Reverend that I was alive and well and that the Lamb of God didst not want to see me just yet! But the Reverend didst not hear me and called on the Holy Spirit to deliver my soul up to heaven!"

"Are you sure that no-one heard you?" Coral asked, stunned by the revelation. She had assumed that if she could hear Jem then everyone else must be able to hear him as well.

"Quite sure! The sermon ended and everyone began to sing the hymn The Lord is My Shepherd Thou Shall Not Want. I heard the sound of loose earth being scattered on my coffin lid. I heard Emmie's muffled sobs and Flossie's full-blown crying and Mother's attempts to comfort them both. Then Father began to weep! I slammed my fists against the coffin lid and didst shout and shout until my throat was hoarse but Father did not hear me and I was buried alive!"

"You poor man!" Coral exclaimed, instinctively snatching hold of Jem's hands and kneading them with the soft inside of her palms.

"I cried until I was hoarse and couldst cry no more. Then after a while I regained my senses and told myself that I wouldst dig my way out and go home to Mother and Father and set everything right!"

"And is that what you did, Jem?"

"I tried! But it was not to be! I levered off each screw with the edge of my thumb-nail. It took so long! It was like trying to prise a winkle from its shell. At last the lid came loose and

I rolled over onto my stomach and didst push upwards with my shoulders. I didst push and push until I emerged from my prison-grave."

Jem caught his breath, re-visiting the harrowing moment. Coral held onto his hand, re-living the moment with him.

"I was lucky Coral that the coffin was made of hazel. I wouldst never have got out hast the coffin been made of solid oak."

"My goodness!"

"By the time I escaped, dawn had broken. I stood at the edge of my grave and gazed down in wonder at the bouquets of flowers strewn across the dew-laden ground. There were red poppies from Emmie and white meadowsweet from Charlie and the boys, blue forget-me-knots from Flossie and sunflowers from Mother." Jem paused, gulping back the salt-tears. "Mother knew how much I loved sunflowers! But after my death Mother never grew them again. Father didst not mind. Father hated sunflowers. He called them Bony's Folly."

"Who's Bony?"

"Napoleon Bonaparte of course," Jem replied, shocked at Coral's ignorance.

"Of course," Coral echoed, feeling incredibly ignorant.

"Then I didst hurry home across the moor. The front door was unlocked so I let myself in. I found Mother kneeling before the fireplace staring at the cold embers. I called out: 'Mother I'm back!' But she didst not hear me. She just stared into the grate, unseeing. So I stepped forwards and placed my hands upon Mother's shoulders meaning to comfort her. At the touch of my hands, she dropped the coal-scuttle onto the hearth and screamed and screamed and screamed! She screamed so loud that I thought I shouldst die all over again from fright."

"How terrible for you!" Coral exclaimed in sympathy.

"Then Father came thundering down the stairs, a heavy iron in his hand. Father's chest collided with mine. He stood stock-still and shouted at me, his voice as hard as nails: 'Be gone Devil! Our son Jem died last night on All Hallow's Eve. May his soul rest in peace. Be gone Devil and allow a poor mother and father to mourn their son's passing!'"

Coral gasped.

"Your father said that?"

"He did," Jem sobbed. "And Mother echoed his every thought."

"And neither of them could see you?"

"They couldst not."

"But they could both **feel** you?"

"Yes! They couldst feel me but they couldst not see or hear me. That is why they did mistake me for an evil spirit. They didst not realise that I was their son."

Coral leant forward tentatively. Then she pressed her lips against his cheek and kissed him tenderly.

"It's OK Jem. I'm here. You're not alone now."

Jem nodded, his eyes filled with still-born tears.

"What did you do next Jem?"

"I ran back to my grave and patted the earth down with the flat of my palms. I didst not want Mother and Father to think that grave-robbers had tooken my corpse. Then I fled. I do not know where I ran to. I just remember running and running until I couldst run no further." Jem gulped and broke off. Then he ran his hands through his hair and continued stoically. "The next day I returned to Saint Merriam's Church in the hope of catching sight of Mother or Father. I knew I couldst not speak to them any more but I might still look at them. But they were not there. So I arranged Mother's sunflowers and Flossie's forget-me-knots in the centre of the grave. Then I said goodbye to each of them in turn because I knew in my heart that they were lost to me from that day forth."

"How heart-breaking for you Jem," Coral murmured disconsolately.

"It was heart-breaking to begin with but it grew easier with time. I returned home every so often and watched Mother polish her copper pans. Hour after hour Mother wouldst scrub those pans! Her tears stained the copper blue, she cried so."

"Poor woman…"

"But it was not all sad, Coral. I watched Flossie grow up into a beautiful young woman with golden hair and cornflower-blue eyes. And once a year - on Flossie's birthday - I would steal into her front garden and leave a sprig of forget-me-knots on Flossie's bedroom windowsill. Even as an old woman Flossie loved forget-me-nots! She would arrange the flowers in a vase in the front window as if she knew that I might come by and admire them."

"And did you?"

"That I did! I wouldst sit on the wall opposite Flossie's cottage and watch her tend her garden. Flossie had the greenest of green fingers! And her sunflowers were the talk of the neighbourhood."

"You mean Bony's Folly was the talk of the neighbourhood!"

"Aye, Bony's Folly!" Jem rejoined, tears of happiness streaming from his eyes.

"Dearest Flossie - she lived to just two weeks short of her eighty-fifth birthday."

"And in what year did she die?" Coral asked.

"1887."

"And you've been alone ever since?"

"That I have."

"Well you shall never be alone again Jem. You've got me now," Coral said softly, squeezing his hand fiercely, wishing that she could see him. She knew that she could never replace Flossie or Emmie but perhaps she could be another kind of sister to him?

Jem looked tenderly at Coral's bandaged face, relieved that she could not see the worry in his eyes.

"That is very kind of thee Coral but I am over two hundred years old. I shall be alive long after thou hast died. I do not think it wise that we become too closely acquainted."

"Let me be the judge of that Jem," Coral replied, determined to be his friend.

"But Coral, thou dost not understand! I may have the outward appearance of a young man but I have the knowledge of an old man, knowledge that I wouldst rather do without!"

"But knowledge is a **good** thing surely?"

"My knowledge is pointless!"

"I disagree. All knowledge is useful. There's always something new to learn," Coral replied. Then she broke off, seized by a new idea. "Just think Jem… If you share your knowledge with me, there's no limit to what you and I might achieve together."

Jem arched his brows sceptically.

"Tis very sweet of thee to say Coral but I fail to see what difference we two canst make ranged against the world's ills. Thou might be an excellent rock-climber but thou art not an Icelandic Goddess imbued with supernatural powers. And I am not the God Thor."

"But you are invisible Jem! There's no limit to what you and I could achieve together if we put our minds to it," Coral said excitedly, imagining all the adventures they could have together. "The only limit is the limit we put on ourselves."

"Coral, I am nothing. I am scarcely worthy of thine company. I didst not even make it to Master Sail-Maker."

"I don't care about your past Jem. I care about our future!"

Then Coral's vivid imagination spiralled away and she imagined all the ways in which Jem's invisibility could be put to good use. They could seed-bomb the motorways and plants tress on derelict land! They could climb up to London and replace the expensive Christmas lights with woven garlands of holly and ivy instead. They could climb to the top of Big Ben and place a Christmas tree on top. They could help the poor and wheel-clamp the selfish! Coral grinned, already a little in love with Jem and in love with all the adventures they could have together.

"We can do so many things Jem! The sky's the limit!"

"Dost thou really mean that?" Jem asked cautiously.

Coral looked so animated that he found it hard to believe that she was injured at all. In fact she looked so dazzlingly brilliant that he feared that she might vanish like the will-o-the wisp and that he would be left alone all over again.

"You saved my life Jem, of course I mean it! I mean every single syllable of every single word I say. Now all you have to do is to remove my bandages then we can go straight home and tell Hazel everything."

Jem gulped nervously. The last thing that he wanted to do was to tell Hazel everything. The truth was that he was also scared stiff lest Coral be left permanently blind. Coral had passed out long before her body had become a human trampoline. But he had not been spared the harrowing details of the gruesome attack. He understood far more than Coral the power of man's iron heel.

CHAPTER EIGHT

The Looking Glass

"Let's get started," Coral said eagerly, her chin tilted upwards so that Jem could remove the strips of bandage stuck to her chin.

"We canst hurry things. We must heat some water up first."

"Is water really necessary?" Coral asked impatiently. "I don't mind if it hurts."

"But **I** mind. Thou hast fair skin. I do not want to risk bruising the layer of new skin."

"How long will the water take to heat?" Coral asked, fiddling with the edge of her pillow, unable to sit still.

"Not long," Jem replied, reminded of Flossie fidgeting in church, fiddling with Emmie's plaits when the pair of them ought to have been praying.

Then he screwed up some rough paper into small tangerine-sized paper-balls. He opened the door of his wood-burning stove and added a sufficient number of balls to form a two inch bed of paper. He placed some kindling on top and struck a match. The paper balls burst into flame.

Jem patiently waited for the kindling to catch light then as soon as he judged the flames to be big enough, he added two beech logs. The wood slowly crackled into life. He closed the door to the stove with a heavy clunk.

"What was that noise?" Coral asked, keen to know everything that Jem was doing. Surely Jem wasn't making a fire in early September? And yet it sounded just like the low drone that a fire makes before it gets going.

"I put some logs into the wood-burner to heat the water," Jem said a little awkwardly, not accustomed to having his every action questioned and remarked upon. It unsettled him somewhat.

"Oh I get it! You've got a wood-burning stove. We used to have a wood-burner in Sheffield. They're great for cooking with. One of my earliest memories is of Dad feeding himself meat and gravy with a huge metal ladle from a pot of stew on the wood-burner. On the subject of food, any chance of a bite to eat? I'm starving."

"I could make thee some arrowroot," Jem replied, only too pleased to delay removing the bandages. "Mother always gave us children arrowroot when we were sickening for something. Catherine virtually lived off the stuff, she was always so poorly."

"What's arrowroot?"

Jem's jaw dropped open in surprise.

"Arrowroot is arrowroot! Surely thou must have tasted arrowroot before?"

"I've never heard of it," Coral replied, unimpressed by the sound of it.

"Arrowroot is made from the root of various plants from the Indies – I can't recall their names – Mother wouldst have known. They still use it in the Abbey kitchens as part of the

Living History exhibit. The starch is very nutritious. It's just what thou needs Coral after thy illness. It'll build thee up! The root is a miracle plant! In medieval times it was used to combat the poison from arrows!"

"What does it taste like?" Coral asked cautiously.

Coral was very particular about her food and the fact that Jem could not tell her the name of the plants the arrowroot came from made her doubly suspicious.

"Like arrowroot!" Jem laughed, the white of his eyes sparkling brightly. "I shall make thee some without delay. Then thou shalt know soon enough."

"How long will it take to make?"

"Ten to fifteen minutes. I have to warm it up on a low heat. It's important not to over-boil the milk," Jem explained, striding over to the sideboard and scooping up a glass bottle of milk from his ice-bucket.

Jem poured the milk into a copper saucepan and added a couple of handfuls of powdered arrowroot. Then he placed the pan on top of the stove and began to stir the liquid with a wooden spoon.

"Jem," Coral asked tentatively, fiddling with her hair.

"Yes?" he replied, concentrating on stirring the thick creamy liquid. "What is it Coral?"

"It's just… I wondered if…" Her voice faded. She twisted a thick lock of hair about her little finger then drew it to her mouth and sucked the ends. It was a disgusting habit she knew but it helped steady her nerves. "I will be able to see when you take the bandages off, won't I?"

The wooden spoon jarred in Jem's hand. He looked up sharply.

"I'm not a physician Coral. But I reckon thine eyesight is safe enough," he lied.

"That's a relief," Coral replied, reassured by Jem's answer. She withdrew the strand of hair from her mouth and wiped the saliva away from her bottom lip. The wet hair lightly brushed against her neck and remained there, stuck to her pale albuminous skin. "The truth is I've scared stiff of going blind. Not that there's anything wrong with being blind. But it would be terribly hard to get used to. Is the arrowroot ready yet?"

"Not quite."

"Good because I've changed my mind. I want to take my bandages off now. The one way to get rid of fear is to face it. So let's do it now!"

Jem's arm jumped involuntarily. But this time he managed to stop the wooden spoon from jumping out of his hand.

"Do you think it wise? The arrowroot is nearly done. It would be a shame to let it go cold."

"Forget the arrowroot! Let's take my bandages off!" Coral said firmly, her mind made up. She leant forwards, keen to get started.

Jem frowned, not sure whether he liked this new assertive Coral. He stopped stirring the mixture and let the wooden spoon rest on the edge of the hot pan. Then he pushed the saucepan to the edge of the hot stove-plate and withdrew to wash his hands.

"What are you doing?" Coral asked impatiently, straining to hear.

"Just give me a few minutes Coral whilst I get all that I need to remove thy bandages properly."

"Of course," Coral replied, listening to Jem work, her mind attuned to his every movement.

Jem gathered together a bowl of warm water, a bottle of soapwort, a sea-sponge, a metal bucket and a towel. He placed the metal bucket on the floor beside Coral's bed. Then he sat down beside her, braced for every eventuality. He loosened his shirt collar, priming himself for the task in hand.

Then without further ado, he added a few drops of soapwort to the water and plunged a golden sea-sponge into the liquid. He waited a few minutes so that the soapwort would permeate the sponge. Then he squeezed tight, removing the excess liquid. His knuckles shone a livid white.

"Now hold still Coral whilst I swab the top layer of bandages with some warm water in order to loosen them."

Coral relaxed the muscles of her face.

"Go ahead Jem. I'm ready."

Jem gently ran the golden sponge across her cheeks.

"That tickles! What on earth are you using?" Coral exclaimed, giggling.

"A sea-sponge," Jem replied, irritated by Coral's giggling.

He had selected the best sea-sponge that he had. He hadst caught it whilst diving off Old Man's Elbow two months back. The sponge was a real beauty. It was certainly no giggling matter!

"You mean an actual sea-sponge from the sea-bed?" Coral queried.

"Yes," Jem said gruffly, retreating back into his shell.

"Really? I've only ever seen photographs of sea-sponges in books. What colour is it?"

"A light gold, tinged with violet."

"And what does it look like? Does it have pin-shaped spicules or star-shaped spicules?"

Jem looked down at the dead creature cupped in his hand and wondered how best to describe it. He was not familiar with Coral's technical vocabulary. Had he shared her knowledge of natural history, he could have told her that its skeleton was formed from complex star-shaped spicules made of silica. But he did not have her vocabulary so he had to make do with his own.

"It looks a bit like a honeycomb."

"Then it's probably a tube sponge. But I like your description better. It's much more imaginative than mine."

Jem's mood softened. Coral's passion for the natural world was infectious. Then he ironed out the creases in his mind and continued with the task in hand.

"Hold still again whilst I remove the remaining ice on thy cheeks."

"Ice? There's ice on my face? No wonder I feel cold!" Coral exclaimed in surprise.

Jem frowned, stung by her criticism. Then he swiftly removed the top layers of wadding to reveal a thin layer of gauze, peppered with tiny pea-sized specks of ice.

"The ice has done a good job of healing thee," Jem commented.

"I'm sure it has," Coral replied. "I don't doubt for a minute that ice works. Hazel swears by a pack of frozen peas!"

Jem's hands froze in mid-task. He stared at Coral in total confusion. Half the time he didn't understand a word she was saying! *Why wouldst anyone in their right mind freeze peas? He ate them only when they were in season.*

But Jem wisely chose not to comment on the frozen peas. Instead he dispelled all thoughts of frozen peas from his mind and started to remove the second layer of wadding to reveal more granules of ice adhered to a layer of silvery gauze underneath. He removed the next layer of gauze and emptied the granules of ice into a tin bucket at his feet. *So far so good…*

"The ice has worked a treat," Jem said confidently, keeping the rest of his thoughts close to his chest. "Thy face is no longer swollen."

"Thanks! Who said your knowledge was useless Jem? All knowledge is useful! And I'm sure the local hospital would never have thought to use ice for six whole weeks like you have!"

Jem smiled awkwardly.

"Don't thank me Coral. Thank Sir Hugh and his ice-house."

"Who's Sir Hugh? He sounds very grand."

Jem stared at Coral agog, astounded that Coral could live on the Hartland peninsular and not have heard of Sir Hugh Stucley, the owner of Hartland Abbey, one of the most beautiful buildings in the whole of North Devon.

"Sir Hugh Stucley is the owner of Hartland Abbey. Thou must have heard of him."

"Sorry Jem, I haven't. But tell me about the ice-house. It sounds much more interesting. Is it sculpted out of ice like the famous Swedish Ice Hotel?"

Jem blinked, even more confused than ever.

"No, it is not a building sculpted out of ice. The ice-house is a large hole in the ground, lined with tiles and filled with blocks of ice. Two hundred years ago the ice-house would have stored all manner of foodstuffs all year round. But Sir Hugh no longer uses the ice-house for his daily needs. He has modern electric freezers to do all that sort of thing in the Abbey kitchens."

"But you **do** use the ice-house because you don't have a freezer!" Coral replied, quick as a flash.

Jem caught his breath, struck by how quickly Coral's mind travelled sideways like a crab.

"Yes, something like that," Jem confessed. "But Sir Hugh likes to keep the ice-house stocked with ice to give the visitors an insight into what life was like in the last century. He calls it Living History."

"A bit like you Jem. You're a piece of living history!" Coral said brightly. "Have you ever met Sir Hugh?"

"Goodness no!" Jem exclaimed, deeply embarrassed by the very idea. "I'm invisible. It is not feasible."

"But Sir Hugh does allow you to live in his beach-hut? You did say that Sir Hugh owns all the land in these parts?"

"He does."

"So Sir Hugh must like you. Otherwise he wouldn't let you live here."

Jem caught his breath. He had never considered Sir Hugh in such a light before.

"Tell more about the beach-hut Jem and how you came to live here," Coral asked, keen to learn more about Jem's mysterious past.

"But what about thy face? I thought thou were in a hurry to remove all the bandages?"

"Can't you talk and remove my bandages at the same time?"

"Goodness no!" Jem exclaimed, shocked by the very idea. "It's best to do one thing at a time and to do it properly rather than trying to do three things at once and making a mess of each one of them. Mother always did one thing at a time and Mother was always right."

"Really? Your mother wouldn't get on with my Mum!" Coral exclaimed, laughing. "Hazel loves nothing better than multi-tasking! In fact she's brilliant at it."

"Multi-what?"

"Never mind, it's a waste of time me telling you. Let's forget about the bandages. Tell me about the beach-hut instead."

"As thou wishes," Jem replied, sitting back in his father's wing-back chair, relieved at the stay of execution. "I have lived in many places - old shepherd huts, hay-barns, a coach-house and a couple of inns. But I never had a permanent place until 1929."

Jem paused as he remembered the first time he saw the building back in the days when Hartland Abbey was host to wonderful parties that had spilled out onto the beach. The beach-hut had been a magnificent building back then, far more opulent than it was now.

"The building was designed in 1920 as a Bathing Pavilion for Gentleman and Lady Bathers. Crowds of fashionable ladies and gentlemen arrived from London dressed in striped bathing costumes and curious swimming caps decorated with rubber flowers. The guests swam all day and danced all night. They brought with them all kinds of exotic animals - parrots, budgerigars and tiny Pekinese lap-dogs. One year a woman brought with her a black puma wearing a diamante collar!"

"A puma?" Coral exclaimed in disbelief. "Are you sure that it wasn't a black Labrador?"

"No, no, it was a puma, I tell thee! But one day the puma escaped. The woman was distraught."

Jem fell silent, lost in thought.

"What happened to the puma?" Coral asked, grinning broadly.

"A search-party was mustered but the puma was ne'er found. Its descendants live on the moor to this day! Hadst thou not heard of the Exmoor big cats?"

"Of course I have Jem. But there aren't any. It's just a myth."

"It's not a myth Coral. It's true!"

"But it can't be! How did the puma breed?"

"With other escaped pumas of course! It was quite popular back in the 1920s for people to own exotic pets and to keep them in their homes. There was no law against it."

Coral listened, unconvinced. But she did not argue the point with Jem. On the contrary, she quite liked the idea that the moors were awash with exotic black pumas all descended from one elegant 1920s ancestor with a diamante collar and her mysterious mate.

"The beach parties were held every summer in the bathing pavilion for nigh on a decade. Then in 1929 there was the Wall Street Crash," Jem continued, his tone suddenly serious. "I don't know what the crash was precisely but it created a lot of hardship throughout the world. It started in the Florida Swamps. People bought land which they hoped couldst be converted into dream seaside homes only they didst not realise that the land they had bought was swampland and that alligators would be their neighbours. The prices went up and up. Everyone thought they were getting richer and richer but in fact they were getting poorer. The land was worthless. As soon as the people discovered the truth, the prices crashed and the ripples couldst be felt all the way across the Atlantic Ocean from the Florida Swamps to Hartland Cove!"

"It sounds familiar," Coral murmured, thinking of the current recessions in Britain and America.

"All the visitors packed up their bags and went back to London. I moved in and have been here ever since. And the black pumas have stayed on as well."

"A likely story!" Coral exclaimed, laughing.

"A true story, I tell thee! There are at least two pumas that live on Exmoor. I've seen them with my own eyes on Docton Moor. And the Wall Street Crash did start with alligators. The books in Hartland Abbey Library say so. Read John Galbraith: The Great Crash, 1929."

Coral stopped laughing and considered the information in the round.

"I like the idea of the alligators Jem. But I've never seen any pumas on the moor and I spend half my time there."

"Then we shall have to agree to disagree."

"I guess so," Coral laughed, still thinking of pumas in diamante collars.

"Shall we remove thine bandages?" Jem asked suddenly, unaccustomed to arguing with Coral.

Coral took a sharp intake of breath, secretly nervous.

"OK then," Coral replied.

Jem lowered his head and carefully peeled away the final layer of silvery gauze that covered Coral's cheeks. Then he carefully removed the compacted wadding from above her eyes. A rush of warm air tickled her cheekbones.

"Goodness. That feels strange. What do I look like?" Coral asked cautiously, her eyes still tightly shut.

Jem studied Coral's face. A pale white scar was just discernible beneath her left eye where Antonia's daisy-tread boot had struck home. But the scar was not at all ugly. In fact it reminded him of a white star, the filaments of light etched across her cheek-bone in neat even diagonals.

"What do I look like, Jem?" Coral repeated impatiently, mentally preparing herself for the worst.

Jem sucked in his cheeks, carefully selecting the right words.

"Thou hast a neat star-shaped scar on thy left cheek. But other than that, thy skin is as good as new."

"Cool. I can pretend it's a tattoo! Now all we have to do is remove the bandages from my eyes."

Jem swallowed.

"I've already removed the bandages above thine eyes Coral."

Coral froze. Crazy chaotic thoughts raced through her brain. Then she took a deep breath and aligned her mind to the new information. *Plenty of people were blind. Being blind wasn't a problem.*

"But a little warm water might help you to open thine eyes," Jem continued, immediately realising what the problem was. "Thy lids appear to be glued together with ointment."

Coral caught her breath with relief. Then she sat quite still whilst Jem delicately dabbed her eyelids with warm water, paying special attention to her left eye.

"What's the ointment made of?"

"Goose-fat and yarrow leaf; the yarrow plant helps the blood to congeal. The Roman Legions called it Soldier's Bloodwort because it worked so well on their blisters."

"I guess the Romans must have suffered a lot from blisters because of all the marching they did!" Coral joked, imagining a line of Roman soldiers all marching in pairs across the British countryside.

130

"Did you make the ointment yourself Jem using a special recipe of your mother's? Or is it a Roman recipe?"

"Neither. I got it from a book by Culpepper called A Historie of Herbal Remedies from the library in Hartland Abbey," Jem replied, removing the last greasy globule of ointment from her eyelashes.

"Try and open thine eyes now," he said softly.

Coral hesitated momentarily. Then she opened her eyes boldly, prepared for every eventuality.

"Canst thou see me?" Jem asked, hoping against hope that Coral would be able to see him.

"You're in focus but so are lots of other squiggly things," Coral remarked happily, wiping the remnants of unctuous yarrow ointment from her eyelids. "That's better," she said gratefully, blinking. "For a moment I thought I had a family of money-spiders walking across my eyeballs," she joked, her blue eyes brighter than ever.

Jem stared in wonder at Coral's dazzling blue eyes. The star-shaped scar on her cheek glinted at him brightly like freshly fallen snow.

"Can I have a mirror please?" Coral asked, keen to see what she looked like.

"A mirror?" Jem repeated, wondering what a mirror might be. "I'm not sure that I have one."

"You must have! You can look in it and see your reflection."

"Oh you mean a looking-glass! There's one just above the wash-stand," Jem said cautiously. Just because he found the star pretty did not mean that Coral would.

But Coral did not exercise similar caution. She leapt out of bed and darted across the bare floor-boards to look at her reflection in the dimpled wash-stand mirror.

"Yikes, that's some scar! If Antonia could see me now she'd be pleased with her handiwork."

"You mean footwork."

Coral looked round sharply.

"I thought you found me unconscious on the beach?"

Jem coloured.

"You lied to me Jem! You promised that you would never lie to me!"

"I didst not lie to thee Coral. I just did not tell thee everything. I thought thou wouldst be angry with me for attacking the other boys."

"You attacked them?" Coral said slowly, her eyes widening.

"I sort of picked them up and threw them. But they landed harder than I expected."

Jem looked down, his face a wall of shame.

"You did all that for me?" Coral asked softly.

Jem nodded.

"Thank you."

"Thou art not angry with me?"

"Why should I be angry with you? They got what they deserved."

"But I threw James straight into Old Man's Elbow! I could have killed him! And I pulled Tom's arm behind his back. I fear I may have broken it."

"It serves him right if you did."

"No Coral, it doesn't! I should not have acted thus. I should have exercised more self-restraint."

"Why? I had no chance against them!"

Jem's jaw softened.

"Why do they hate thee so much?"

Coral shrugged her shoulders.

"Does there **have** to be a reason?"

"Yes there does!"

The veins in his forehead pulsed. His jaw locked in anger. *There had to be a reason. He had watched a pretty sixteen year old girl with long brown hair try to stamp the eyesight out of another pretty teenage girl with long blonde hair! There **had** to be a reason! He would go insane if there were not a reason!*

"There has to be a reason Coral. I've lived through too many wars and seen far too much suffering for there not to be a reason. I've seen the bloody Field Hospitals of the Napoleonic War! I've seen the opium addicts of the 1860s. I've seen the amputees and victims of the First and Second World Wars. And I've seen Antonia jump on your face Coral and try to make mince-meat of it!" Jem exploded.

He slammed his fist into the wall, furious with himself for being so impotent.

"Stop it Jem! Antonia's not worth it."

"Yes she is! Every child is worth it. But children canst become cruel if neglected." Jem unclenched his fist and looked at Coral with soulful, searching eyes. "Perhaps Antonia has been neglected by her parents?"

"Antonia neglected? Are you kidding? All Antonia has to do is click her fingers and her Daddy will come running and buy her whatever she wants."

"Gifts are no substitute for love."

"Antonia gets plenty of love! Her Mum dotes on her. The plain fact of the matter is that Antonia **enjoys** hurting people. Some people just do. There's no rhyme or reason behind it, just good old-fashioned malice."

The word 'old-fashioned' struck Jem like an arrow through the chest.

"Do you really think so?" he asked falteringly.

"I **know** so."

"No. I cannot agree with thee Coral."

"Why not? It's not difficult to understand. Tom, Kim, James and Antonia worked themselves up into a frenzy and kicked me. That's what mobs do."

"But why Coral? There hast to be a **reason.**"

"Sure, there is. It's called human nature. Why else do you think we're destroying this beautiful green planet of ours? Human-beings have the capacity to destroy. Only in the long run once we've destroyed every last green thing on this planet, nature will have the last laugh. The human race will become extinct. New trees and species will evolve from the ashes and the cycle of life will begin all over again. And who knows, future species of intelligent life may be less selfish than us! Now there's a thought to hold onto."

Jem stared at Coral speechless. Coral smiled at him appeasingly. He looked so sad. She almost wished she had kept her thoughts to herself. Her eyes travelled along the deep grooves of his furrowed brow, down the bridge of his nose to his pinched lips. Then she leant forwards and kissed him on the forehead. She smiled sweetly.

"Maybe it's time I told you how my father died, Jem… John was a peaceful, law-abiding man. But he was knocked off his motorbike one day by a soft-top Mini. Maybe the car-driver was too scared to stop. Whatever the whys and wherefores, John died alone by the side of the road. How stupid and senseless is that?"

Jem stared at Coral dumbly, too shocked to speak.

"The reality is that when you go out of the front door, Jem, **stuff** happens. The day you are born, Jem, **stuff** happens. Where ever you are, Jem, **stuff** happens. Now you can stay inside and lock yourself away from the world or you can go outside and face it. My dad went out and faced it. He died because he just happened to be in the wrong place at the wrong time. I was in the wrong place at the wrong time and the same thing nearly happened to me only luckily **you** were on hand to rescue me."

Liquid silence filled the little room. Coral kissed Jem lightly on the neck. He blushed. Coral swiftly turned away and withdrew to the sideboard. Her eyes alighted upon the Honesty seeds in the clay bowl and she smiled, pleased that she had been brave enough to kiss him. Honesty: it was always the best policy.

"This place is amazing Jem! You're amazing Jem! I never thought my first boy-friend would be a ghost!"

Jem's eyes flashed from topaz to black opal.

"I am **not** a ghost!" he thundered. "I eat, drink and sleep just like you! The only difference is that I've been doing so for over two hundred years."

Jem turned and fled. At the water's edge he dived into the waves and swam and swam until he could swim no more.

Coral stood in the open doorway, aghast. *What had she just done?*

CHAPTER NINE

Sir Aubrey

"Jem come back! I didn't mean what I just said," Coral shouted, chasing after him across the burning hot sand. "Jem…"

Coral squinted into the bright blue sky but the sun bludgeoned her eyeballs rendering her momentarily blind.

Salt tears streamed from her tear-ducts as she was assaulted on three sides by the glare from the sun, sea and sand. She retreated, her toes curled to prevent the underside of her feet from getting scorched by the hot pebbles.

Once back in the cool of Jem's hut, Coral rifled through his wardrobe, searching for something more practical to wear. She exchanged her frilly dress-shirt for a functional denim shirt with a wide collar. The denim shirt worked well as a dress fastened at the waist with a belt. She coiled Jem's leather belt twice about her waist and secured it with a knot. Then she scoured the floor for something to put on her feet. Jem's shoes were far too big for her, so she was forced to improvise. She stepped into a pillow-case, turned down the sides so that they formed stiff protective flaps and fastened her 'pillow-boot' halfway up the calves with rope from Jem's desk-drawer. She repeated the process with a second pillow-case. Then she grabbed a peaked cap from the coat-stand and headed back outside, determined to win back Jem.

Jem sat down at the base of Old Man's Elbow staring grimly at the raised ribbons of sand created by the receding tide. The bank of dimpled sand was dotted with tiny finger-sized holes. Next to each hole were tiny circular strings of sandy fecal matter - indicating a lugworm nursery. A collection of blue mussels adhered to an isolated boulder of black schist rock closeby. A dead anemone languished in a small rock-pool, its claret coloured hairs smothered in wet sand.

Coral drew level with Jem and stood at the water's edge.

"I'm sorry Jem. I didn't mean to upset you just now by calling you a ghost. You're not a ghost. You're different, that's all."

Jem turned his head towards her and glared, his eyes a wall of flame.

"Go away," he said hoarsely, tiny bubbles of foam coating his bottom lip.

Coral hesitated, shocked by his manner. Then she drew a deep breath and spoke.

"I'm sorry Jem. I didn't mean to hurt your feelings."

"Go away!" Jem snapped, standing up angrily. Then he turned and headed back up the beach, his hands screwed into fists.

"Jem, please hear me out. I didn't mean to call you a ghost. It just slipped out. It was stupid of me!" Coral called after him.

Jem reached the top-shore and vaulted the stone-stile into Hartland Wood. Then he started up the steep wooded track towards Hartland Abbey. *He needed time on his own to think.*

"Jem stop! Wait for me!" Coral shouted, giving chase as best she could in her pillow-case boots. But the makeshift footwear kept slipping off and she was forced to stop several times to re-tie them. "Please Jem! This is stupid! Stop and talk," Coral called repeatedly.

But Jem did not heed Coral's pleas for conciliation. Instead he passed through the metal gate into the Abbey grounds and cut a diagonal path across the manicured lawn. Then he darted up the exterior stone staircase into the Abbey, much to the displeasure of the resident male peacock who responded to Jem's sudden appearance by spreading its tail-feathers wide and puffing up its neck aggressively.

The Abbey door clicked shut behind Jem. The peacock performed a victory parade on the lawn.

Safe in the confines of the library, Jem relaxed. The smell of parchment paper mingled with that of recently lit candle-wax. He imbibed the cocktail of unusual smells then sat down at a window-seat, thankful to be alone at last.

Outside in the Abbey grounds, all was not so peaceful. Coral arrived at the edge of the Abbey lawn and was immediately spotted by Mrs. Julia Phipps, a woman of considerable girth and with the lung capacity of a Dreadnought battleship.

"It's her, the missing Devon school-girl!" Mrs. Phipps bellowed in ear-splitting tones, charging across the lawn towards a startled Coral.

"Julia darling, let's not be too hasty. You can't be sure it's the right girl," Mr. Phipps said soothingly, jogging to keep up with his wife.

A thin, middle-aged man with a balding pate and moon-glasses, Mr. Phipps had the air of man much put upon.

"Nonsense Donald, it's her I tell you! The Missing Devon School Girl!" Julia said scathingly. "Sound the alarm! Phone the police! Do something manly for once in your life Donald."

Donald took a sharp intake of breath, cursing the capacity of Somerset cider to make a grown man bend down on one knee and propose marriage. But there was no going back now. He was trapped in a life of matrimony or until such time as Julia decided to relinquish all claim to him.

"We really can't be sure, dearest."

"Yes we can Donald! Stop standing there like a lemon and do something!"

"Don't fret Julia. But let's try and be a bit quieter, shall we? We don't want to scare the girl, do we?"

"The girl's not scared. You're the one who's scared Dad!" a stocky boy scoffed contemptuously, chocolate biscuit crumbs smeared all over his bottom lip.

The boy shoved another biscuit into his mouth and ground his teeth together, glaring at his father with unconcealed contempt.

"Call the police Donald!" Mrs. Phipps commanded, her considerable cleavage wobbling like two vanilla blancmanges in her eagerness to apprehend Coral.

"Mum's right. You can tell the girl's guilty by the way she's looking at us. Mum's rumbled her!" the boy boasted, wondering whether he ought to rugby-tackle Coral. She hardly seemed worth it. One puff of wind would blow her over.

Coral stared despairingly at Julia's intimidating bulk and fierce piggy-brown eyes, then across to the boy's vacant grin. Fight or flight? Neither approach appealed to her. Maybe she should try talking to them?

However Coral was not granted the opportunity to test dialogue as the boy suddenly bounded forwards and made a grab for her.

Fortunately Coral was far too quick for him. She spun round on the balls of her feet and sprinted away towards the duck pond.

"Quick Donald, don't just stand there like a wet dishcloth!" Julia wailed. "Help Daniel catch her!"

The unkind jibe was sufficient to spur Donald to action but not on the course Julia had intended. He sprinted after Daniel and more by accident than by design, succeeded in wrestling his son to the ground in the best limp-wristed rugby tackle of all time.

Daniel lay sprawled on his stomach like a beached whale. Donald staggered to his feet and opened his arms wide, forming a human-shield between Coral and Julia who now rumbled towards them both like an angry black rhino.

"Quick Coral run! Take the back steps into the rear of the Abbey. You can work your way to the front from there," Donald shouted, arms spread-eagled like a starfish.

Then an almighty splash as both Julia and Donald fell backwards into the Abbey pond.

Coral did not hang around to see what would happen next. She sprinted up the rear staircase into the Abbey.

Once inside she caught her breath and proceeded along the dimly-lit corridors until she reached the heart of the building. A shaft of orange light shot through the heraldic windows above her. The next minute she was standing on tiptoes staring up at the portrait of an old man with a toothbrush moustache and eyes that glinted like stars.

"Donald! How could you?" Julia shouted angrily, clambering out of the pond, her lace knickers splattered with spots of blue-green algae.

The peacock took one look at Julia's undergarments and opened his tail-feathers and began parading up and down the lawn trumpeting his superiority.

Meanwhile a bedraggled Donald crawled out of the pond, green duckweed draped about his ears like funky foam ear-phones.

"Donald! I have never, ever, been so humiliated in my entire life!" Julia bellowed angrily. Sir Aubrey coughed. Julia spun round and came face to face with Sir Aubrey's diminutive figure. "Who on earth are you?"

"I might ask the same question of you Madam?" Sir Aubrey enquired politely.

"What the devil? Where in the deuce did you spring from?" Julia demanded hotly.

"I have been here all along Madam, although you appear to have only just spotted me," Sir Aubrey replied, stepping forward and performing a low bow.

Then Sir Aubrey took a step back and straightened his cravat. Fastidious by nature, Sir Aubrey took considerable care with his appearance. Today he was dressed in his best plum-coloured waistcoat and white dress-shirt; a diamond tie-pin sparkled in the centre of his cerise silk cravat. He wore blue stockings and silver breeches. On his feet he sported ruby-studded shoes with a delicate two-inch heel. On his head he wore a white powdered wig, the curls pulled back into a short pony-tail.

"I am delighted to see your little family have enjoyed your picnic lunch in my Walled Garden. But might I ask you to refrain from raising your voice quite so loudly? It disturbs the peacocks. Once they get roused and start whooping, there's no stopping them. It can take days to calm them down."

"What? How? Who?" Julia said mechanically, her jaw opening and shutting like a target on a fairground shooting range.

"Sir Aubrey at your service," the cunning old ghost replied, his grey eyes twinkling at her like pearl drops.

Sir Aubrey inclined his head and examined the ring on the little finger of his left hand. The fire opal glinted in the sunlight, hinting at all manner of possibilities.

"Sir Aubrey of Hartland Abbey? It's an honour, an absolute honour to meet you!" Julia exclaimed extravagantly. Then she spun round and berated her husband unkindly. "Donald, why didn't you tell me we were on private land?"

"I think that you will find from looking at the ordnance survey map located in the top left-hand side of your husband's ruck-sack that you have accidentally departed from the coastal path," Sir Aubrey replied, smiling at her disingenuously. "But no matter, I can set you on the right track easily enough. But all in good time, all in good time. First, please allow me to give you a tour of the Abbey. Having availed yourself of my Walled Garden, you may as well see the rest of the property. And we can stop off at the laundry on the way to get you some dry clothes."

"Thank you Your Lordship!" Julia exclaimed.

"And if you would be so kind as to extricate your son from my ornamental redcurrant bushes, I would be most appreciative."

"Stop that Dan," Donald scolded, not so easily deceived by Sir Aubrey as his wife, but happy to go along with Sir Aubrey for the time-being.

"And please leave your mobiles on the sundial to dry out. They probably won't work after their little dip in the pond but it's always best to be on the safe side, don't you think? I would hate to think that one of you might accidentally telephone the police with ill-gotten information about a certain Devon school girl."

Sir Aubrey then gave Mr and Mrs. Phipps the kind of meaningful stare that only Mr. Phipps was clever enough to understand. Then he led the family off to the servant's quarters, having seemingly forgotten all about the proposed tour of the Abbey.

CHAPTER TEN

The Library

The library door opened. Jem looked up in alarm as two pairs of feet slid seamlessly across the polished floorboards, one set clad in pointed leather shoes with ruby buttons, the other wearing what looked like his mother's starched pillow-cases.

Jem blanched. What on earth was Coral doing in the library? And who was she with? If he didn't know better he would say the ruby-encrusted shoes belonged to Sir Aubrey. But what on earth wouldst Coral be doing with Sir Aubrey? And why were they both tiptoeing down the aisle as if they were both up to no good?

The deep boom of a woman's foghorn voice sounded from the kitchens below. Coral and Sir Aubrey exchanged meaningful glances.

"Don't worry Coral. That infernal woman can't follow us up here. But even so, it is all so terribly tedious of her."

Coral smiled as if she understood exactly what Sir Aubrey meant. He led the way down the aisle of books until they came to a small, semi-circular seating alcove directly facing the front lawn. Daylight gleamed through the heraldic windows, casting coloured light on the window-seats. Sir Aubrey made a bee-line for the alcove and sat down, beckoning Coral to do likewise with a curl of his hand.

"What a beautiful view," Coral remarked, kneeling on the cushioned seating and peering out of the window.

The peacock continued to parade up and down the lawn with its magnificent tail-feathers splayed, whilst three disinterested pea-hens gorged themselves on redcurrants in the shrubbery.

"Isn't it just?" Sir Aubrey rejoined, his pale eyes sparkling like silver sixpences.

Then the diminutive ghost twisted his fire-opal ring once round his little finger. The ring made a light hissing sound. He slipped the ring off his finger, drew a pair of half-moon reading glasses from his waistcoat pocket and inspected the ring at close-quarters. Then he smiled a secretive smile, slipped the ring back on his little finger and placed his hands on his knees. The ring flashed briefly a deep magenta, and then faded back to its usual opaque orange.

"Won't you join us Jem?" Sir Aubrey said crisply, his eyes locked onto the back of the heavy King James Bible in Jem's hands.

The bible hit the table with an unholy thud as Jem abruptly let go of it.

"Yes please come and sit with us Jem. We can't fight for ever," Coral pleaded. "And stop pretending we're not here. We can both see you whether you like it or not."

"Thou canst see me? Both of thee?" Jem exclaimed, shocked.

"Indeed we can!" Sir Aubrey trilled brightly. "Delighted to meet you Jem, I've been meaning to introduce myself to you for quite some time. But you've always been so deeply engrossed in one book or other that I've not wanted to interrupt you," Sir Aubrey said cordially, keen to be on good terms with Jem.

The diminutive ghost floated a few feet up into the air and gave a low bow.

Jem's jaw dropped open.

"It must be a lot for you to take in," Coral remarked, smiling at Jem kindly.

Sir Aubrey performed a mini-pirouette in mid-air. Golden sparks shot out from his waistcoat pockets. Then he put his hand to his breast and bowed.

"I do so love to dance a minuet or a quadrille! I try to keep up with the latest dances. I'm not that keen on the waltz. It's a bit Teutonic for my taste. But I'm **in love** with the flamenco!" Sir Aubrey said ebulliently, thrusting his right arm in the air and curling his castanet fingers into an arc.

Then Sir Aubrey clicked his heels together and a flash of red flame shot out from his ruby-encrusted shoes.

Coral laughed. Jem stared at Sir Aubrey's shoes, speechless.

"Alas, I'm not as light on my feet as I used to be," Sir Aubrey confessed, lowering his arms, slightly out of breath. He pointed to his left knee and tapped it lightly. "Gout. Old age catches up with us all. Even ghosts!"

Then Sir Aubrey threw back his head and laughed a rich caviar laugh. Jem stared at Sir Aubrey dumbfounded. Coral smiled. Then the elderly ghost heaved a great melancholy sigh and his jaw set rigid. He stared past Jem and Coral as his mind travelled back in time to the Regency ballrooms of his youth.

Beautiful young girls dressed in elegant batiste gowns danced the night away, a strip of coloured ribbon tied beneath their shallow breasts. Young men danced beside them, suitably light-headed and light of heart. Everyone was so young, so happy and carefree!

Sir Aubrey sighed longingly. He tinkered with the end of his ponytail. Then his skin faded to an alabaster white as he remembered the Battle of Waterloo and the revolution in men's fashion that followed. After the famous show-down between Napoleon and Wellington on June 18th 1815, common sailor's trousers banished breeches forever! Sir Aubrey ran a delicate hand down the edge of his breeches. Who would ever have believed it?

Sombre men in tall hats took centre-stage, marking an end to periwigs and bouffon hair. Heavy velvet evening-dresses trimmed with swansdown filled the ballrooms. The men buttoned up and no longer danced freely. At dinner, the guests sat as stiff as pokers in their Wellington hats, Wellington bonnets and Wellington jackets made from twilled sarsnet. Outside in the street, Gentlemen loped along in the London fog cloaked in heavy Wellington mantles. The whole world became stiff and formal and Duke of Wellington mad.

The Regency parties ended and the first rumblings of the industrial revolution took hold. By the 1840s railways traversed the British countryside. Sir Aubrey had been happy to die and become a ghost. His death had been an insignificant death from the coughing disease consumption, not a brave hero's death like Nelson's at Trafalgar. But death had allowed him to return to the dreams of his youth. He had been spared the Machine Age. He had remained a young romantic fool happily dancing quadrilles in his mind forever!

"Sir Aubrey?" Coral said softly, wondering why he had frozen as still as a statue.

Sir Aubrey smiled faintly. There was nothing quite like an English summer and nothing quite like English girls dancing in the rain! The young people of today dancing in the rain at Glastonbury, reminded him of the Regency girls of his youth dancing the quadrille at a Country Fayre.

"Sir Aubrey, are you alright? You look dreadfully pale," Coral asked anxiously as Sir Aubrey's clothes drained of all colour.

A swirling white mist filled the room. All that remained of Sir Aubrey was his ring. It floated in the air: the ring of Kitty, his one true love.

"Sir Aubrey!" Coral exclaimed. "Sir Aubrey come back!"

Suddenly there was a burst of golden sparks. The swirling mass re-configured into the shape and substantial presence of Sir Aubrey. The elderly ghost smiled at Coral benignly, his skin still a pale white, his clothes a milky opal.

"Sorry my dear child, I did not mean to frighten you. I hadn't gone far. I was still here in spirit. A part of me is always here."

"Do you want to sit down?" Coral asked, still concerned about his welfare. "You're still awfully pale."

"I'm fine!" Sir Aubrey exclaimed ebulliently, snapping back to life with a starburst smile and click of the heels.

He shot back to his window-seat and sat down. Then he straightened his neck-tie, fingered his tie-pin and checked the curls of his hair. His fire-opal ring flashed a brilliant orange. His clothes burst back into their full range of colour: maroons, blues, violets and brilliant crimsons.

"Do join us Jem!" Sir Aubrey urged, patting the sumptuous red cushion beside him. "Bring the King James Bible with you if you want. I've always had a soft spot for good King James. He took a keen interest in witches! Did you know that Shakespeare wrote the play Macbeth especially for him?"

"No I didn't," Jem replied, bemused.

"Ah yes, King James was no fool! But enough of King James! Come and sit with us Jem. You have nothing to fear. After all, you and I both have all the time in the world."

"You and I?" Jem repeated, crossing the room with the bible held close to his chest, a look of bewilderment etched across his brow.

"Quite so," Sir Aubrey replied, smiling conspiratorially.

"Shall I explain Sir Aubrey?" Coral interrupted. "Or do you want to?"

"No, no, you go ahead, dear girl. I'm feeling awfully tired after that gruesome half hour with Mr. and Mrs. Phipps and their odious son. How that poor man puts up with that woman God only knows!"

"Mr. and Mrs. Phipps?" Jem repeated, his puzzlement growing.

"Mrs. Julia Phipps spotted me on the croquet lawn," Coral explained. "She immediately screamed at the top of her voice that I was the Missing Devon School Girl and tried to arrest me! I can only assume that she thought that I had run away from home and needed apprehending."

"Quite so, quite so," Sir Aubrey chimed in agreement.

"But Hartland Abbey is closed to the public on Mondays," Jem interrupted, wondering how the Phipps family had come to be in the Abbey grounds in the first place.

"That's what I thought!" Sir Aubrey exclaimed, rolling his eyes heavenward. "Only Mrs. Phipps is clearly a law unto herself! Fancied a picnic in the Walled Garden, the meddlesome busybody! And she had the audacity to put on airs and graces as if she owned the place. No matter, I soon put her straight. I pledged not to prosecute her for trespass provided she did not breathe a word about Coral's presence here to the press."

"And she agreed?" Jem asked dubiously.

"In the end," Sir Aubrey said wearily. "But it took some time. At one point Mrs. Phipps threatened to arrest **me** for having abducted Coral!" Sir Aubrey added indignantly. "The ridiculous woman! I wish the Marquis of Queensbury were still in residence. He could teach her a thing or two about manners!"

"The Marquis of Queensbury?" Jem repeated, even more confused than ever.

"Quite so. Only the Marquis is currently haunting the Houses of Parliament and having such a good time poking fun at the MPs that he really can't spare the time," Sir Aubrey added gleefully.

"The Marquis of Queensbury? The famous gentleman boxer? But he hast been dead for over a century," Jem argued.

"His ghost hasn't!" Sir Aubrey replied. "And who else would have the nerve to leak to the newspapers the MPs Expenses Scandal? The Marquis knows a thing or two about duck-islands and moats I can tell you."

"Sorry. But I do not understand thee," Jem replied, none the wiser.

"You don't need to understand Jem!" Sir Aubrey replied, laughing. "The important fact is this: Mrs. Julia Phipps will not go to the police because she is frightened of being prosecuted for trespass. What is more, she is currently staring goggle-eyed at a plate of cream scones in the kitchen, too frightened to eat the tiniest mouthful."

"So we are safe?" Jem asked uncertainly.

"As safe as houses!" Sir Aubrey replied happily.

"And how long hast thou known about my existence, Sir Aubrey?" Jem asked.

"For as long as you've been able to see me old chum!" Sir Aubrey replied, his eyes brimming with mischief. "Two hundred odd years, I should hazard a guess."

Jem's jaw dropped open for the third time in the space of a few hours.

"I still don't understand," Jem said anxiously, at a total loss.

"It's like this Jem," Coral said kindly, her voice as soft as a lamb's fleece. "Sir Aubrey is the type of ghost that I wrongly accused you of being. He really can walk through glass – in and out of mirrors – and do all the kind of things that **real** ghosts can do. But he can't manipulate objects like you and I can. He really **is** a ghost, just like his good friend the Marquis of Queensbury is a ghost. But **you're** totally different. You're a Sentient Corporal Entity."

"A what?" Jem repeated, his cheeks reddening.

"A Sentient Corporal Entity," Sir Aubrey repeated. "I've only met a couple in my time. They're incredibly rare."

"In other words you're special Jem! You're in a half-way place, somewhere in-between the spirit world and the ordinary world that I inhabit," Coral explained.

"A Sentient Corporal Entity?" Jem repeated, not sure whether he liked the description or not.

"Don't worry!" Coral exclaimed, reading his mind. "Just be pleased that you now know what you are."

"Why should I be pleased?" Jem said sullenly, still annoyed with her for having called him a ghost.

"Good heavens, young man. Show some manners!" Sir Aubrey exclaimed, startled by Jem's rudeness. "The young girl made a perfectly natural mistake in calling you a ghost and should be forgiven."

"That's a matter of opinion," Jem said grudgingly.

"Dear boy, how ungrateful can you get?" Sir Aubrey demanded, springing to his feet outraged. "You have a solid corporal form that continues to need food and water whereas I am but a spirit of the air condemned to consume nothing but water molecules for eternity! **I** have not eaten a decent square meal for two centuries whereas **you** regularly tuck into the succulent sweet-heart cabbages in the Walled Garden without so much as a moment's bye your leave! It's quite scandalous how ungrateful you are. Not to mention all the raspberries you help yourself to! I'd give my eye-teeth to taste a raspberry again!"

Jem glowered.

"Hast thou been spying on me, Sir Aubrey?"

"Good heavens no! I have far more interesting things to do with my time than spy on **you** Master Jem. The source of my knowledge is Edward the Head Gardener. Edward knows all about your little escapades. He's forever talking about the mysterious visitor that likes to lift baby gem lettuces in the dead of night. Edward holds forth at the Red Lion most nights, waxing lyrical on the mystery of his disappearing parsnips and fraudulent French beans."

"I shall try to be more careful in future," Jem said solemnly. "I didst not realise the Head Gardener saw me."

"Oh don't worry about Edward. He sees everything," Sir Aubrey replied, grinning from cheek-to-cheek. "As do I, Jem!

I've always had eyes in the back of my head even **before** I was a ghost."

"And how many people can see us both?" Jem asked nervously, the full implications of Sir Aubrey's revelation only just sinking in.

"That's an impossible question to answer," Sir Aubrey replied. "The spirit world is a confusing place at the best of times. Your guess is as good as mine dear boy."

"I still do not understand!" Jem thundered, looking accusingly at both Sir Aubrey and Coral.

"Dear me, what **more** is there to understand?" Sir Aubrey asked wearily.

"Canst the Phipps family see me?" Jem demanded.

Jem had always assumed that he was invisible to everybody. The idea that he might be visible to more people than he had ever considered possible genuinely terrified him.

"Indubitably," Sir Aubrey replied matter-of-factly. "But don't worry. We shan't set Julia Phipps loose on you, shall we Coral?" he added with a churlish grin. "Rest assured Jem, the vast majority of the adult population **cannot** see ghosts. They are far too unimaginative. But children can and often do."

"Art thou saying that Mr and Mrs. Phipps and their son Daniel can all see ghosts?" Jem asked bluntly.

"Absolutely," Coral replied. "All three members of the Phipps family possess a vivid imagination and therefore have the ability to see ghosts."

"But crucially when they first saw me, they did not realise that I was a ghost," Sir Aubrey explained, picking up the story. "They all thought that I was the rightful owner of Hartland Abbey. Indeed, everything was going fine until Mrs. Phipps changed her mind about keeping quiet and decided to arrest me! Even though she is a woman of very little brain, she soon realised that something was wrong when every time she lunged at me all she could catch hold of was thin air. I soon realised that the only way I was going to get any peace and quiet was to scare them all into silence. So I introduced Coral to them as the Ghost of the Missing Devon School Girl."

"All I had to do was to pretend to take a bite from a scone and to place it back on the plate uneaten," Coral explained, taking up the narrative. "Then Sir Aubrey floated up through the ceiling to scare them and re-appeared through the tablecloth! You should have seen their faces! It was so funny!" Coral giggled, a little bit of Sir Aubrey's devilment clearly having rubbed off on her. "But the ruse worked brilliantly and Julia Phipps stopped screaming and sat still for a change."

"But surely the Phipps family will now go to the police and tell them all about us?" Jem asked anxiously, his logical mind methodically working its way through all the assembled facts. "They promised not to go to the authorities for fear of being sued for trespass by Sir Hugh Stucley, the real owner of Hartland Abbey. But now that they know that Sir Aubrey is a ghost, what's stopping them from going to the police straight away?"

"Because they can't go to the police and say that they're seen two ghosts in Hartland Abbey without making themselves look like complete idiots!" Coral replied, laughing. "Besides, right now Mrs. Phipps is too scared to say anything to anybody."

Jem swallowed hard, trying to dispel from his mind the memory of the witch-hunt two centuries ago when he had had the misfortune to be spotted by a visitor to Hartland. At that time a large proportion of the British public believed in ghosts.

The village had united to hound him out of existence with every farming implement, scythe, gun, stick and stone available to them!

There was so much that Coral did not understand about the history of prejudice and he was loathe to tell her about it; some stories were so dark they were best left buried in the past where they belonged.

"Jem, please stop being angry with me. You must forgive me for having called you a ghost," Coral said quietly, the perpendicular line in her forehead pronounced.

Jem's cheeks coloured. Coral's blue eyes pleaded with a lustrous intensity that it was impossible to ignore.

But before Jem could say or do anything, Sir Aubrey sprang to his feet and floated up into the air and smiled at them enigmatically.

"Ah the trials and tribulations of young love! I have been in love many times in my life but that first, intense, arrow-piercing love affair is **always** the most memorable. Even if it does invariably end in tears!"

Coral burst into fits of giggles, not in the least bit embarrassed by Sir Aubrey's sudden outburst. There was something incredibly tongue-in-cheek about Sir Aubrey that made her take what he said with a pinch of salt.

Sir Aubrey blanched, hurt that Coral did not take him seriously. Inwardly his heart yearned to extol the power of love to heal the deepest of wounds. His ring flashed magenta. He drew it to his lips and kissed it. *Kitty my love where are you?*

"Thou art mistaken, Sir Aubrey," Jem said gruffly. "Coral and I are just good friends."

Sir Aubrey shook his head defiantly.

"Mistaken? Nonsense! I'm always right in affairs of the heart," Sir Aubrey exclaimed, crossing his arms emphatically.

Coral sprang to her feet, deciding that now was the time to intervene.

"I've had enough of you two bickering. I need to go home to Shell Cottage and tell Hazel that I'm OK. And you, Sir Aubrey, need to go downstairs and show the Phipps family home. You can't leave them locked in the kitchen in soaking wet clothes a moment longer. It simply isn't kind," Coral concluded with a steely smile.

"As you wish," Sir Aubrey replied, bowing low. "But I insist you take the horse and carriage to Shell Cottage. It's too far to walk." He turned to address Jem. "I take it that you know how to handle a carriage and horses young man?"

"I know enough…"

"Then take the trap from the stable. No-one will miss it. But you'll have to be quick about it. A driverless carriage might cause quite a stir if someone spots you."

"Excuse me, but aren't you both forgetting somebody?" Coral said indignantly. "I know how to ride a wild Exmoor pony. I'm sure I can manage a horse and trap."

"Well I'd be damned! A lady carriage-driver! Bravo young lady, bravo!" Sir Aubrey exclaimed, clapping his hands in praise.

Jem glowered.

"Do not curse in front of a lady Sir Aubrey!"

"Oh honestly, dear boy, why do you insist on being so old-fashioned? Damnation is hardly a swear word these days. And isn't it time you learnt to speak the Queen's English? All these 'thees' and 'thous' and 'hadsts' and 'wouldsts' are driving me to distraction. It's not as if you now how to use them correctly either. Your grammar is all over the place!"

157

"Actually, that's a good point Sir Aubrey," Coral commented. "How come you were both born in the eighteenth century but you each speak so differently?"

"Oh that's easy to explain young lady. I am a gentleman, educated in three tongues – English, Latin and French – whilst Master Jem here speaks with a faint Devonshire accent of the time, overlaid with biblical phraseology. Self-taught I believe."

Jem blushed.

Sir Aubrey grinned.

"And now if you would both follow me, I shall lead you to the stable-yard. Young lady, your carriage awaits…"

CHAPTER ELEVEN

Home Sweet Home

The smell of fresh hay and pungent horsy breath assailed Jem's nostrils as he entered the Abbey stables. The two mares greeted him with nuzzling heads and welcoming snorts. They knew Jem from his numerous visits to the Walled Garden to collect vegetables and fruit.

On the way back home Jem would often stop at the stables to give Delilah and Flaxen the odd carrot top or two. In return, the mares did not breathe a word to anyone about the straw Jem secretly 'borrowed' to protect the leaves of his young strawberry plants from marauding earwigs. Instead the shrewd horses turned a blind eye, looking forward to a handful of fresh Devon strawberries come the end of June.

Jem led the two medium sized mares out of the stables towards the little trap and harnessed them securely. Coral jumped up into the driver's seat and eagerly took the reins. He sat down beside her, trying to mask his concern that the horses might disobey an unknown handler.

Jem need not have worried. With a ruffle of their manes and a gentle tug on the reins, Coral immediately took control. The horses set off at a steady trot down the long, majestic drive. The sun shone through the magnificent beech trees, the smooth brown trunks glistening in the afternoon sun.

They soon reached Wild Country Lane and started down it towards Pancake Hollow.

The hazel and beech hedgerows were bursting with wild clematis and pink shrub roses, all bound together by the rapier grip of the wild brambles.

Flaxen, the senior of the two horses, was harnessed to the right-hand side of the carriage on the road side. Meanwhile her skittish daughter Delilah was assigned to the left. Delilah needed a regular reminder with a sharp tug of the reins to check her stride and stay close to the hedgerow.

"Not too fast Coral," Jem cautioned as Delilah made a break for freedom on the open road.

"It's OK, the horses are fine!" Coral replied, secretly not too certain how to slow the carriage down.

However the mares seemed to have a momentum of their own. Coral decided to trust Flaxen's gut instinct and not to worry too much about their speed. Indeed, if the truth be told, Coral was not a seasoned rider at all. But an eagerness to muck out the donkey stables at Saunton Sands had earned her lessons from old Bernie Witherspoon, the Donkey Man.

Now approaching eighty years of age with crippling arthritis in his lower back, Bernie was more than happy to let the kid with the moonshine laugh clean out his stables in return for a lesson or two.

Bernie had taught Coral the basics. The inkpot ponies had taught her the rest. A gentle tap on the fetlock got the ponies from a walk to a trot. A tickle of the spine and a promise of fresh king cups got the ponies loping across the bell heather at a steady canter. But Coral had never mastered a gallop or a controlled stop.

The inkpot ponies tended to stop when they wanted, generally where there was some good pasture. The beach donkeys always stopped at the edge of the sand-dunes in the shade.

"If we're lucky we shan't meet anybody coming the other way," Jem commented, brows puckered.

"We'll be lucky," Coral replied happily. "One more hill and we'll be in Pancake Hollow. You'll be able to see the spiral chimney of Shell Cottage any second now."

"Thou livest there?" Jem exclaimed, surprised. "I've always wondered who didst live in the house with the twisted witch's chimney."

"You've got a nerve Jem, likening my chimney to a witch's broomstick, coming from some-one offended at being called a ghost!" Coral exclaimed, flashing him an artful smile.

"That's different," Jem replied awkwardly.

"I don't see that it is. Besides, I didn't mean to offend you when I called you a ghost."

"I know thou didst not."

"Hazel says offence should never be taken unless intended."

Jem raised his eyebrows.

"Surely Coral that is the whole point about offence? People do not usually set out to offend others. I know that thou didst not intend to hurt my feelings by calling me a ghost but thou didst still offend me."

"But you shouldn't have been offended!" Coral argued, refusing to back down. "I was just describing you in the only words I knew. How was I to know that the word 'ghost' would offend you? I did not intentionally set out to offend you."

"And thy point is?"

"That we shouldn't jump to conclusions about anything!"

"I guess there's merit in what thou sayest," Jem replied, not sure if there was a disagreement between them or not.

Coral had the awkward habit of talking so very fast that he ended up agreeing with her before he had had sufficient time to properly reflect upon what she had just said. He was not sure whether this was a good or bad thing. All he knew for certain was that Coral would make a very successful Justice of the Peace.

"Look, Shell Cottage!" Coral exclaimed excitedly.

The pretty pink and brown tiled roof of Shell Cottage glistened in the afternoon sun like swirls of hot toffee and pink sugar-candy. Meanwhile its spiral chimney provided a comfortable perch for a pair of portly woodpigeons.

"Not so fast Coral. We don't want to turn the carriage over!"

"Stop worrying Jem. I've never known such a worrier, your every other word is don't, watch out or be careful."

"That's because there is an awful lot to worry about," Jem replied, brows furrowed. "People are unpredictable. Accidents do not just happen. Careless people **make** them happen."

"True. But people are also like onions, there are so many different layers to them, we really shouldn't jump to conclusions about them too quickly," Coral replied, relieved that the two mares had finally decided to slow down as they descended the steep slope into Pancake Hollow. "Take my mum Hazel. She wants to be called by her first name Hazel and not to be called

Mum. Now most women don't have a problem with being called Mum but Hazel does. However deep-down, Hazel still wants to be thought of as my mum. She just doesn't want to be called Mum out-loud."

Jem scratched his head. Hazel sounded a lot like Flossie with her very long-winded and devious explanations as to why there was burnt caramel in the saucepan and neat squares of perfectly good caramel hidden in her dress pocket.

"In fact Hazel's view is quite straight-forward," Coral continued, getting into her stride. "Hazel believes in total equality between men and women. She thinks that the label 'Mum' masks a woman's true identity and that the term 'Dad' masks a man's true identity. Get it?"

"I think so," Jem said slowly. "But I don't agree."

"No-one's asking you to agree Jem!" Coral exclaimed. "My grandmother totally disagrees with Hazel. The last thing Nan wants is to be considered equal to men. As far as Nan is concerned she's infinitely **superior**. Nan is quite happy to let Grandad work in Bristol all day whilst she busies herself at home doing whatever she pleases. Nan would far sooner make home-made jam and do exciting things like bungee-jumping than be a wage-slave like Grandad! In fact Nan thinks that middle-class career women are mad. They had a cushy deal and now they've gone and squandered it."

"Thy grandmother is lucky. My grandmother hadst no choice but to work or she'd have gone hungry," Jem remarked, wondering what 'bungee-jumping' entailed.

Coral tugged hard on the reins realising that she had overstepped the mark.

"Here we are, Jem, Shell Cottage!"

"Careful!" Jem shouted nervously as Coral steered the little gig towards a grass verge adjacent to a farm track and skidded to a halt.

"I think the gig will be OK here, we're not blocking the lane," Coral said, leaning forwards and giving both horses a stroke on the side of the neck. "Thank you girls for behaving so well: I'll fetch you a carrot each from the garden for your pains."

Jem watched Coral disappear around the back of Shell Cottage. She re-emerged carrying two fine orange carrots with green feathery tops, her hands dusted with red clay earth.

"Your grandmother sounds quite a character," Jem remarked, taking a carrot and shaking off the mud before feeding it to Flaxen whilst Coral fed the other carrot to Delilah. "What didst thou say thy grandmother does apart from making fudge? Bungee…?"

"Bungee-jumping!"

"And what exactly is that?"

"Well, basically you hurl yourself head-first off the top of a bridge suspended by a piece of elastic," Coral replied, grinning at Jem's horrified expression.

"But why?" Jem asked, goggle-eyed.

"For fun!"

"I'd sooner stick to fishing or diving," Jem remarked sceptically, wondering how many people liked to bungee-jump.

"Actually Jem, whilst we're on the subject of fishing and diving, I thought I might tell Hazel that I got injured diving off Old Man's Elbow. I don't want her to know that I was beaten up by Antonia. Is that OK by you Jem?"

"What?" Jem exclaimed, appalled. "But they attacked you! They might have killed you."

The thought of Antonia and James getting away scot-free was simply too much for Jem to stomach. He wanted them brought to account.

"But they **didn't** kill me," Coral said calmly, stroking Delilah's black mane.

"But they could have blinded you!" Jem remonstrated, too angry to stroke Flaxen.

The wise old mare backed away from him, wary of his temper.

"But they didn't blind me Jem. I can see perfectly OK."

"That's not the point. They must be brought to justice. Commonsense and morality demand it."

Coral smiled a wintry smile.

"Commonsense is thin on the ground Jem. And there's no such thing as a universal morality. Everything is relative."

"All the more reason to reassert a common morality based on the law of the land!"

"It won't work Jem. People are too divided on what the law should say."

"But those callous ragamuffins must not be allowed to get away with it!"

"Forget about them Jem. I want to protect Hazel. She's only just got over John's death. If Hazel were to find out what happened to me, it would destroy her."

Jem sucked in his cheeks, trying to maintain his sangfroid. Then he relaxed his jaw and continued speaking.

"I acknowledge that thy mother has been through a lot Coral. But Antonia and James still need to be punished. If they think that they can get away with murder, maybe next time they will."

"No Jem, I don't think so. They scared themselves. They won't be that violent ever again - not Kim, Tom or Antonia."

"And James?"

Coral hesitated.

"Not even James."

"Thou dost not sound certain."

"I'm as certain as I can be," Coral replied. "So Jem, will you promise not to tell Hazel what happened?"

"I shan't tell Hazel what happened because I shan't meet her," Jem replied gruffly.

Coral's face fell.

"Please come with me Jem. I need your support. You can't run out on me now!"

"I'm not running out on thee Coral! I'm invisible, I cannot come with you. Cowardice has nothing to do with it."

"But Hazel **might** be able to see you…"

"If Hazel can see me then I shall tell her everything. I will not lie to her, Coral, not even for thee!" Jem said hoarsely, wishing that they had never started this conversation.

The door to Shell Cottage opened suddenly. Hazel sprinted across the lawn, tears spilling forth from her luminous grey eyes.

"Coral! Coral! You're back! I **knew** you were alive!"

Hazel flung her arms about Coral and clasped her tightly to her chest. Then she ran her bony hands repeatedly through her daughter's unkempt hair, her blunt nails catching on Coral's tangled, honeycomb ends.

Delilah whinnied loudly, struggling to break free from the little gig.

"Where ever did you get those horses from?" Hazel asked, surprised. She drew back and looked directly into Coral's face. Then she gasped in horror as the star-shaped scar registered.

"My God, whatever have you done to yourself Coral?"

"It's a long story," Coral replied.

"Then tell me! Come and sit down on the verandah and tell me immediately," Hazel instructed imperiously, grabbing Coral by the arm and frog-marching her over to the verandah to sit down. "What happened?"

Jem struggled to calm Delilah whilst Hazel interrogated Coral about where she had been for the past six weeks. But the black mare did not take kindly to having an invisible groom and made life extremely difficult for him.

Meanwhile Coral proceeded to construct a fabulous piece of fiction which Jem could only marvel at. According to Coral's version of events, she had taken the train to Newquay for the day and ended up at the Sunrise Festival. By the time the last band had finished their set, it had been too late for her to take the last train home so she had crashed out in a tipi owned by a girl called Vicky from Wells.

The next day, the festival was soon in full swing and one music festival led to another and before Coral knew it she was on the road, first with Vicky and her brother Nick in their bright yellow campervan; then with a group of New Age travellers who lived in authentic gypsy wagons with painted shutters and old-fashioned wooden wheels.

Coral then explained how she had finally fallen out with her fellow travellers over the treatment of their horses. The travellers loved their animals well enough but skimped on the basics. The horses were fed well but they badly needed to see a blacksmith to be re-shod. Added to that, the long hours on the road had really begun to take a toll on the animals' health.

Finally Coral had decided to do a runner in the little gig, taking the two mares with her. She promised Hazel that she would return them as soon as possible. In the meantime the horses would be fine at the Abbey stables.

Jem marvelled at Hazel's willingness to believe Coral's far-fetched story. Then he reflected that the mind often sees only what it wants to see and that it can take the truth much longer to register.

"But even so, you should have telephoned me Coral!" Hazel admonished, clasping the bottom of Coral's chin and looking her squarely in the eye. "I've been worried sick."

"I know. I'm sorry Hazel."

"Just promise me that you'll never run off like that again. If there's a problem, tell me and we can work it out. Do you promise?"

"I promise."

"Good. And for my part, I promise not to crowd you," Hazel replied, looking directly into Coral's contrite blue eyes. She smiled tenderly. "Goodness, you've been left with one hell of a scar beneath your left eye. Whatever did you do to yourself? You're lucky not to have had your eye out. What happened? Did you spike your cheek on a bramble or something? Did you fall off one of the horses whilst exercising them?"

"Yes. I fell off Delilah and landed in a hedgerow. I snagged my cheek on a wild shrub rose," Coral replied, substituting the shrub rose for Antonia's synthetic daisy-tread.

Hazel craned forward in John's white wicker chair and examined the smooth scar on their daughter's face. Then she ran her index finger along Coral's left cheek-bone, down the bridge of her nose, up to that high forehead with the deep indention running like a spine of a leaf across it. Finally her finger travelled down to those cherry blossom lips, forever pursed in contemplation.

Then Hazel stood up abruptly, satisfied that she had got her daughter back.

"Let's go inside darling. You look exhausted," Hazel said decisively. Then she glanced down at Coral's pillow-case shoes. "What on earth have you got on your feet darling?"

"Pillow-cases. Don't ask – it's a long story."

"I can imagine."

Smiling, Hazel put her arm around her daughter's shoulders and led her into the cool, comfortable interior of Shell Cottage.

Jem watched protectively as they disappeared inside Shell Cottage. Then he stroked Delilah's flank, trying to keep her calm. But the young mare was restless by nature. He knew that she would not be happy harnessed to the gig for much longer. He quickly gave her a handful of meadowsweet and left her grazing on the roadside verge.

Then he pushed open the pretty kissing-gate and stepped through the arch of wild clematis into the front garden of Shell Cottage. He started down the herring-bone path towards the verandah. *Just one peak inside the house would satisfy his curiosity and put his mind at rest.* If he saw Hazel and Coral deep in animated conversation then he would know that all was well.

Jem tiptoed along the verandah. Garlands of honeysuckle brushed against his elbows as he passed beneath the fragrant bowers. Bees clustered about the honeysuckle, gorging on the sweet nectar of the delicate pink and white tubular flowers. He paused outside the bay-window, cupped his right hand to his ear and leant forwards to listen.

But Jem only had time to glimpse two silhouettes seated by the fireside when there was a loud snapping sound behind him as Delilah broke free from her harness and bolted headlong through the gate into the garden.

Flaxen immediately reared up on her hind-legs. Beaded bubbles appeared at the mare's mouth as she strained to free herself from her bridle, desperate to join Delilah in the flowerbed nibbling the tender young shoots.

"Whoa! Easy does it Flaxen my lovely. Let me unclip thee. Then I'll take thee down to join thy daughter in the garden," Jem said softly, shepherding the fearful grey through the front gate onto the lawn.

Jem darted back to the gig, thankful that he had had the presence of mind to bring a couple of leather head-collars with him from the Abbey Stables. A sixth sense had told him that things might not go to plan and that he needed to be prepared for every eventuality.

Then his face fell as he realised that he had two head-collars but only one lead-rope. The other lead-rope must have fallen off the gig when they flew round the corners too fast. He would just have to improvise. The first horse he had to bring into line was Delilah. Flaxen ought not to pose so much of a problem.

Jem duly returned to the garden and approached Delilah. She was busy eating the grass at the foot of an apple tree. Every so often she reached up with her neck and nibbled the leaves of a nearby thorn tree. The thorn tree was no more than five feet high but its twisted branches were covered in lethal inch-long thorns. Delilah cleverly circumnavigated the thorns, concentrating on the tiny half-penny sized leaves. A swathe of pretty harebells tickled her hooves, the delicate bell-shaped flowers cast in the shape of pixie bonnets.

"Easy does it Delilah, my lovely," Jem whispered softly, slipping a head-collar over her head without too much difficulty. "Let me tie thee to the apple tree. Then thou canst continue to munch the grass in safety," Jem murmured, attaching a guide-rope to her head-collar then securing the other end of the rope to the apple tree.

He now scanned the garden for a means of securing Flaxen. The yellow cord of the washing-line might work. He carefully untied the washing-line from the hook on the exterior wall of Shell Cottage and approached Flaxen. The mare paused momentarily whilst he slotted the head-collar over her neck but the tasty cardoons in the border interested her far more than the yellow line.

Jem smiled, satisfied with a job well done. Then he returned to his window vantage-point. He froze, shocked by the change in the scene before him. Hazel's jaw was locked in anger. Coral's eyes brimmed with tears. Both women were in the throes of a volatile argument.

"There's nothing the matter with the horses! Something must have scared them. But they're alright now," Coral said tearfully.

"And how do they come to be in my garden?" Hazel demanded, angrily gesturing towards the front lawn.

Coral averted her eyes.

"It's not what you think Mum."

"Don't presume to know what I think young lady!"

"Sorry Mum."

"And stop calling me Mum! My name is Hazel. Two horses do not un-harness themselves of their own accord and enter my garden unaided! Some-one else must have assisted them."

Coral gulped guiltily.

"You're right Mum. I lied to you. I'm sorry."

Hazel's angry grey eyes mellowed into a passionate entreaty for the truth. She kneaded her long skirt twixt her liver-spotted hands. Lying did not become Coral; it became nobody.

"Thank you Coral. Now I'd like you to tell me the truth. Just tell me everything. Don't leave out any details. However insignificant they may seem to you, they might be significant to me. I won't be angry with you. I promise."

Coral wiped the tears from her eyes, cornered. Her lips opened but no words issued forth. *How could she tell the truth?* The truth had no place in their conversation. The truth was something **other**.

"I can't Mum! I'd like to tell you but you wouldn't believe me if I did," Coral exclaimed tearfully, furious with herself for not having anticipated such an outcome.

Delilah had been difficult to handle from the start. If she had only let Jem drive the gig then none of this would have happened. But she had been so cocky and confident that nothing could go wrong, and she had so much wanted to prove to Jem that a twenty-first century girl could hold her own with any boy!

"Try me," Hazel said sharply. "The truth can't hurt us anymore than we're hurting now. I know half the story already, so you may as well tell me the rest. You're not alone, are you Coral? Who else was in that carriage with you?" Hazel demanded, her eyes like vitreous glass.

Silence.

Hazel marched over to the window and peered outside in the direction of the herbaceous border with its row of imperious red hollyhocks, magnificent cardoons and purple ornamental thistles. As Hazel drew back the curtains, Coral caught a fleeting glimpse of Jem's face pressed up against the window-pane.

"His name is Jem! He's a friend. I met him at the Sunrise Festival. He helped me with the horses."

"Is that all he did?" Hazel asked quietly, letting go of the muslin curtain and turning away from the window.

Jem's face vanished from view. Coral gulped.

Hazel stared at Coral long and hard, waiting for a direct answer.

"OK Mum if you must know, Jem nursed my wounds with soapwort flowers and bloodwort tincture."

"Bloodwort? Don't talk gibberish! I've had enough of your flights of fancy! You sound just like my mother with her crazy home-made remedies."

"It's not gibberish! If Jem hadn't used bloodwort, my face would still be in a terrible state. You've no idea how badly cut and bruised I was when he found me!"

"Found you? Where did this Jem person find you?"

"Nothing. Forget what I just said."

"Tell me the truth Coral **now**! Or do I have to go outside and find this Jem person myself and drag him in here by the scruff of the neck to sort this all out once and for all?" Hazel bellowed, the veins in her temples pulsing. "Well then, what's it to be Coral? I'm waiting for an answer!"

The door opened. A light draught drifted down the hallway. The country air was laced with the scent of apple blossom and the strong stench of horse sweat.

Hazel froze in her armchair, her clear grey eyes locked onto the thin strip of blue sky that was visible through the open doorway.

"Come in," Hazel said crisply, her voice steel-tipped.

There was no reply.

"Show yourself!" Hazel demanded, standing up and stepping lightly onto the ragged jute rug.

Jem entered the room and smiled at Coral appeasingly.

"Sorry about the horses Coral. I couldn't control them."

"It's OK Jem. I understand," Coral whispered, disappointed that Hazel could not see Jem.

"Where is he Coral? I know you can see him. I'm not stupid," Hazel demanded, her eyes locked onto the jute rug. She had vacuumed the rug this morning and it had not been rucked up then. But it was rucked up now...

"On the rug," Coral replied, stunned by her mother's insight. "Thank you darling. It's nice to be told the truth for a change."

Then Hazel spun round, grabbed an ornamental vase from the sideboard and slammed it down hard on what she hoped was Jem's head.

"Mum, stop it! Jem isn't dangerous!" Coral shouted as a dazed Jem staggered backwards, fragments of broken blue and white china lodged in his hair.

174

"Jem rescued me from Antonia and the rest of her gang. They're the ones who were trying to hurt me, not Jem! If it hadn't been for Jem, I'd be dead!"

Hazel's body locked rigid. She tried to say something but couldn't. The colour drained from her face. She took a few steps back and sat down on the sofa. Her eyes welled with tears. She put her hand to her throat and clasped it tightly, smothering her fire-coral necklace with her thin palm.

"Antonia hurt you?" Hazel said in a ghostly voice. "Why didn't you tell me?"

Coral gulped.

"I was too scared to tell you."

Hazel nodded. Then she tugged once with her fingers and ripped off her neck-lace. Tiny coral beads scattered in all directions.

"I'm to blame. I'm to blame for everything," Hazel said quietly, her voice like smouldering hot coals. "We should have stayed in Sheffield. I should have let you grow up like an ordinary teenager instead of creating this magical, fairy-tale world. Everything is my fault."

Then Hazel broke off and kneaded her denim skirt with her hot hands, working the stiff material up and down with the balls of her palms. Then she stabbed her right thigh with her left elbow and fell still.

"My only defence is that after John's death I didn't want you to worry about money and earning a living when you grew up," Hazel continued softly, the self-pity banished from her voice. "So I taught you how to make shell necklaces and showed you how to paint with water-colours, oils, gouache and pastels. I encouraged you to make crazy textile creations - twisting, drawing, sewing - the list was endless. I took you rock-climbing, fossil-hunting, everything-ing... But the mistake I made is that I didn't just **show** you. I **trapped** you inside a world of your imagination. It is little wonder that you can't relate to kids your own age. Sooner or later someone was bound to pick on you."

"No!" Coral shouted, stepping forward and cradling Hazel's convulsed body in her arms. "I wanted to do all those crazy creative things! I still do. But you're right in some ways. I'm not finding the transition to adult-hood easy. But I'll always be your creative daughter Coral and you'll always be my mum Hazel. **Because that is who and what we are!** And hey, how many mums would have the presence of mind to strike a man on the head with a vase? A man that they can't even see! Mum, you're cooler than the Devil Who Wears Prada whether you want to be or not!"

Hazel wiped the tears from her cheeks with the back of her hands.

"That's very sweet of you to say darling."

"It's not sweet. It's the truth."

Jem stood motionless and watched intently as mother and daughter sat down on the sofa, oblivious of his presence. He thought of little Flossie with her hot squares of fudge stuffed in her calico apron pockets and dearest Mother with her bunches of lavender draped over the fire to dry and he reckoned that the world hadn't changed so very much. There were only two basic kinds of people: those with open minds and hearts and those who are inward-looking and closed.

Perhaps being a Sentient Corporal Entity wasn't such a bad thing after all? He got to witness every shade of life and was by far the richer for it.

CHAPTER TWELVE

Danger

The sound of the horses braying in alarm broke the mood of subdued silence in Shell Cottage. Jem and Coral rushed to the window and looked out. Sudbury Court was ablaze! They hastened outside to calm the horses.

The terrified mares raked the bark of the trees with their front hooves, their nostrils flared fearfully in recognition of the killer-smoke.

"Flaxen stay! Delilah, stay!" Jem said firmly.

But this was one battle that Jem could not win. Neither firm commands nor soothing words were going to calm either horse.

Hazel remained indoors, stunned by Coral's revelation. *Had she heard correctly?* Antonia had attacked Coral and left her for dead? *It was inconceivable! Unbelievable! And totally unforgivable…*

Outside, Coral froze on the lawn, her eyes locked onto the wisps of black smoke that curled and twisted about the red-brick walls of the Tudor Manor House.

Initially the smoke appeared manageable – like the lone puffs of a camp fire – but in the space of a few minutes the plumes of sinewy smoke had quadrupled in number, rendering the sky a pall of black.

The horses grew more and more nervous. The whites of their eyes seemed to double in size as the danger drew nearer. Flaxen reared up on her hind-legs, trying to free herself from the plastic washing-line cord. Delilah drummed the ground with her front hooves. The young black mare lowered her head and pulled hard on the guide-rope, the only thing binding her to the apple tree. The rope was strong but not tough enough to withstand so much pressure. The lower branches of the apple tree shook. Apples rained down to the ground.

Spooked by the sudden shower of heavy green apples, Delilah strained again and this time she broke free. She bolted straight through the open gate and galloped back up the lane towards Hartland Abbey, dragging the guide-rope behind her.

Flaxen whinnied plaintively, desperate to follow Delilah to freedom. Rivulets of water snaked across the elderly mare's white neck as her whole body broke out in a cold sweat. Coral could not bear the sight a moment longer and ignoring Jem's shouts of warning, darted forwards to free the mare.

"Easy Flaxen, easy does it," Coral said softly, untying the yellow cord that bound her. "Off you go girl! Go home to Hartland Abbey and safety!"

Flaxen flew through the garden gate, out of Pancake Hollow onto the moors.

Jem and Coral watched her go. Then they turned and stared in horror at the blazing inferno that engulfed the Tudor Manor House.

Sudbury Court was about a mile away as the crow flies. However in the illuminated evening sky it looked alarmingly close. The black mushroom cloud was headed in their direction and threatened to engulf the entire Hartland peninsular.

Hazel appeared at the cottage window and stared unseeingly at the pall of black. Her jaw locked, her loose hands lightly pummelled the edge of her cheesecloth skirt.

Then she turned and slowly walked back to the sofa and sat down, lost in her own private thoughts.

"We need to check that someone has alerted the Fire-Brigade," Coral said swiftly, making eye-contact with Jem.

He nodded, in total agreement. Then he followed Coral into the living-room of Shell Cottage.

Hazel did not register their presence. She sat perched on the edge of the sofa, her eyes glazed, her spindle-thin legs crossed, her brows knotted in thought.

Coral ran round the back of the sofa to the writing bureau, seized the black plastic handset of the retro 1950s telephone and rapidly punched the dirty grey keys.

"Hello. I need the Fire Brigade."

"What's your post code?" the woman on the end of the line enquired.

"It doesn't matter. The fire isn't here, it's at…"

The line went dead.

"Hello? Damn! I've been cut off!" Coral exclaimed, punching the numbers 999 again.

Jem's jaw locked in fury. He spun round and glared at the indentation in the cotton sofa where Hazel had been sitting moments earlier.

"The lines aren't down Coral. Thy mother has cut the connection," Jem said furiously, seizing the pair of sewing scissors out of Hazel's pincer-like fingers.

"Hazel! What did you do that for? Sudbury Court is on fire!" Coral exclaimed in disbelief.

"Let it burn," Hazel replied, her lips pinched, her agate eyes burning with a deep hatred.

"But Antonia's grandmother lives in Sudbury Court! She's an old lady!"

"Then she'll have to move quickly," Hazel rejoined, her eyes hard, her jaw as tough as millstone grit.

"You can't mean that Hazel! Just because Antonia beat me up doesn't mean that her grandmother deserves to die on my account!"

Hazel remained silent. But the tight lips and wild eyes said everything that needed to be said.

"Coral, do you have one of those telephones without wires?" Jem said urgently, scouring the room for any electronic device that might be what they needed.

"Yes but I don't have any credit," Coral replied. Then her voice trailed off and her eyes locked onto her mother's handbag.

But Hazel second-guessed Coral. A freckled hand latched onto the mobile and lobbed it straight into the fish tank. There was a loud splash followed by a heavy thud as the mobile hit the bottom of the glass tank, sending shockwaves throughout the water. The angel-fish dispersed in a blur of beaded yellow and black bubbles.

Jem rammed his fist into the tank and pulled out the mobile. But it was too late: the mechanism was already dead.

"What is it with thy modern machines? Why do they not work in water?" Jem exclaimed, thinking back to his beloved wind-up radio that Tom had so cruelly tossed into the sea.

"Mum, why did you do that?" Coral shouted, distraught. "Why? Two wrongs don't make a right!"

"True. But it makes me feel good."

"What?" Coral exclaimed in disbelief. "You don't mean that Mum. You can't…" Coral stammered, backing away in disgust, unable to look at those dull, expressionless eyes. They were not her mother's eyes. They were someone else's. Phlegm filled her lungs. She swallowed. "Wait for me Jem, I'm coming with you!"

Coral started across the jute rug into the vestibule. Jem shook his head, barring her way.

"No Coral. It's too dangerous to come with me. Go to Hartland Abbey on foot and sound the alarm. I'll make my way cross-country to Sudbury Court and see what help I can give. Being invisible won't hinder me for a change. If anything it might make my life easier."

Coral hesitated. She wanted to go with him but she could see the sense in their splitting up. Jem would be able to travel much faster alone. She would only slow him down.

"OK Jem. I'll do as you say. But be careful. The flames can still burn you."

"I know," he replied solemnly. "I'll be careful."

Coral nodded. Then she impulsively darted forwards and planted a kiss on his cheek. Then she drew back, her blue eyes brimming with love.

"After I've raised the alarm, I'll make my way to Sudbury Court with re-enforcements. Don't try and stop me. I promise to be careful."

Their eyes met. Jem nodded grimly, knowing that he could not control her.

Coral was a free spirit, fired by one thing only: her conscience.

The wind rose. The black clouds of smoke raced across the heath-land. The abrasive wind licked the back of their necks. Coral's long hair blew across her face. She parted the twisted strands of hair with her fingers and stared out across the heather with a deep sense of foreboding. The horizon was a blur of black smoke and razor-shell flames. Time was running out for those unfortunate souls trapped inside Sudbury Court.

"Coral! Come back!" Hazel called shrilly.

Hazel darted across the lawn, her dainty slippered feet sinking into the moss-covered turf. "Come back Coral! I beg of you!" Hazel repeated, catching hold of Coral's tensed arm. "Please darling. There's no need to go anywhere. There's bound to be fire-engines on the way."

"Keep out of it Hazel! I'm not listening to your crazy ideas one moment longer!" Coral shouted, distraught. Then she turned swiftly on her heels and marched away.

Hazel froze, caught in the crossfire of her own making. Then her eyes registered the state of Coral's clothing and she started forwards again with renewed purpose.

"Coral wait! You can't go dressed as you are. You need to wrap up warm. Night is falling. Here, take my fleece…"

Coral blanked out Hazel's voice and carried on regardless.

Hazel stopped on the far edge of the lawn, her arms outstretched, her pale blue fleece hanging limply off the edge of her brittle wrists. Her eyes traced an image of despair in the air. She lowered her arms, defeated.

CHAPTER THIRTEEN

The Inferno

Jem set off across the moor running as fast as he could over the tussocks of grass and low lying gorse. To the west lay the open sea, to the south Hartland Abbey and Pancake Hollow, due north the raging inferno of Sudbury Court.

After ten gruelling minutes, Jem reached a barrier of barbed-wire. An angry hand-painted wooden sign shouted at him not to proceed: "DANGER! KEEP OUT!"

He had arrived at the southern-most tip of Blind Man's Folly, a small gully bounded on three sides by peat bog. The only way to avoid the peat bog was to pass through the gully. According to local folklore you had to either be blind or mad to enter the gully and if you weren't blind when you went in, you would definitely be blind when you came out the other side.

A few yards further along, the Countryside Commission had erected a far more welcoming signboard detailing the local fauna and flora. There were illustrations of snakes-head fritillaries and willow warblers, plus a detailed map of the terrain and suggested routes around the treacherous bog.

Jem ignored the advice of both signboards and boldly entered the gully. Sheer black granite rocks rose up on all sides. The ground was strewn with car-shaped boulders covered in rich green moss, the texture smooth and soft like a snooker table. The edges of the gully were vertical. Spindle-berry trees grew out from the vertical cracks, the topside of their branches covered in patches of green moss. Moisture hung in the air. Jem proceeded with caution across the velvet bottom of the gully, mindful of the many sunken hollows, their slit-like entrances hidden by tussocks of knot grass and self-seeded gorse.

The land levelled and the gully gradually opened out. Jem had arrived at the edge of a large area of wetland. Tall tussocks of bleached grass rose up from between pools of still chicory-coloured water. Jem leapt from tussock to tussock, mindful not to slip into the stagnant pools. Globules of glutinous red clay sprayed his trouser bottoms every time he jumped. The going got tougher. The pools of glutinous sludge widened and became harder to avoid. Soon his trouser-bottoms were wet through.

Jem gritted his teeth and pressed on regardless. Even if it meant wading through the watery clay up to his knees, he was determined to take the quickest route to the besieged building. He was just thankful that he had managed to convince Coral to head for Hartland Abbey. Blind Man's Gully was no place for a girl, even one as high spirited as Coral.

Back at Shell Cottage events were unfolding fast. Coral rushed back upstairs to her bedroom and changed into a pair of old jeans and a grey hoodie. Then she rummaged in the spare room for Hazel's old motorbike boots. She tossed aside a skateboard, a rolled-up beach-mat and a couple of flat, deflated beach balls. She waded through a stack of supermarket bags containing old tennis balls, plastic shuttle-cocks and snorkelling equipment. Then she stubbed her toe on the corner of an ancient ottoman trunk, on top of which lay two wooden badminton racquets dating from John's childhood days at Sheffield Grammar School.

Coral paused and studied the racquets, struck by their warped shape. The heads were twisted, Janus-style; one side faced the past and the other side faced an uncertain future.

Then she cast the racquets aside and dug deeper beneath the bags of old dressing-up clothes, unearthing as she went boxes containing all manner of obsolete objects, including a bag of used light bulbs, the vitreous globes stained a sooty black.

She knocked over a black lacquered box. Out tumbled row upon row of hand-painted lead soldiers, dressed in cobalt blue trousers and matching tunics with white piping and white epaulettes. The soldiers wore flat-topped hats with green plumes. Shaky handwriting on a piece of crumpled brown paper catalogued the contents: "l'uniforme et les armes des soldats du Premier Empire." Coral stuffed the soldiers back into the box, stung back into action. Where were Hazel's boots? They had to be here somewhere!

A cob-spider hung lifeless in its own web, a decomposing wasp in its grip. They had both died a pyrrhic death. Then right in the corner, squashed up in between the wardrobe and the ottoman, Coral spotted Hazel's old biker boots!

Coral quickly wiped away the cobwebs from the boots and pulled them on. The leather was stiff and cold but the boots fitted perfectly. She flexed her toes and bent her knees, familiarising herself with the feel of the heavy-weight leather encasing her shins. These boots were just what she needed. They would provide her with the protection she need at Sudbury Court.

Coral quietly thanked John for his spirited nature and hoped that she would be able to live up to his expectations of her. Then she grudgingly thanked Hazel for having been bold enough to ride pillion with him on the back of his Triumph Thunderbird.

Downstairs Coral skidded to a halt, confronted by Hazel's pitiful figure, both shoulders hunched, a pair of stout walking boots held fast in her bony hands.

Neither woman spoke. Hazel was too shocked at the sight of her old motorcycle boots on Coral's feet to speak. Coral was still too angry with her mother to say anything.

Outside a horse brayed in alarm. Both women slowly turned towards the sound. Coral's heart pounded. She rushed outside, unwilling to look her mother in the eye. Hazel stepped aside, crest-fallen.

Flaxen stood in the middle of the lawn, her white coat drenched in sweat and splattered with red clay. The mare's eyes were dilated. Her saliva-beaded tongue and drooping jowls indicated that she was badly dehydrated. She was also spooked out of her mind.

"Flaxen? What on earth are you doing back here?" Coral asked, walking slowly towards the panting mare.

Coral extended a placatory hand. The mare snorted and raked the lawn feebly with her front hooves. Coral studied the mare carefully. Why had she come back? Was she injured? Or was the road to Hartland Abbey blocked by emergency vehicles? Had the panic spread to the surrounding countryside meaning that Flaxen had been too freaked out to find a route home to the Abbey stables? All three scenarios were distinctly possible.

The sound of light footsteps on the herringbone path behind her...

"Coral, I'm so sorry! I didn't mean what I said earlier. Of course I don't want Antonia's grandmother to get hurt. Heaven forbid. Please darling, let me help you," Hazel said softly, her expression contrite.

Coral froze with her hand held out towards Flaxen. The mare snorted. Coral's cheeks flushed crimson. Then Coral turned slowly round and stared harshly into her mother's haunted eyes.

Hazel flinched under Coral's clinical scrutiny. She stood rigid, her auburn hair stuck to her cheeks, the curls flat. John's old leather motorcycle jacket was cradled tightly to her breast. Her tear-stained cheeks glistened in the dimming light, the freckles magnified, the dark circles beneath her eyes pronounced.

Silence. Hazel caught her breath and waited on tenterhooks for Coral to speak. The silence deepened. Hazel gulped and took a hesitant step forward. All was still. Hazel took another tentative step forward. She finally paused a few feet from Coral. Then she slowly extended her right hand towards her daughter in supplication.

"Please Coral, forgive me."

Coral's heart crumpled. She seized hold of Hazel's brittle hand and squeezed it tightly. Then with the flat of her thumbs she tenderly caressed those bony knuckles and fat brown freckles with those large black sunspots.

"I don't know what came over me darling. I don't want anyone to die, at Sudbury Court or any place else..." Hazel exclaimed fitfully.

"It's OK Mum. I believe you. It's all in the past now."

"Wear this – it's your father's – the leather will keep you warm and protect you from…"

Hazel broke off, reluctant to finish the sentence.

"Thank you," Coral replied tenderly, scooping the jacket out of her mother's poker arms and slipping it on.

Coral zipped up the front of her father's 1950s-style leather-jacket then pressed the brass poppers down with the flat of her thumb. Then she ran her fingers lightly over her father's old motorcycle club badge depicting a Triumph Tiger, its mouth wide-open in mid-roar. The roaring tiger was more than just a badge. It was a right of passage.

Hazel watched as Coral's youthful fingers caressed the insignia. Fresh tears spilled from Hazel's pale eyes as she remembered John sitting on a stool in his cluttered workshop, stitching the Triumph badge in place with gold metallic thread.

Then Flaxen snorted again as if trying to tell them both something. The gold thread shimmered then was gone. Hazel looked up and smiled a shy, transient smile.

"Maybe if I get some meadowsweet from the hedgerow we can calm the mare down?" she suggested softly, her voice like a wind rushing through a reed bed. "You'll get to Hartland Abbey much quicker if you ride Coral. That's if you feel well enough? If not, I could go myself."

"It's OK Mum, I'll be fine," Coral replied, smiling.

"You'll have to ride bare-back. Can you manage that?" Hazel pressed, bending down and snapping off a few stems of meadowsweet from the base of the dry-stone wall.

"Of course! Stop worrying."

"Here, Coral, you feed Flaxen. She knows you better than me," Hazel prompted, proffering the fluffy meadowsweet with its tiny white flowers.

Coral took the meadowsweet from her mother's rough-hewn hands and approached the mare cautiously.

Flaxen opened her mouth partially; her tongue whipped sideways. Then she hooked the meadowsweet over her tongue and began to chew.

Soon Flaxen was feeding greedily on the feathery white flowers and zingy green stems packed with sugary goodness.

"You're right Hazel! Flaxen loves it. Actually, could you get me some more and maybe a bowl of water? Flaxen is terribly dehydrated."

"I won't be a tick," Hazel replied, darting around the side of the house in search of some more meadowsweet and a bucket of fresh water from the water-butt.

Flaxen was soon calm enough for Coral to mount her without a problem. The mare slowly curled back her head, checking the identity of her new rider. Then she snorted her consent.

Hazel led the mare diagonally across the lawn, out through the rosebud archway onto the country lane. Suddenly Flaxen lurched sideways and seized a mouthful of delicious dandelion leaves from the roadside verge.

"Stop it, you greedy thing!" Coral laughed, relieved that Flaxen was no longer fretful and was far more interested in eating dandelions.

"Are you sure you're going to be OK riding without a saddle?" Hazel double-checked.

"I'll be fine Mum. I'm wearing Dad's jacket and your boots, what more could I need?" Coral asked, smiling kindly, her crescent lips curled. Then she leant forwards and put her arms firmly around Flaxen's mane.

Coral kicked once with her heel.

"See you later Mum! I mean Hazel!" Coral yelled as with a burst of speed Flaxen shot up the lane out of Pancake Hollow. "Don't worry about a thing!"

"Be careful my darling. I love you so very much, far more than you shall ever know," Hazel murmured faintly, her voice filling the tumultuous sky with raindrop-like notes.

Then Hazel turned and stared across the smoke-grey moor towards the leaping flames that encased the five hundred year old Elizabethan Hall in a ring of fire. Hazel gasped in horror, filled with compassion for those trapped within its four turrets. The whole place was a tinder-box that had just been lit! Heaven help those inside…

A scene of mayhem confronted Jem at Sudbury Court. Men scrambled like ants about the burning edifice as it rained down blocks of scorched grey stone and red brick. The ancient oak frames collapsed one after another and were violently consumed in a wall of flames.

The Fire Brigade had not yet arrived. Men were running back and forth with pails of water. A group of hard-nosed farmers directed a couple of hoses at the front porch but the paltry jets of water made little inroads into the advancing flames. The men were fighting a losing battle and knew it.

Grey smoke billowed forth from the upstairs windows of the beleaguered building. On the fourth floor a girl's head could just be made out, the face contorted into a terrified scream.

Jem sprinted straight through the front entrance and disappeared into the burning wreck. He headed straight for the fourth floor and the trapped girl.

Suddenly a second girl, a blue scarf protecting her nose and mouth, appeared at the window. The girl moved with purpose and inner steel. Within seconds she had carefully bound the nose and mouth of the first girl with a band of material.

"Keep the scarf over your mouth!" Antonia instructed. "And try not to breathe in the smoke."

Antonia knew that the scarf would probably not do a lot to help but she wanted Kim to concentrate on breathing rather than panicking.

"It's no good Toni! We're going to die!" Kim wailed hysterically.

"No you're not going to die! Just keep the scarf over your mouth! You're inhaling smoke you stupid idiot!" Antonia snapped.

Suddenly there was a loud crack. Antonia pushed Kim sideways just in the nick of time. Seconds later the keystone collapsed. The stone window-casement disintegrated before their very eyes. Flames from the floor below shot upwards, causing a menacing up-draught.

"We're going to die!" Kim screamed hysterically, paralysed by fear.

"No we're not. We're going to get out of here. But only if you shut up and do exactly as I say!" Antonia shouted, her eyes like molten lava. She seized Kim roughly by the collar of her denim jacket. "Listen to me Kim. We're going to make our way back along this corridor and down the rear staircase. Do you understand?"

"But we can't! The corridor is on fire! Everything's on fire!"

The sound of flesh striking flesh as Antonia delivered a searing blow to Kim's face. Then she grabbed Kim by both arms and hauled her roughly down the corridor.

"No! I can't!" Kim screamed, wrenching herself free and collapsing onto her knees.

She curled up tightly into a ball.

"Get up!" Antonia bellowed angrily.

Antonia seized Kim by the shoulders and dragged her forcibly along the corridor. The hot parquet wood scorched Kim's knees. Half-way along Antonia paused, exhausted.

"Get up!" Antonia gasped, her voice jagged-edged. Sweat poured from her face, her razor-sharp fringe glued to her forehead.

Kim did not answer. She stared past Antonia, her eyes mesmerised by the leaping flames that licked the topmost remaining walls of the floor below.

Antonia grabbed Kim about the wrists and pulled her to a standing position.

"Now walk!" Antonia ordered, her top lip curled into a menacing sneer.

Kim stared at Antonia with terrified eyes. Then she nodded her head mechanically.

Antonia led the way down the corridor. Kim followed, her eyes locked onto Antonia's long pony-tail plait which swayed back and forth like a hypnotist's pendulum. Every so often Antonia stopped and listened for any unusual sounds that might indicate that a piece of the building was about to collapse and give way. Plumes of dark grey smoke poured out from beneath the closed bedroom doors on either side of the corridor. The wispy fingers snatched at both girls' ankles in swift, biting movements. Kim began to cough. Then without warning, she darted sideways and grabbed onto one of the brass door-handles.

Kim howled in pain then let go, the top layer of her skin adhered to the scorching brass door-knob.

"Idiot! Don't touch the door-knobs!" Antonia barked savagely. "You mustn't open any doors or you'll allow more air into the side rooms which will feed the flames and let smoke into the corridor. Do you understand?"

"Sorry Toni. I didn't know," Kim garbled, clutching her burnt hand.

"Let me have a look at that," Antonia said gently, taking hold of Kim's right arm and inspecting her hand. "Jesus! That must hurt. Stand still, whilst I bind your palm."

Antonia quickly removed the protective blue kerchief from her face and tore the material in two. She took one half and carefully wrapped it about Kim's burnt palm.

Then she turned Kim's hand over and tied the material in a tough double-knot just above the knuckles.

"That should hold."

"Thanks," Kim replied, her voice monotone, stunned by the gnawing pain that dug deep into her palm and radiated out along the bones to her five fingers.

Meanwhile Antonia quickly made herself a replacement face mask with the remaining scrap of material and assessed their surroundings.

"Right then Kim, let's get out of here! This place is beginning to annoy me!"

But even as the girls bravely progressed along the fourth floor corridor, the manor house was falling down about them.

The ceiling in a room somewhere close-by thundered to the ground and a hole appeared on the left-hand side of the corridor wall, a mere three metres from where they were standing. Red flames gleamed through. Kim stared at the gap in the wall, struck dumb.

Antonia grabbed the terrified girl about the waist and yanked her back from the incipient flames. Then they both sprinted down the corridor, arms linked, headed for the far staircase.

However at the top of the stairs, they careered to a halt, assailed once more by smoke and billowing black dust. Seconds later a huge block of ceiling plaster rained to the ground in front of them, totally blocking the staircase. The white particles settled. The exit downstairs was blocked. The flames had been kept at bay but their way downstairs was now barred. They were trapped on the fourth floor with no way out other than by jumping.

"We can't get out! We're going to die!" Kim screamed hysterically.

"No we're not! We're just going to have to improvise," Antonia shouted, secretly relieved that they had not taken the staircase. Had they descended by that route they would have been toast in seconds.

Thinking fast, Antonia gripped Kim firmly by the forearm and led her back along the corridor to the new gap in the wall. Antonia craned forwards and peered through the jagged hole into the chasm below. Her face lit up. A large segment of ceiling plaster had fallen onto the Doric stone pillars of the ground floor ballroom. There was a still a way out.

The Greek Revival Ballroom was the only room in the entire building that was new, commissioned by Lady Hortensia when the old Tudor long gallery had succumbed to death-watch beetle. The Doric pillars had been the central feature of the new ballroom. Although the floorboards of the first and second floors were now a ball of fire, the magnificent stone pillars were still standing. What is more, a block of white plaster, about three metres wide and five metres long, was balanced on top of the pillars, forming the perfect landing-pad. Critically Antonia realised that the plaster was not yet on fire. If they jumped down onto it then they should still be able to scramble along the edge and make their way to the second floor window. It was the only option open to them but it was do-able if they kept their wits about them.

"We're going to die! We killed Coral and now we're going to have to pay for it with our own lives!" Kim screamed hysterically, terrified by the sight of the flames on the ground floor.

Then she collapsed to the ground and curled up into a ball, her head buried in her arms.

"Shut up! You haven't killed anybody!" Antonia shouted, seizing Kim by the head and jerking her chin upwards. She looked directly into Kim's terrified eyes. "Repeat after me, Kim: I haven't killed anybody."

"Yes I have! I killed Coral! We both did!"

"No we did not!" Antonia bellowed in Kim's face. Then she caught her breath and withdrew. Her nails fingered the end of her ponytail restlessly. "I'm not proud of what we did Kim. It was wrong. But we did not kill Coral. You **must** believe me."

"I can't," Kim sobbed, revisited by her recurrent nightmares.

"Stop feeling sorry for yourself Kim! I **can** and I **will** get you out of here! But you must co-operate with me!" Antonia exclaimed, frustrated.

Antonia took a few deep breaths. It was hard work being kind. Then she squatted down on the ground next to Kim and tried another approach.

"You see that block of plaster down there Kim - the one that looks like a piece of Christmas cake icing?"

Kim peered over the edge of her knees. She nodded warily.

"All we have to do is jump down onto the plaster-block. Then we can work our way along it to the second floor windows and safety," Antonia said gently, reaching forwards and putting an arm about Kim's back. She kneaded the back of Kim's sweat-shirt.

Kim flinched. Then she shuffled forwards on her bottom, freeing herself from Antonia's unwelcome embrace. She peered warily through the gap in the wall.

"I don't know… I think I can do it."

"Brilliant!" Antonia exclaimed, exulted. "Now Kim, do you think you can stand up for me?"

Kim stood up.

"Fantastic Kim! Now when I give the word, we're going to jump. Together. Will you do that for me?" Antonia coaxed.

Kim did not answer.

Antonia pulled back the curtain of mouse-coloured hair framing Kim's face and stroked her cheek with the underside of her red lacquered thumb. Antonia swallowed, filled with remorse for having treated Kim so badly. The kid was young, impressionable and deep-down, incredibly sweet.

However as Antonia's mood softened, Kim's mood hardened. Kim eyed Antonia's chipped nails suspiciously. The red varnish was tarnished and the thumb-nail split revealing delicate flesh underneath. Then Kim flinched, remembering all the times Antonia had lashed out with those very same nails.

"It's not far Kim. It looks much further than it is. But we can do it, I promise!" Antonia said purposefully, her eyes brimming with confidence, her brown eyes speckled with bits of luminous gold.

Suddenly Kim made up her mind. She was fed up with being Antonia's lap-dog, expected to perform whatever trick Antonia devised for her.

"I'm not jumping!" Kim said shrilly, twisting out of Antonia's arms and blundering back down the corridor into a wall of smoke.

"Have it your own way then!" Antonia shouted angrily, hurt by Kim's rebuttal. "But remember, I tried to help you! Don't say that I didn't want to help you! Don't say I didn't try!"

Antonia took one last look at Kim then she stepped forwards and peered through the hole in the wall at the chasm beyond. The plaster-block was still there but more of the fourth floor ceiling had collapsed. Large chunks of plaster lay strewn across the floor like isolated icebergs. The flames continued to roar on the first floor but the absence of drapery and furnishings in the ballroom meant that there was still a way out **if** she held her nerve.

Antonia narrowed her eyes and calculated the distance. She would have to jump about five metres. She took three sharp breaths, summoning up the confidence to jump. Then for the first time in her life Antonia thought of somebody other than herself. She glanced back at Kim's tiny figure curled up in a ball, waiting to die, and had a change of heart.

"Kim! Come on! We can do this!" Antonia shouted. "I can save us both!"

Kim was curled up tightly in a ball, her head between her elbows, her forehead resting against the splintered floorboards.

"Kim! Please! Trust me!" Antonia screamed, starting back down the corridor.

But as Antonia drew near to Kim, the floorboards in front gave way in one sickening chain reaction. Clouds of dust and smoke swirled upwards. Blinded, Antonia leapt to safety just in time. When the clouds of dust had settled, a gap of ten metres separated the two girls, the corridor guillotined in two.

Antonia stared across the chasm, distraught. Kim was still curled up in a foetal position. Bits of grey plasterboard peppered her pretty mouse-coloured hair. Her body was still. Antonia turned away. A lone tear rolled out of her left eye and speared her cheek. Then with the last ounces of strength left inside her, Antonia launched herself towards the block of dirty-white plaster below.

Coral flew into the court-yard of Charlings Farm at a gallop. She slowed to a trot, then a steady walk and dismounted. She led Flaxen into the court-yard and knocked on the door of the ramshackle farm. The blazing remains of Sudbury Court were in full view of the farmstead but Flaxen did not appear unsettled; whatever had spooked her earlier had receded from her memory and the wily old mare now trusted Coral implicitly.

The front door to the farm-house opened a few inches and a sickly-looking woman with a toddler in her arms peered out fearfully.

"Nothing's happened to Tom has it?" the woman asked anxiously.

"Not to my knowledge. Is Tom your husband?"

"Yes!" the woman exclaimed, flinging the door wide open. "He went to help fight the flames over at Sudbury. He's not hurt is he?"

"I'm afraid I don't know. I'm on my way over there right now to see if I can offer any assistance. I just stopped by to ask if I could leave my horse in one of your barns. If I ride any closer to Sudbury the flames will spook her."

"As you like… The stables are just off to your right, past the hay-barn. Be sure to ask after Tom for me. Tom Williams of Charlings Farm…"

"Of course. It's as good as done," Coral replied. "Thanks for your help. I'll take Flaxen round to the stables then I'll be on my way."

"Wait! Wild Country Lane is blocked. Take the foot-path. The road is up at Cross-Keys - a burst water-main - that's why the fire-engines haven't been able to get through. The poor lads are ferrying the water through in buckets!"

Coral thanked the farmer's wife and set off along the foot-path on the last stage of her journey.

The going was slow. The wind was far stronger than she anticipated and the light was fading fast. Coral shuddered at the thought of bodies being charcoaled to dust in the darkness. Then she dispelled the morbid picture from her mind and told herself that everything was going to turn out alright, that the emergency services would soon fix the burst water-main and quell the flames. Man's strength was his ingenuity and ability to come back from the brink.

Coral arrived at the crest of the hill and stared down at the manor house in horror. She swallowed hard, devastated. She had arrived too late.

The building was a skeletal version of its former self. The front façade was a wall of flame. The four towers held fast, the bricks intact but the roof of each tower had gone. Flames roared through each aperture suggesting that the inside of the towers had been gutted.

Steeling herself for the worst, Coral walked down the ridge of the hill towards the building. People appeared to be congregating around the back. The fire-crew had arrived and with a selection of spray jets and hoses, were attempting to ward off the advancing flames.

Her first thought was to find Jem. He might not be able to die like ordinary people but he was still at risk of getting badly burnt. The thought of his being trapped inside the building, injured but invisible to the naked eye, didn't bear thinking about! She had to go inside and find him right away.

Coral knew the lay-out of the manor house reasonably well. Lady Hortensia often used the Good Earth to provide the catering for various dinner parties and functions held at the Court. On these occasions Coral helped her mother ferry trays of food from their car through to the manor house kitchens. Coral felt pretty confident of being able to navigate the rear of the property.

Buoyed up by her new plan of action, she sprinted round to the back staircase. Then she stopped in her tracks, her hopes in tatters.

The back staircase was a wall of flame. Two firemen were tackling the staircase with hoses but they were making little progress. Another group of determined men were successfully directing jets of water onto the flames on the ground floor and were beginning to make headway.

All was not lost.

Coral paused to focus. Then with a surge of energy, she sprinted past the second group of firemen into the remains of the ballroom.

The firemen's incredulous warning shouts fell on death ears as Coral nimbly threaded her way through the burning debris, head bowed, the hood of her sweat-shirt pulled protectively over her head. She headed straight for a four-foot high chunk of ceiling plaster lying in the centre of the ballroom floor and climbed up onto it to get a better look at her surroundings.

"Jem! Jem where are you? Can you hear me?"

Footsteps sounded directly behind her as a fireman shouted at her to retreat. Coral twisted round and stared into his livid, bloodshot eyes. The look of alarm in his face was such that she considered giving up and climbing back down to safety when suddenly she spied a hole in the side of the wall several floors above her. There was a body lying curled up on the floor! Then Coral let out another gasp of surprise as she spotted two pink boots poking out over the edge of a plaster-block.

"Antonia? Antonia is that you?" Coral shouted, turning back towards the fireman to tell him what she had seen but the fireman was no longer there.

Her eyes returned to those distinctive dirty pink Doc Martens. It was definitely Antonia. But how on earth had she got up there? And was she alive or dead?

Panic seized Coral. If the flames didn't kill Antonia, the smoke soon would!

The next moment there was a loud crack and the rear left-hand tower of Sudbury Court collapsed, bringing the last surviving staircase down with it. Plaster and ceiling timbers came thundering to the ground. The remaining firemen sprinted to safety just in time. There was now no way up to the first floor. The two individuals trapped upstairs were doomed to certain death.

Unless…

Coral stared up at the Doric pillars, deep in thought. The wedge of plaster on which Antonia was lying was balanced across two stone pillars.

She narrowed her eyes, making sure that she was not imagining things. The pillars were not actually the main support. A pair of wooden floor joists ran the length of the second floor and provided the critical structural support for the plaster-block upon which Antonia was lying. The smouldering joists would be difficult to avoid. But if she were careful and kept her wits about her, she should be able to circumnavigate them and avoid getting burnt. Crucially the joists had only recently caught fire and were burning slowly because of their great girth. It was worth a try. And she could not live with herself if she did not try to rescue Antonia.

Coral calmly assessed the lie of the land. If she were to climb up one of the stone pillars she could, in theory, reach the plaster-block. Of course if she applied too much weight to either column she risked bringing the plaster-block crashing to the ground and Antonia with it. On the other hand, if she did nothing, and Antonia remained trapped on the second floor, there was no way out for her except in a coffin.

"Hold on Antonia! I'm coming up to get you!" Coral called up to the prone body.

Then Coral jumped down from her vantage point and darted towards the first pillar, thankful that the firemen had done such a good job of bringing the flames in the ballroom under control.

She probed the base of the pillar with her boot, testing how hot the stone was. Her wet metal toe-cap hissed on contact with the hot stone. Climbing was going to be painful. But if she could climb the Giant's Elbow, she could climb this pillar.

Coral shut her eyes and mentally prepared herself for the climb. When she was ready, she opened her eyes, her vision unimpaired by doubt or fear. She pulled the sleeves of her hoodie down over her wrists, wishing that she had had the presence of mind to bring some leather gloves with her. Then she paused. She had not checked the internal pockets…

She unzipped her father's jacket and thrust her hand deep into the inside pocket and pulled out one of his old motorbike gloves. She tried the other internal pocket and another leather gauntlet appeared from inside the rumpled lining. Luck was on her side!

Now reasonably protected, Coral placed a leather-clad palm onto the side of the stone pillar and clamped her fingers tight. The stone was warm but the heat was tolerable. She started to climb, pulling her legs up behind her like a monkey.

Suddenly a shot of burning pain flared across her waist as she unwittingly raised her arms too high above her, exposing her midriff to the hot pillar. She righted her clothing as best she could and pressed on, taking much smaller, crab-like movements.

Eventually she got to the top of the twenty foot pillar and caught her breath, resisting the temptation to rest. Now all she had to do was catch hold of the block of ceiling plaster to her right.

More by luck, than by judgement, Coral managed to twist backwards so that she was hanging upside down like a giant sloth. She hooked her knees around the ceiling joist and proceeded along it as quickly as she could.

In a burst of some ten seconds she had exchanged the smouldering wooden joist for the plaster-block. She rolled over onto her side and lay there panting, her eyes tightly closed. Then she spat away the smuts from her mouth, opened her eyes and came face to face with Antonia lying sprawled beside her.

Coral slid forward on her belly and checked Antonia's pulse at the neck. Antonia was breathing! A surge of happiness exploded inside Coral. She'd got to Antonia in time. She slid further forward and gently cupped Antonia's heavy head in her hands.

Antonia's dark eyelashes quivered. Then she slowly opened her chestnut eyes and stared up at Coral with the expression of someone who has just been wakened from a bad dream.

"Coral? What in the hell are you doing here?"

"Rescuing you!" Coral replied, gripping Antonia's right arm and gently pulling her up into a sitting position.

Antonia wobbled slightly. There was not that much room for the two girls on the plaster-block.

"But why?" Antonia asked, rubbing her temples, not sure whether this was really happening or whether she was dreaming.

"Because I want to!" Coral snapped impatiently. "Now's not the time to argue. We can't hang around. The ceiling joist could collapse any moment. Where are the others?"

"Kim's upstairs on the fourth floor landing. She was too frightened to jump."

"That's who I saw!" Coral exclaimed. "Is there any way we can get up to her?"

"Don't be crazy! I tried to get Kim to jump but she wouldn't. The corridor collapsed between us. You can't reach her. I tried but it's no longer possible."

"We can't just leave her!" Coral replied stubbornly. "I'm going to see if I can get to her by crawling along the ceiling joist."

"Don't! You'll be committing suicide!" Antonia shouted. "It's not worth the risk."

"Kim **is** worth the risk," Coral replied, her voice even.

"Look, we've got to get out of here," Antonia gasped, kneeling up with difficulty and starting to shuffle up the plaster towards the window. But after a few feet she cried out in pain and fell forwards clutching her left knee.

Coral had to make a quick spur of the moment decision. Kim may or may not be alive. Antonia was alive but too injured to make it to the second floor window unaided.

"OK. I'm coming with you Antonia," Coral said briskly, placing her arm around Antonia's left shoulder.

They began to crawl painstakingly forward towards the row of three lattice windows.

Coral examined the diamond-shaped panes, not really understanding what she was looking at. The metal had melted. Black streaks of molten metal had spread across the glass.

"The window is too hot to touch. I'll have to use my boots," Coral said decisively, lying down on her back next to Antonia on the edge of the plaster.

Coral pulled the hood of her sweat-shirt over her eyes to protect them. Then she shut her eyes and kicked.

Some of the glass shattered but the lattice window-frames held firm.

"Move aside Coral, I'll do it!" Antonia said, deeply aware of the irony of her offer of help.

"But your knee's injured Toni."

"Then it's about to get injured some more!"

A smash of breaking glass as Antonia's daisy-tread soles smashed effortlessly through the glass lattice-panes.

The way ahead was clear.

"One, two, three, jump!" both girls shouted in unison as they leapt to safety.

Coral could not remember landing on the lawn. She slowly came to, vaguely aware of Antonia's presence. Then a blur of men in yellow jackets and hard hats veered into her line of vision, yelling to everyone to stand clear because the old lady was about to collapse at any moment.

"What's about to collapse?" Coral asked weakly.

"The east tower," Antonia replied as they were both transferred to stretchers and carried across the lawn towards the waiting ambulances.

The smell of men's hot breath; Coral blinked at the white interior of the ambulance, totally disorientated.

"Are we in an ambulance or outside it?" Coral asked groggily, her head still muzzy after her fall.

Before Antonia could reply, there was a loud crack as the last remaining ballroom ceiling-joist finally thundered to the ground.

"No! Jem!" Coral screamed in terror.

She leapt out of the ambulance and sprinted back towards the wreckage, determined to rescue Jem.

"Coral come back! Kim must be dead from the smoke by now," Antonia shouted after her.

But all Coral could think about was Jem. Head-down, she sprinted towards the wrecked building, her heart set on one thing and one thing only: finding Jem.

Coral knew that as long as Kim remained trapped inside the burning wreckage, Jem would strive to free her. She must help him. Only she could see Jem, therefore only she stood any chance of finding him.

Antonia charged after Coral, snatching unsuccessfully at her flailing arms; then she stopped and stared in horror as Coral raced through the white metal archway of the conservatory into the cauldron of certain death.

"Come back Coral! It's useless!" Antonia shouted fearfully.

But Coral's long corkscrew hair dissolved into the citrus trees in a blur of green, orange and grey. Then a tongue of flame as the peach trees in the conservatory caught alight followed by the acrid smell of burning lemons. It was only a matter of time before the metal archway above Coral's head gave way.

The debris from the collapsed central tower slid down onto the conservatory roof. There was an ear-splitting crack and the metal conservatory roof gave way. The glass panes shattered. Shards of glass burst into the air like exploding disco-balls.

"No! Coral!" Antonia screamed, distraught. She stared aghast at the space where once the conservatory arch had been.

Seconds later Tom appeared on the lawn, eyes wild with fear.

"Antonia! What are you doing here?" he exclaimed, relieved to see that she was not injured. "James is in the back of the ambulance. You'd better go to him. He's lost his left leg. He keeps screaming that he wants to go back into the burning building to get it."

Antonia ignored Tom. Instead she stared at the collapsed conservatory, her jaw locked in horror.

"Why?" Antonia murmured under her breath soulfully. "Why did you do that Coral? You didn't have to," Antonia sobbed, hot tears streaming down her face.

"What are you going on about?" Tom demanded, bewildered. "Did you hear what I said about James? He's lost his leg and needs you."

"To hell with James!" Antonia rasped, wiping her cheeks brusquely with her dirty cotton sleeve. "Why did Coral have to die? Why did she have to try and save Kim? If anyone deserves to be dead it's **me** not Coral!"

"What are you going on about?" Tom snapped irritably. "Kim's fine. Someone dragged her out just before the ballroom roof caved in. How they did it, God only knows. Kim's in the second ambulance being treated for shock."

"But that's impossible!" Antonia exclaimed, spinning round to face Tom for the first time.

She stared at him quizzically. Then the glimmer of understanding spread across her face as the final pieces of the jigsaw puzzle slotted together and she understood what had really happened: Coral had not gone into the building to find Kim but to find the mysterious inhabitant of Hartland Cove.

More shouting and confusion ensued as Jem charged through the body of on-lookers causing shouts of consternation and disbelief in his wake. He hurled himself into the collapsed conservatory and started to fling hot shards of glass and metal into the air with his bare hands. Antonia watched as brick and glass flew in all directions. The incredulous fire-fighters stared at the missiles, rigid with fear.

Antonia alone understood that Jem was burrowing through the mound of rubble, determined to get to Coral, the girl he loved.

"What is that?" Tom asked slowly.

"It's him, you blithering idiot!"

"Who's him?" Tom replied dully, unable to make sense of what he could see.

"The invisible occupant of the beach-hut!" Antonia said impatiently. "He rescued James. Then he rescued Kim. And now he's trying to rescue Coral. Only it's too late. Coral can't have survived that collapse," Antonia said sadly, hot tears rolling down her ash-coated face.

Then a loud shriek rent the air that was neither human nor animal but took the form of a surge of such powerful energy that everyone in the crowd felt it although they did not know what it was that they felt.

The energy coursed through Antonia's body and she suddenly understood more than she would have believed it was possible to understand about the true meaning and nature of love.

L O V E

Antonia spelt it in the air. She spelt it in her mind. She spelt it in her heart. And then she wept more deeply than she had ever known it was possible to weep.

The last of the burning brick and stone was cast asunder. Jem emerged from the wreckage, Coral's dead body cradled in his arms. Her skin and hair was covered in a thin layer of matt-grey ash. Tiny jewel-shaped shards of glass decorated her temples like fairy-lights.

The startled on-lookers stared in wonder as Coral's ethereal form floated across the charcoaled grass towards the moor.

"Toni? What's happening?" Tom quaked in fear as Coral's body floated towards the sea.

"Do I really have to explain it to you, Tom? The invisible owner of the fishing-net that you so thoughtlessly threw into the sea, has just carried the dead body of Coral, the girl whom you and I beat senseless, from the wreckage. And the shock-wave that you felt just now was his grief at the loss of the girl he loved!" Antonia replied calmly, her tears combining with the ash in the air to create a veil of silence.

Time stood still.

Then a loud thud as Tom fainted for the second time in the space of two hours. The first occasion was when he had accidentally spilled some milk into the electric toaster whilst trying to eat cereal, fry bacon and make a cup of coffee at the same time. This misguided action had caused an electric short-circuit. The power had cut out.

Tom had immediately gone upstairs to locate the trip-switch, forgetting all about the bacon that he had left frying in hot oil in the kitchen. It was only a matter of time before the frying-pan caught alight, then the table-cloth, and finally Lady Hortensia's kitchen curtains. The rest was history.

Antonia stared down at Tom's inert body, filled with contempt. Then she turned and started back towards the row of emergency vehicles, determined to help protect Jem's identity. If she were clever, she ought to be able to contain the secret of the Hartland Ghost.

She would tell the journalists that an unknown recluse had retrieved Coral's body from the burning wreckage and that he did not wish to be identified. She would deny all knowledge of the floating body and suggest that the crowd had imagined it all in a fit of collective hysteria. She might not be able to undo all the harm her selfish actions had caused but she **could** help preserve the public peace. It was her duty and her responsibility.

Antonia rubbed her hands together then marched boldly towards the assembled television cameras prepared to do battle. It was the very least that she could do for Jem and Coral.

CHAPTER FOURTEEN

The Meadow

A young couple sat under a group of orange trees in a small citrus grove. A bunch of freshly picked lavender rested in the woman's lap. The man smiled at the woman lovingly, a coral necklace held fast in the palm of his hand. Then with great care he opened the fragile silver clasp with his long, arrow-tipped fingers.

"Fire coral - *corallium rubrum* - from the Sea of Japan. It's extremely rare," the man said quietly as he fastened the necklace about the woman's swallow neck.

"Thank you darling. It's beautiful," the woman replied. "I love coral. It's so delicate. But also much tougher than it looks."

"A bit like you!" the man replied, laughing.

"No, not like me!" the woman protested, suspicious of the man's intentions. "I'm not in the least bit tough. And I certainly don't have your bravery John. But if we were ever to have a daughter, she's bound to have a bit of both us in her, so maybe we should call her Coral?"

"Whatever you want Hazel. Your wish is my desire!"

The citrus grove melted away and Coral found herself lying in a bed of long meadow grass populated by wild flowers. There was brilliant lion's bane, delicate ladies' smock, sly snakes-head fritillary and bold king-cups. And amongst the meadow of flowers were the hardy inkpot ponies, their lustrous eyes glowing with everlasting warmth.

Coral blinked. *Where was she?* She had absolutely no idea. But the grass was very comfortable and the fluffy seed-heads of the rosebay-willow herb made the perfect pillow. She could lie here forever on her meadow mattress! Well perhaps not forever. But she might lie here awhile and gather her strength.

The church bells rang out across the rocky headland. The sky was a slate grey, the sea a deep turtle-blue. The mourners arrived in twos and threes, dressed in the very brightest colours in strict accordance with Hazel's wishes. Hazel had decided that Coral's funeral should be a celebration of all that was good and positive about Coral's life, not a melancholy affair.

Hazel looked resplendent in a ruby red dress, John's fire-coral necklace caressing her collar-bone. The errant strands of grey had vanished from her normally tired-looking head of hair and in their place sat a fine set of bright auburn curls. Hazel looked positively radiant as she clutched a bouquet of red and yellow Gaillardias - the sunset flower - to her chest.

The tiny chapel was situated right on the edge of the heath overlooking the sea. The single-storey building had white-washed walls and a simple stone floor inlaid with grave-stones. A series of three stained-glass windows depicting the Lamb of God, the Good Samaritan and the Lilies of the Field comprised the only ornamentation in the building.

However an abundance of flowers filled every alcove. Garlands of wild honey-suckle had been draped along the front of the pews. Dried salmon pink hops were suspended from the entrance porch. Magnificent white lilies stood pride of place in a tall fluted glass vase, positioned directly adjacent to the baptism font. The air was heavy with the scent of the countryside.

"Madam, if you would be so kind as to take a seat in the front pew," the vicar said kindly; a young man with cherubic red cheeks. He was dressed in black. A band of stiff white card encased his neck like a halo of light.

The young vicar led Hazel down the narrow aisle of the plain Non-Conformist Chapel. They reached the front row and the vicar politely paused and waited for Hazel to take a seat. Hazel smiled at the token of friendship and sat down.

As a non church-goer and a person of no particular faith, Hazel had been surprised by the ease with which she had been able to persuade the young vicar to allow Coral's funeral to take place in his tiny out-of-the-way chapel on the edge of the moor. Hazel cast her mind back to the conversation she had had with him but a few days earlier.

"I have to warn you, Reverend, I don't know what Coral's beliefs were, or if she had any. All I know is that she was a child of nature and it is my sincerest wish that she should be buried close to the moor and the sea that she loved."

"Of course Coral can be buried here in our churchyard!" the young vicar replied softly, his eyes dancing with vitality. "Coral was not unknown to me. I have often spied her on the moor. I try to spend the greater part of my ministry watching over **all** my flock - those who come to church every Sunday and especially those who do not. I have often had the pleasure of watching

Coral feed the Exmoor ponies. I once helped her deliver a foal. It's all in day's work for a twenty-first century vicar!" the young man laughed heartily, his love-affair with life so tangible that Hazel could taste it. "It is only right and proper that Coral should be buried here in this churchyard close to all that she loved. The issue of faith ends here."

A lone tear now rolled down Hazel's cheeks as she considered the implications of the vicar's open-mindedness.

Then the sound of heavy footsteps as Antonia entered the chapel dressed in a snow-white dress, her brown hair cut short into a boyish crop. She wore no make-up at all but still looked striking. About her wrist she wore a delicate daisy-chain made especially for her by Kim.

Hazel watched quietly as Antonia sat down in the front row. Hazel did not take exception to Antonia's decision to sit in such a prominent position. Indeed, she didn't expect someone like Antonia to choose anywhere other than the front row. The important point was that Coral would have wanted Antonia to attend her funeral; now, more than ever, tolerance and mutual understanding were paramount. Grief could not bring Coral back from the dead but it could bind those left behind closer together.

More footsteps as the rest of the congregation arrived in dribs and drabs. Kim was the next to enter. She walked cautiously down the central aisle dressed in turquoise blue, her long layered skirt redolent of the rippling ocean waves. She moved hesitantly, her tawny grey eyes fixed on the stone floor.

Kim was accompanied by a nervous-looking Tom. He wore his father's emerald green suit in keeping with Kim's nautical theme. His expression was subdued and wan. There was no hint of the hard-knuckled boy whose fists had once punched so hard that his own blood as well as Coral's had cruelly spilled from them.

Tom and Kim sat down in the sixth row, their leaf-like hands folded together in complicit communion. Tom looked up nervously and unintentionally caught the vicar's eye. A rush of pink spread rapidly across Tom's cheeks like a late flowering shrub rose. Hazel read into Tom's blush the fact that the young lad was afraid of the easy-going vicar with his ready smile and piercing green eyes.

Throughout proceedings Sir Aubrey stood on the altar steps giving each mourner's outfit marks out of ten. Had poor Tom been able to see Sir Aubrey, he would probably have fainted on the spot! But luckily for Tom he was saved this embarrassment by his inability to see the irreverent ghost dressed in his best black velvet frock-coat, gold breeches, silver shoes and a moonbeam-cravat!

The sound of squeaking metal wheels as James was pushed down the aisle in a wheelchair by his poker-faced father. Lady Hortensia walked directly next to James's wheelchair, keeping an eagle-eye on the direction of the insubordinate wheels. A formidable six feet tall, Lady Hortensia was dressed in a canary yellow trouser-suit befitting a woman with such a sunny disposition and an intense love of life. Indeed, it was due to Lady Hortensia's considerable influence that James had been extracted against his wishes from his hospital bed. (Her brother was the surgeon who had successfully operated on the remains of James's leg).

The fact that James was still in considerable pain and recovering from surgery did not make the slightest bit of difference to Lady Hortensia whose sense of right and wrong ran deep. It was at her ancestral home where the tragedy had happened and therefore on her watch. She took on board full responsibility for all that had occurred, especially the misguided behaviour of her grand-daughter Antonia, whose friends' carelessness had caused the fire in the first place.

James's father wheeled the wheelchair right to the front of the church and parked it near to the pulpit, adjacent to Coral's willow coffin. A whiskered man with very little hair, he sat down in the fifth row next to a pillar and lowered his head, hoping to keep a low profile. For the first time in his life, the smart London lawyer felt embarrassed to be seen wearing his usual smart grey. Everyone else was dressed in bright colours. He glowered at his son James, furious with him for not having communicated the dress code prior to leaving the house.

Meanwhile James ran a heavily bandaged hand through his heavy brown hair wishing that his wheelchair had not been parked so close to Coral's coffin in full display of the rest of the congregation. A tartan blanket covered his lap and solitary leg. He began to wish that the blanket covered him whole.

The last of the congregation sat down. They consisted of a handful of Coral's school teachers - Mr Knot, a short man with thick black spectacles who taught Biology; Mr Rush, the Head of Sixth Form, who perched on the edge of his seat like a whippet at the starting-block; and gooky Miss Glass dressed in a swirl of primary colours, all layered one on top of each other like a cartoon cake. Needless to say, Miss Glass taught Textile Art.

Miss Harper, the sprightly local ballet school Principal, made a well-timed late entrance. Well into her seventies and still holding dance-classes for toddlers through to teenagers in Bude United Reformed Church Hall every Saturday, she walked briskly to a middle aisle and sat down. Her pianist Miss Stride, a genteel lady with a white bun and her head permanently locked at a forty-five degree angle, followed slowly behind with the aid of her guide-dog Pippa, a fat white Labrador with wistful brown eyes. How Miss Stride still managed to play the piano was little short of miraculous but miracles do happen in these out of the way places and no-one feels the need to pass comment on them because they are accepted as a routine day-to-day occurrence.

A smattering of prefects and school office-holders that Coral barely knew, also attended. A large question-mark hung in the air as the individual members of the congregation all pondered the same question: who actually was Coral?

There was a general feeling of ignorance that permeated the congregation with the exception of the elderly Donkey Man from Saunton Sands who sat in the back row, dressed in a jaunty red, yellow and green check-suit. He fingered his pork-pie hat with the same attention to detail that he had listened to Coral's tales of adventures along the coast, and the old man knew Coral as well as it is possible to know another human-being. It was all in detail. The detail was where you had to look. He smiled, his puffy pink cheeks covered in freckles.

The ceremony began. Everyone except James listened attentively to the vicar's welcoming address. James sullenly eyeballed the stone tablet on the floor before him. The tablet listed the names of all those young men from Hartland who had died whilst serving their country in the Great War. James did not pause for one moment to consider the sacrifice of those young teenage soldiers, many of whom had been but a few years older than he was now. But then James never did think of anyone other than himself and his own personal needs. It would take far more than the death of Coral and the destruction of Sudbury Court for James to change his ways. Right now all his thoughts were centred on his own personal sacrifice – namely his left leg – and his desire to get back to hospital as quickly as possible to ensure continued treatment of the withered stump that remained.

The vicar finished his address and sat down. The room fell silent as a young woman with frizzy hennaed hair walked solemnly up to the pulpit, an oboe held tightly in her ebony hands. She smiled an effervescent smile. Then with her profile silhouetted against the stained-glass windows, she began to play.

The music echoed about the tiny chapel. Sir Aubrey floated down to the young musician's side, enchanted. He tilted his head on one side, his arms crossed and his tongue clicking in time with the melody. The music wafted out of the tiny chapel onto the heath. The inkpot ponies paused momentarily to listen. Then they shook their manes, lowered their heads and continued nibbling the jewelled black bilberries.

The oboist finished playing and returned to her seat in the chancel. The young vicar sprung to his feet and addressed the congregation with an intensity that was palpable.

"We are gathered here today to mark the passing of Coral, a vibrant young woman whose zest for life and passion for the natural world was an inspiration to all who knew her! Although not a practising Christian, Coral embodied the

Christian spirit of compassion. I remember the first time I met Coral on the moor. She was trying to free a young hedgehog tangled up in the plastic rings that hold a regular six-pack of beer together.

Coral's passion for animal welfare extended to a passion for **all** our welfare as evidenced by her decision to enter Sudbury Court in an attempt to rescue those trapped inside. We shall never know what went through Coral's mind in those last closing moments of her life. We shall never know whether she made peace with God or that which she perceived God to be. However we can say that Coral's actions were in keeping with the teachings of Saint Francis of Assisi. Coral believed that mankind should share the world with all living creatures and not subordinate them to our will.

Finally, Coral's passion for nature was complimented by her love of art. In many ways Coral's paintings of nature were an expression of her inner soul. It is that soul which we remember here today."

The vicar fell silent. He studied the congregation thoughtfully. He spoke no more on the subject of the after-life, heaven or hell.

"If you would like to turn your hymn books to page 202, we shall sing the well-known hymn, All Things Bright and Beautiful. It is a tune that I have often heard Coral singing whilst picking wild whortleberries on the heath," the vicar confided in his firm but melodious voice.

The organist began to play. The congregation's voices swelled into an uplifting anthem to nature. Blessed with perfect pitch, Kim's voice soared above the other voices like a skylark in June: pure, sweet and innocent.

Jem quietly slipped into the back of the chapel. He had fought shy of coming to the funeral, not feeling able to trust himself to remain composed. But now, as the words of his favourite hymn soared to the rafters, Jem entered the chapel unnoticed. He tiptoed quietly to the far side of the back row and stood beneath the stained-glass painting depicting the lilies of the field. Kim's pure voice soared higher and higher. Jem opened his mouth and joined in the chorus: "All things bright and beautiful the Lord God made them all."

Coral lay blissfully in her willow bed. She listened to a nightingale singing. Then she heard the low buzz of electric-blue damsel-flies as they hovered above the village pond, their diaphanous wings beating rapidly at twenty-five beats per second. Then Coral started as she heard another sound - one she knew intimately - the rhythmic beating of her heart-beat. She put her hand to her chest… Nothing! There was no heart-beat! Fear gripped her. She raised both hands above her head and began to explore her environment. She was not lying on the grass beside the village pond as she had thought but entombed in a reed-like basket!

Then everything came flooding back to her in a kaleidoscope of Klimt-like images. She saw afresh Antonia's pink boots lying on the edge of the plaster. She saw the leaping flames and the exploding glass of the conservatory roof as it crashed down all about her. The pop of a lemon exploding, then nothing; she could remember no more.

Kim's beautiful voice soared to the rafters, her soprano voice several octaves above the others. Coral sank back into her willow bed and listened to Kim's singing. It must be Kim's heart-beat that she could hear. Jem must have succeeded in rescuing Kim from the fourth floor after all. Coral smiled to herself, content that Kim was alive. People like Kim deserved a second chance.

Coral contentedly listened to Kim's singing. She ran her cold hands along the inside of the willow casket and came to the conclusion that she must be in church attending her own funeral. There was no other explanation. And on the basis of the evidence available, she must be a ghost like Sir Aubrey.

The idea of being a ghost did not frighten her. The idea of being dead did not frighten her either. On the contrary, Coral accepted the reality of her present situation with a stoicism born from experience.

The one person Coral felt for was Hazel. It was hard to contemplate her sorrow. Hazel was in a wretched place and there was nothing that she could do to comfort her. All that she could do was prepare for life as a ghost. It couldn't be that hard, surely? Sir Aubrey always looked so happy. And maybe once she had mastered the art of being a ghost, she could visit Shell Cottage and keep a watchful eye over Hazel; that was the best that she could hope for.

Then Coral started with surprise as she heard a second heart-beat, louder than Kim's. The thunderous heart-beat grew louder and louder, dominating the congregation. Whom did it belong to?

Then as Jem's voice soared with Kim's, Coral let out a little gasp of delight as she realised whose heart-beat she could hear. It was Jem's heart, beating as loud and strong as only his heart could!

Tentatively she raised her right hand and probed her willow coffin with her finger-tips, wanting to take a look at Jem. Then she let out a gasp of surprise as the tips of fingers pierced through the top of the woven coffin. She quickly withdrew her hand, hoping that no-one had spotted her. She did not want to start a panic at her own funeral. Where was Sir Aubrey? She longed to speak to him. She could really do with his advice right now! He was bound to be in the church somewhere. Sir Aubrey would never pass up the chance of a good singsong. The question was this: would Sir Aubrey be able to hear her voice above the noise of everyone else's singing?

"Psst! Sir Aubrey can you hear me?"

James looked up sharply, interrupted from his self-indulgent thoughts by the sound of someone whispering close-by. He glared at Lady Hortensia, assuming that she must have whispered something fatuous to his father. Only people of her rank were arrogant enough to talk in church. He had always hated Lady Hortensia; and now that Antonia was no longer the heir to a vast country estate but the heir to a bowl of ashes, he saw no future in maintaining any relations with her either, especially as Antonia had cut her hair so short that she looked like a choir-boy.

"Sir Aubrey? Are you out there?" Coral repeated urgently.

James intensified his glare. Women over fifty should not be allowed to wear canary yellow. The woman looked ridiculous dressed in submarine yellow with garish jumbo gold earrings and a gigantic crocodile-skin handbag. And as for her yellow trouser-suit, it made her look like a lump of 3-D Lego!

"Sir Aubrey! Can you hear me?" Coral whispered louder still.

But Sir Aubrey did not hear Coral. He might have been able to hear Coral had he not been so busy dancing a jig in the baptism font, justifying his actions on the grounds that it was a non-conformist chapel and that the progressive young vicar would not be offended.

Jem, in stark contrast with the irreverent ghost, conducted himself with God-fearing duty. He felt obligated by his own conscience, and his upbringing, to honour Coral by wearing black. However Jem did not wear a dull unimaginative undertaker's black. He wore the bluish-black of a cormorant's wings and of bulbous seaweed at low tide; the black of the charcoal-burner's dying art and of Wordsworth's dark and mysterious Lake District tarns.

The choir fell silent. The oboist took to her feet again. As the young woman played, Jem tiptoed down the aisle, keen to take a closer look at Coral's beautifully woven coffin before it was transported from the chapel and lowered into the cold earth. He drew level with the coffin and looked down at the woven fronds. The craftsmanship was first-rate. He smiled, his spirits gladdened by the knowledge that the hand-made coffin did Coral justice. *The sail-makers of eighteenth century Hartland wouldst have admired the magnificent stitching!*

Then an oak-apple formed in Jem's throat and he gazed down sadly at the woven casket, finding it hard to believe that Coral was dead. Coral did not *feel* dead. He had known instinctively when Mother, Father and dearest Flossie had died. But he had not had the same feeling with Coral. He reached out and ran his tremulous hand across the woven casket, feeling with his finger-tips every twist and knot in the willow. The coffin did not *feel* dead either. The willow felt alive. Coral felt alive. It was as if he could feel her warm breath permeating through the willow fronds!

It made no sense!

The oboist finished playing and sat down in the chancel next to the ruddy-faced choir-master with his blue button eyes. Then the vicar led the congregation in the Lord's Prayer. Coral tensed inside the coffin as she heard Jem's booming fog-horn voice sound directly above her head.

"Jem can you hear me?"

But Jem could not hear Coral for the simple reason that Coral was speaking in her mind and had not yet learnt how to forge her body to her will and use her vocal chords. She had still to learn how to be a ghost and for the time-being she was very much like an infant child that has not yet mastered the power of speech.

The prayer ended and the last of the A-men incantations rang out, deep, low and strong. The vicar surveyed the congregation with his piercing green eyes. Then he stepped forward and spoke in a commanding voice that sent a shiver down Jem's spine.

"Let all our transgressions be forgotten. Let us pledge to turn over a new leaf and start afresh."

Tom shuddered. Kim gripped his arm in trepidation. Silence as the disparate congregation considered the instruction. The vicar held his breath. Then his cheeks relaxed into their more familiar cherubic demeanour.

"We may now proceed to the churchyard for Coral's burial. Everyone is welcome by the grave-side, not just family members. Hazel has asked me to remind you that you are all invited to cast a keep-sake into Coral's open grave. I believe that Hazel has in mind simple tokens of love, such as a friendship bracelet, an old photograph or perhaps a handwritten note. Nothing elaborate, just something simple that will decompose over time."

The pall-bearers now stepped forward and carried Coral's willow casket down the stone aisle, out through the tiled daub and mortar porch, into the pretty churchyard of the cliff-top chapel.

Coral let out a gasp of surprise as her body was lifted upwards.

"Sir Aubrey? Can you hear me? Sir Aubrey! Where are you when I need you? Sir Aubrey!"

But Sir Aubrey was far too self-absorbed to hear Coral. He had taken himself off to the churchyard and was currently sitting on a gravestone singing Greensleeves whilst polishing his shoes with a dandelion puff. Three delicate dog-violets poked out of his top pocket in lieu of a handkerchief.

Coral could just make out the silvery notes of Sir Aubrey's ethereal voice and relaxed. Her anxieties melted away and she realised that there was no great rush for her to get out of the coffin. After all, she had all the time in the world now that she was a ghost like Sir Aubrey!

The most important thing to do was to remain calm and not to cause a commotion by her sudden appearance. She did not know how many people in the congregation might be able to see ghosts. Clearly it was going to be tricky learning how to be a sensitive ghost who always kept the needs of others foremost in her mind.

Sir Aubrey finished polishing his shoes and looked up at the pall-bearers. The colour drained from his face. He did not want to see Coral buried. *The idea was too painful to contemplate! Coral had been such a sweet child. He had been so looking forward to getting to know her. It was tragic.*

He floated through the chapel porch into the empty building. He paused before the painting of the Good Samaritan and made the sign of the cross. Then he escaped to the vestry and gazed longingly at the communion wine. *How he wished that he could raise a glass in Coral's memory!*

A small group of mourners collected around Coral's graveside. Hazel stooped down and placed her fire-coral necklace on the top of Coral's willow casket. Then everyone watched as Coral's body was lowered slowly into the hollow grave.

The vicar then silently signalled to the assembled mourners, indicating with a curl of the hand that they could now cast their respective keepsakes into the grave.

Antonia was the first to come forward. She stepped daintily to the lip of the hollow. Then she opened her cupped hand to reveal a small pink heart cut from the leather of one of her Doc Marten boots. She shut her eyes and said a few private words. Then she let go of the heart and withdrew, her skin glistening like a white rosebud just opened.

Kim now edged forward and cast a pair of hand-sewn starfish earrings into the hollow grave. Tom followed with a swan's feather. Tom watched pensively as the feather floated slowly downwards in eddying curves and he let go of his cowardice and vowed to stand up for what is right from now on, instead of being bullied into silence by peer pressure.

Then came the sound of metal wheels cutting a rude path through the long grass as James was pushed up to the graveside against his will by a determined Lady Hortensia. James scowled at the other mourners, wishing that he was able-bodied. He looked enviously at Tom's skinny albino frame and wished that he could have one of his legs. Tom was no athlete. What right did he have to keep both his legs?

Lady Hortensia stepped forwards energetically, a miniature leather book held in her chubby hand. The book was a mere two inches wide and three inches long, and entitled 'Visions of Light' by the Edwardian poet J.G. Whittier.

Then Lady Hortensia cleared her throat and began to recite an excerpt from the narrative poem:

"But nature is not solitude
She crowds us with her thronging wood;
Her many hands reach out to us,
Her many tongues are garrulous;
Perpetual riddles of surprise
She offers to our ears and eyes.
She will not leave our senses still
But drags them captive at her will;
And making earth too great for heaven,
She hides the Giver in the given.
The task was thine to mould and fashion
Life's plastic newness into grace;
To make the boyish heart heroic,
And light with thought the maiden's face.
Sweetly here upon thee grew
The lesson which that beauty gave,
The ideal of the pure and true
In earth and sky and gliding wave."

Lady Hortensia shut the tiny book. Then she stooped forward and carefully placed the book on top of the woven casket. James watched, tempted to push the old battle-axe into the grave.

The vicar then signalled to the pall-bearers that they could commence covering Coral's grave with fresh earth. Coral lay back in her willow-herb bed and listened to the sound of the freshly tilled earth being scattered on top of her coffin.

Suddenly Lady Hortensia stepped forward and held up her hand.

"Stop! James hasn't donated a keepsake," Lacy Hortensia boomed. "Get up James. It's time you showed some respect for the dead."

"Get up? But I can't get up! I've just had my leg amputated."

"And your point is? Plenty of our soldiers serving in Afghanistan have had both their legs amputated. Surely you can manage to stand on one leg for a few moments?"

"But I haven't bought anything to put into Coral's grave. There's no point in me standing up," James remonstrated, his pinched cheeks revealing a mixture of self-pity and conceit.

"Then you'll just have to donate your watch."

"What? What are you mad? It's a Rolex! My Dad bought it for me for my sixteenth birthday!"

"You're far too young to own a Rolex," Lady Hortensia snorted with disdain, snatching the watch from his wrist and tossing it into the open grave.

"What in the hell do you think you're doing?" James exploded, lunging forwards, determined to get his Rolex back.

"Ah, so you're discovered that you can move after all James. You can push the wheelchair. It'll do you good to exercise your one good leg," Lady Hortensia said crisply, smiling at him with her leonine eyes. Suddenly canary-yellow seemed the perfect colour for her after all. Only a woman of her stature could get away with wearing canary yellow and still put the fear of God up James. He fell silent, too angry to speak. But he made no attempt to retrieve his precious Rolex.

Coral lay back on her willow-herb bed and listened as the last of the fresh earth was scattered on top of her coffin. Then she relaxed into herself, looking forward to the moment when she would finally be able to float up out of her coffin and surprise Sir Aubrey and Jem.

The mourners laid bouquets of flowers on top of the grave and departed one by one. The churchyard emptied. Hazel remained by the edge of the grave, the last person in the churchyard. She listened for the sound of the metal kissing-gate snapping shut. Now suddenly alone, she erupted into a volcano of acrid tears that burnt her cheeks. Time stilled. Hazel's breathing returned to an even keel. She bit her lips, ashamed of her extravagant tears. Then she turned and walked briskly back to the porch where the kind-hearted young vicar patiently waited for her with a ready smile and a listening ear, keen to comfort her as best he could.

Inside the willow casket, Coral blinked in confusion. Her eyelashes were wet for some reason. Raindrops landed on her forehead making the front strands of her hair damp. She frowned, puzzled. She couldn't hear any rain. And even if it were raining, surely the rain could not penetrate the willow fronds so quickly?

The air inside the woven casket grew more and more stuffy and Coral gradually realised that what she had imagined to be raindrops were in fact droplets of perspiration. *If only Sir Aubrey were around to explain everything to her!* She needed his advice on how to prepare for life as a ghost. But Sir Aubrey still did not come to pay his respects at her graveside.

Instead Jem arrived, carrying a sprig of lavender clutched in his smudged hands. He had spent a long time wrestling with his conscience, berating himself a thousand times for his negligence. *He should not have trusted Coral to remain outside the burning edifice of Sudbury Court. He should have realised that she would brave the flames to try and rescue Kim and Antonia!* Tears erupted from Jem's eyes. They coursed down his cheeks like arrows.

Frowning, he checked himself and laid the sprig of lavender at the foot of Coral's grave. Then he knelt down amongst all the bouquets of flowers and inhaled the sweet aroma of a summer meadow.

Fresh tears flowed down Jem's cheeks. This time he did not try to fight them. He stopped feeling embarrassed. He no longer thought it unmanly to weep. On the contrary, for the first time in two hundred years, he actually understood that it was mature to show ones emotions instead of fighting to keep them under lock and key.

Exhausted, Jem lay down at Coral's graveside and cradled her unseen body in his invisible arms. He continued to lie there all day. Daylight gave way to dusk. Flames of fire-coral flared out from behind the strips of charcoal-grey cloud on the horizon. Then the wind rose and blew away the last remnants of grey cloud revealing a blood-red sunset. There was one last flash of fire-coral and night fell like a stone.

The sea mist rolled in from the west and filled every corner of the graveyard with its cold, cloying tendrils. The mist soothed Jem's brow and wiped away his tears. Finally sleep enveloped him. Coral lay quite still in her willow grave and listened to the sound of Jem's snoring. A wave of relief rushed through her. She relaxed a little, thankful that Jem was no longer crying but at rest.

Then Coral shivered in her meadow bed, beginning to feel bitterly cold for the first time since her death. She was surprised at this discovery. It had never crossed her mind that ghosts might feel the cold. She would never have guessed it from Sir Aubrey. He always seemed so bright and warm and hearty. Where **was** Sir Aubrey? She really needed him right now.

Jem woke early the next morning at Coral's graveside, his body chilled to the bone.

He sat up stiffly and blinked at the bouquets of flowers coated with dew-drops. Then he sighed. He had dreamt that Coral was sleeping in his beach-hut and that hot arrowroot bubbled away on the top of his wood-burner. *But it must have been a dream.*

The scratching sound of the church-gate dragging on the stone-path; Jem looked up abruptly. It was Hazel. He frowned. He did not want to be reacquainted with Hazel's turbulent grief. It was hard enough coping with his own.

"Good-bye Coral. I'll be back to visit you this evening," he said hurriedly, his voice crackling with emotion. Then he turned and fled.

Coral tried to raise her arms and legs to go after him but for some reason her body felt too heavy to move.

"Come back Jem!" Coral called out desperately. "Don't go! I love you."

But the sound of his thundering heart-beat grew quieter and quieter. He leapt over the stone wall onto the moor.

"Jem! Come back!" Coral shouted hoarsely.

Jem's booming heart-beat grew fainter and fainter until it was no longer audible. Coral shivered in her willow bed, feeling more and more desolate with every passing moment. She should have spoken to Jem earlier! She should have slipped out of her grave hours ago and woken him up when she still had the energy to do so.

But she had felt so comfortable in her meadow bed and there hadn't seemed to be any great hurry to get out of the churchyard whilst Jem was asleep above her. Also she had wanted him to rest after his exertions fighting the flames at Sudbury Court. So she had done nothing and as a direct consequence of her inaction, Jem was now gone! And now for some strange reason she felt so terribly cold that she no longer had the strength to raise her arm, never mind sit up and go after Jem! She burst into tears, distraught.

"Sir Aubrey where are you when I need you? Sir Aubrey!"

CHAPTER FIFTEEN

Help is at Hand

Hazel arrived at the graveside. Her skin had lost yesterday's lustre and her hair was back to its usual flat lifeless structure. Ordinary life had returned after yesterday's church service. Only for Hazel, ordinary life had lost its meaning because there was one vital missing element: Coral.

Inside her coffin, Coral listened miserably as Hazel wept and talked at the same time, her mind going round and round in vicious circles. Every now and then Hazel would catch her breath and sound as if she was suffocating, choked by her own sobs. It was heartbreaking to hear! And the more distressed Hazel became, the sadder Coral felt, until the tips of Coral's fingers began to turn blue with the cold.

"Hazel! Mum! Can you hear me?"

But Hazel could not hear Coral. All she could hear was the monotonous moan of the distant waves lapping against the northerly shore. Grief enveloped her, dulling her hearing, cutting off all links to the outside world.

"Mum! I love you!" Coral cried out, helplessly.

Then with a great effort Coral managed to raise her left hand. She pressed her palm against the layer of willow directly above her chest. At first she met with success. Her hand passed through the woven willow fronds. But then it connected with hard clay earth. Her strength departed and her arm collapsed back down by her side, a dead-weight.

The sound of receding footsteps as Hazel walked slowly back across the wet grass. Then the scraping of metal against metal as Hazel struggled to lift the latch of the rusty metal gate. The mechanism snapped back savagely, biting her fingers.

"Hazel! Mum!" Coral called out, her tongue numb with cold.

Then a cloud of loneliness hit her and she began to despair. How much longer was she going to remain trapped inside this coffin unable to get out unaided? Where was Sir Aubrey?

The wind whistled over the moor. Coral listened miserably to the wind's melancholy lament. She shivered, stung by the biting cold. Her teeth chattered. What was happening to her? She clasped her arms about her ribcage and hugged herself in a last-ditched effort to keep warm.

Directly above the churchyard a male peregrine called to its mate as the pair glided along the cliff-tops utilising the hot thermals. The female spotted a young hare and swooped low over the bracken, her talons pared. The hare twisted left then right weaving in and out of the sharp yellow gorse. At the last moment the hare bolted down a burrow to safety. The female peregrine let out a shrill cry of disappointment then soared upwards to join her mate.

Then another sharp note echoed across the heath. The sound of an A-sharp as sprightly Sir Aubrey skipped across the bell-heather singing to himself:

"What shall we do with the drunken sailor? What shall we do with the drunken sailor? What shall we do with the drunken sailor early in the morning? Put him in the long boat till he's sober! Put him in the long boat till he's sober! Put him in the long boat till he's sober early in the morning!"

Sir Aubrey sprang from tussock to tussock, his hands in the pockets of his tail-coat, dressed in emerald green breeches and a matching orange waistcoat.

"Sir Aubrey? Sir Aubrey is that you?" Coral whispered weakly, her voice faint.

She craned her head upwards so that her hair touched the roof of her willow casket. Every muscle in her neck jarred with pain at the effort but she fought against the stiffness in her joints and managed to raise her head a few inches.

"Sir Aubrey! It's me Coral! Can you hear me?"

Sir Aubrey stopped singing. He spun round a full three hundred and sixty degrees and listened hard. Coral called again. Sir Aubrey leapt into the air with delight.

"Of course I can hear you my dear child!" Sir Aubrey exclaimed happily. "Well I never! A ghost just like me! Wonders will never cease!" Sir Aubrey exclaimed again, floating into the churchyard then down through the hard clay earth to sit alongside Coral in her willow bed.

His iridescent eyes sparkled at Coral brightly, casting waves of rainbow light about the interior of the willow coffin.

"Sir Aubrey! Thank God I've found you!" Coral exclaimed in relief. "I was beginning to think that you had disappeared off the face of this earth! Or else that you had gone to Parliament with your friend the Marquis of Queensberry to poke fun at the lazy MPs," Coral added brightly, trying to hide the fact that she was shivering with cold. "Didn't you hear me calling out to you in church yesterday?"

"Sorry no! It must be the wax in my ears!" Sir Aubrey replied disingenuously, taking a feather quill out of his breast pocket and pretending to clean his ear canals with it.

"But that's impossible Sir Aubrey! You can't have wax in your ears. You're a ghost. You don't have any substance!"

"The saltwater combines with the oxygen in the air and solidifies in my ear canals," Sir Aubrey blithely replied.

"Nonsense! I don't believe one word of it!" Coral replied, laughing, her teeth chattering as she did so.

"If you don't believe me, you can ask my good friend The Marquis of Queensbury. He suffers from terrible rhinitis when he's in London. All that smog in the summer months causes havoc with his nasal passages!"

Coral smiled. Oxygen could not turn into wax. But smog might well make a person's nose run and cause breathing difficulties. She let the matter drop. She was too cold to argue the point.

"Have you seen Jem by any chance Sir Aubrey?"

"I'm afraid not. Should I have?"

"He was here about an hour ago. I tried talking to him but he couldn't hear me. Then Hazel visited me. She couldn't hear me either! I tried to push my way up out of the grave to comfort her but I couldn't for some reason. My fingers passed through the willow casket but then they came up against solid brick clay.

And one other thing, Sir Aubrey, I feel so terribly, terribly cold! What ever is wrong with me, Sir Aubrey? Why can only you hear me? And why can't I float up to the surface like you can? And is it normal to feel so cold?"

Sir Aubrey rubbed his chin thoughtfully. But Sir Aubrey was never without an answer for long.

"It sounds to me as if you've allowed yourself to get too cold by thinking sad thoughts. What you need to do is to think happy and uplifting thoughts. You should soon start to feel warmer and be able to float upwards through the compacted clay."

"Say that again, I have to be happy in order to warm myself up?"

"Quite so! Why do you think that I dance and laugh so much? A ghost needs to keep moving and be joyful in order to stay warm. And only once a ghost is warm can he glide through solid objects. You appear to have got yourself stuck inside your own grave."

"That would explain it," Coral replied weakly.

"The trouble is that you **think** too much Coral! You've listened to everyone crying and allowed yourself to get too sad. It's hardly surprising that you're so stiff. What you need to do now is to imagine how happy Jem will feel when he discovers that you have returned from the dead."

"So I am definitely dead? There's no chance that I'm still alive but just too cold and weak to shift the heavy clay?" Coral asked forlornly.

"Indubitably! You're as dead as a door-post!"

"In that case how can you be so sure that Jem will be able to see and hear me? He didn't hear me earlier. So why should he be able to see me?"

"Of course he will be able to see you! If Jem can see and hear **me**, then he will be able to see and hear you. Do stop worrying Coral. Everything's going to be just dandy."

Coral considered Sir Aubrey's opinion but made no reply. She wanted to believe him but sometimes in life what one wants is not attainable.

"Do you think that Jem will be able to touch me?"

Sir Aubrey glanced down at his fire-opal ring and studied his reflection in it.

"No I'm afraid not. Ghosts are intangible. His hands will go right through your body now that you're a ghost. Having said that, I must confess that you are behaving rather oddly for a ghost!"

"Oddly? What do you mean by oddly?"

"Well you look incredibly cold but you really shouldn't be as cold as you are! Not with me here to cheer you up! It's most unnatural. Sir Aubrey can warm the coldest of hearts! It is in my genes and in my nature!"

"Maybe you're losing your touch," Coral replied, laughing in spite of her discomfort.

"Dear me! I hope not!" Sir Aubrey exclaimed, mortified at the thought. "Perhaps there is more to this coldness of yours than meets the eye. Perhaps you're not a ghost after all, maybe you're a…"

His voice broke off.

"Maybe I'm a what?" Coral demanded impatiently.

"Maybe you're in some sort of half-way house like Jem…"

"Is that really possible?" Coral asked, trying not to get too excited.

"Everything is possible! To a degree," Sir Aubrey replied, thinking of the last time he saw the ghost of a pig fly past him. Ghost pigs can fly, unlike their living counterparts.

"Well let's find out," Coral said eagerly. "Shall we try shaking hands? If my hand doesn't pass through your hand then we will know that I'm not a ghost."

"That won't work. **My hand** passes through everything, remember! It'll pass through your hand straightaway irrespective of whether you're a ghost or not. No, there's only one method and it's so obvious that I really feel quite embarrassed that I didn't think of it earlier," Sir Aubrey confessed. "Can you feel your heart beating?"

"It wasn't beating earlier when I was in the church."

"Yes but now! Can you feel it beating now?"

"I can't feel anything. My body's all numb with cold," Coral replied miserably.

"In that case, if it would not be too indelicate to ask, would you allow me to listen for the sound of your heart-beat? It will involve my passing through your, erm, breast-plate, then through your ribcage to the seat of your heart."

"Sure. But wouldn't it be easier to take my pulse?"

"I can't apply any pressure to your vein Coral, my hands go through matter," Sir Aubrey repeated patiently. "I can just about manage to catch a dandelion-puff blowing in the wind but I can't actually pick one myself.

"Sorry. I'm not thinking straight. I'm too cold," Coral confessed. She paused then asked bravely. "Will it hurt?"

"Will what hurt?"

"Will your head hurt me when it passes through my ribcage to get to my heart?"

"Goodness no! Ghosts cannot cause or feel pain. Although we can scare the living daylights out of someone we don't like!" Sir Aubrey quipped, grinning at her devilishly. "But as rule we only pick on grown-ups. It's much more fun to tease them."

"Honestly Sir Aubrey, you're impossible!" Coral remarked, laughing weakly.

"That's the general idea!" Sir Aubrey chuckled exuberantly.

Then Sir Aubrey's laughter gave way to silence and deep concentration.

Coral tensed as he tilted his head towards her…

Sir Aubrey's face grew still, his jaw taut and visceral. He took a deep breath and passed his skull straight through her cotton dress, through her muscle, skin and bone, down through the zigzag chambers of her ribcage towards the inner chamber of her heart. He pressed his ear against her aorta and listened for the sound of a heart-beat.

"By Jove! No wonder you can't float out of your grave. You're not a ghost at all!" Sir Aubrey exclaimed joyfully. "You're a Sentient Corporal Entity!"

"You mean I'm like Jem?" Coral asked excitedly.

"Precisely so!"

"But since when? I couldn't hear my heart-beat earlier in church. I swear it! It doesn't make sense."

"Of course it makes sense! Everything always makes sense if one looks hard enough!" Sir Aubrey assured her, grinning at her ecstatically. "You probably couldn't hear your heart-beat earlier because you were in the transition stage. Or, you had wax in your ears!"

They both laughed.

"So what do we do now, Sir Aubrey?"

"We're just going to have to get you out of here the old-fashioned way, with a spade."

"But we don't have a spade."

"Quite so! And even if we did, the handle would pass straight through my hands!" Sir Aubrey twittered.

"So what are we going to do?" Coral asked anxiously, her voice hoarse as her whole neck began to seize up from cold.

The last vestiges of heat began to ebb away from her like the receding tide. Her teeth began to chatter violently. She tried to smile as instructed but her lips refused to obey her commands. She began to think that she would never get out of her miserable coffin and that she was condemned to spend the rest of her life buried under the ground.

"I'm going to fetch Jem," Sir Aubrey said decisively. "He can't have gone far. I shan't be long. Remember: think warm happy thoughts and you'll soon warm up."

"But I'm **not** a ghost Sir Aubrey. I won't warm up!"

"Try all the same. You're a half-ghost remember, so maybe you can keep **half** of your body warm? Smile Coral! Think of hot scones with butter and jam! Think of cheese on toast with apple chutney! Think of jugged hare and roast beef…"

"Enough Sir Aubrey! I get the general idea. Now go!"

Sir Aubrey nodded. Then in one tremendous, acrobatic bound, Sir Aubrey shot back up through the earth into the stillness of the morning.

Sunlight glanced off his moonbeam cravat. Another ray of sunlight alighted on the plum tree in the corner of the graveyard. Sir Aubrey took a running leap and landed on the lowest bough of the plum tree. His soles slipped through the outer layer of silvery brown bark. Then he hovered momentarily on a pincushion of air directly above the pale green leaves and clusters of fruit.

He squinted greedily at the juicy plums, wishing that he were able to eat them. Then he glided up, up, to the topmost crown of the tree and stared out across the moor-land, sifting the brown from the black, the purple from the deep reds, casting his net far and wide in his search for Jem.

Then a flush of pale pink spread across Sir Aubrey's face as he spied the lone figure of Jem seated at the foot of the oak trees at Two-Tree Junction. Of course! Jem was bound to be at Two-Tree Junction, a magical place of healing and peace. It was the most sensible place to be.

CHAPTER SIXTEEN

A New Beginning

Jem sat cross-legged on the ground, his eyes closed. His back rested against the conjoined tree trunks. A necklace of dark green leaves encircled his shoulders. The underside of each leaf was pale and matt, borne on hairy shoots. The leaves tickled the back of his neck but did not bother him. He felt at home. Two-Tree Junction was the place he always went to in order to clear his mind and tend his soul: a place of profound peace.

The young oak saplings had first caught his eye two centuries ago when he was up on the moor with Flossie and Mother. Napoleon had been victorious in battles across Europe. Jem secretly admired the young Corsican officer who had risen through the ranks to lead his country. But Father had been outraged! They had exchanged angry words. Jem had marched up onto the moor in a huff and joined Mother and Flossie picking bilberries. It was then that Jem first saw the tiny saplings… He remembered looking down at them and thinking that they wouldst never make it to adult-hood in such a windswept place.

But the tiny saplings had had other ideas! By the time they were four years old they had assumed an almost human form. Flossie adored them, calling them her 'dancing faeries.' She would drag him up onto the heath and lead him in a merry dance about the trees, singing 'ring-a-ring of roses' at the top of her butterscotch voice. Round and round they danced together, getting dizzier and dizzier until they collapsed to the ground in a fit of giggles. "And we all fall down!"

As the trees grew, Jem collected sticks for kindling and blossom for Mother. He would watch enchanted as Flossie separated the delicate flower petals and set her 'fairy boats' to sail in a saucer of water. It was beautiful magic: the magic of nature and all things innocent.

Five years passed and the oak trees grew stout; their backs curved eastwards, battered into shape by the Atlantic gales. There wasn't sufficient space for two mature oak trees on such a small plot so something clever had to happen and nothing is cleverer than Mother Nature!

The trunks of the two trees fused together and the branches interlocked, creating a curious-shaped tree that bore a striking resemblance to an old man resting his elbows on a walking-stick. The head of the old man was a raised fungal growth located ten feet from the ground on the fattest section of the trunk. A curious oak-apple poked out of the side of the old man's mouth like a pipe.

The oak-apple pipe had always fascinated Jem! Oak-apples are not edible but are a kind of excrescence produced on the oak tree by gall-flies. The oak-apples can be found growing at the end of brittle twigs. They are round and small like golden marbles with a tiny pin-prick hole in the side made by the gall-fly.

Flossie once tried to make an oak-apple necklace by threading yarn through the little pin-prick holes but the tough oak-apples refused to let her needle pass through. It was Nature's way of saying: "Enough! Don't mess with me!"

Jem suddenly stopped reminiscing. He could not make up his mind what to do for the best. He felt lost. He could see no way forward.

Then he slipped his hand in his trouser pocket and pulled out a golden oak-apple. He stared at the tiny oak-apple wishing it could talk and tell him what to do. He had never felt as lonely as he felt now!

It had been his intention to bury the oak-apple in Coral's grave but on seeing Hazel place her fire-coral necklace on top of the willow coffin, he had changed his mind.

It wouldst have been impertinent to mimic an act of devotion twixt mother and daughter. Besides, the oak-apple did not do Coral justice. Nothing could do Coral justice. If he couldst reach up to the heavens with a scalpel and remove a section of blue sky and give it to Coral as a present then that would be different! But he could not. He did not have the know-how.

He could think of nothing else to give Coral of any consequence. Indeed, the more he considered Hazel's request that Coral be buried with keep-sakes, the more he questioned the validity of the idea.

Life was eternal. Possessions were transient. What need did Coral have of possessions in the After-Life? It seemed all very mystical. But then again, God worked in mysterious ways.

Then Jem remembered Antonia's solemn face as she cast her leather heart into Coral's grave and he understood that in that small act of devotion Antonia had discovered a kinder and gentler part of herself.

The only festering sore was James. The boy's vanity and arrogance was sickening! But time was a great leveller. *Perhaps life in a wheelchair dependent on the kindness of others wouldst teach James humility?*

*

The silvery notes of Sir Aubrey's voice echoed across the heath. Jem looked up and met Sir Aubrey's luminous gaze.

"Hello Jem dear chap!" Sir Aubrey said brightly, floating down to greet him. He sat down on a stone in the bell-heather, a thin layer of shimmering air separating his clothes from the hard surface of the rock.

Then he smoothed down the back of his purple frockcoat so as not to crease the velvet. The fact that the velvet coat could not be creased and was an elaborate montage of coloured air was of no consequence to Sir Aubrey. Old habits die hard and as far as Sir Aubrey was concerned Manners Maketh the Man.

"Good Morning Sir Aubrey. What brings thee here?" Jem asked politely.

"You my dear chap!" Sir Aubrey trilled exuberantly, his eyes dancing in their sockets like glittery fish scales. "I need your help."

Jem sighed forlornly.

"I'm afraid that I canst be of little help to thee, Sir Aubrey. My heart is heavy. I will be poor company for thee."

"No matter! It is not your company that I seek but your manpower. And as to your heart, it shall be as right as rain in an hour or two."

"Sir Aubrey, I warn thee! I am not in the mood to have my feelings trifled with!" Jem said angrily, his knuckles curled into fists, his eyes dark and threatening.

"Steady on, there's no need to be so touchy. You're lucky Jem to have a heart old chap! I'd love to have a heart like yours, even if it does cause you pain every now and again. It's a cold, hard life being a ghost I can tell you! You're lucky that you have blood in your veins to circulate!" Sir Aubrey exclaimed, his coat turning a violent red.

Sir Aubrey's clothes changed colour according to his mood and right now the mild mannered ghost was thoroughly miffed. Indeed, he was so acutely offended by Jem's attitude that his entire set of stockings, garter and frockcoat burst into flames of orange light.

Jem's jaw dropped open, taken aback by Sir Aubrey's transformation.

"I apologise Sir Aubrey. I didst not mean to hurt thy feelings," Jem replied with difficulty, his voice thick with emotion after a night spent grieving for Coral. "Thou always appear to be so merry. I didst not credit thee with deep feelings."

"Not many people do," Sir Aubrey replied, his frockcoat now a riotous red. "People never stop to think how the poor ghost feels when they scream in our ears! It's spine-chilling the sound some women can make when they set their minds to it! And the men aren't much better either, stamping about like demented cavemen just because I happen to have paid them a visit!"

"Thou couldst try being nice to people instead of spending your time haunting their houses," Jem remarked, suppressing a smile.

"You've missed the point entirely! Just because we ghosts don't have hearts of flesh doesn't mean that we can't feel anything. We still have hearts. In fact our hearts are terribly vulnerable, prone to frost-bite and all kinds of disorders of the nervous system."

"I'm beginning to understand," Jem replied, trying hard to contain a smile.

The one good thing about Sir Aubrey was the fact that he could always be relied upon to provoke a man to action. Jem stood up and ran his hands through his dishevelled hair.

"I give in! Sir Aubrey, how can I help thee? Thou came to fetch me for a reason. What is the reason?"

"There's important work to be done!" Sir Aubrey exclaimed excitedly. "And only you can do it! No other man has the sufficient strength to perform the task required and not be scared out of his wits!"

"And what is it that thou dost want me to do?" Jem asked patiently, amused by Sir Aubrey's extravagant theatrics. Brevity was not one of Sir Aubrey's strong points.

"Oh. Don't you know?" Sir Aubrey replied, genuinely surprised. "I thought I'd already told you. Dear me, I'm losing my memory in old age. We have serious business to do and we can't waste one moment longer!"

"And the business is?"

"Why we have to get Coral out of her grave before she dies a death of cold!"

Jem froze. His eyes flashed. His right hand curled into a fist. *If Sir Aubrey was lying to him he would wring his neck, he…* He stared at Sir Aubrey long and hard, trying to divine the truth. Then he slowly unfurled his hand and let it flop back down to his side.

There was a stillness in Sir Aubrey's gaze that confirmed he was telling the truth.

"Coral's alive?" Jem asked, his voice tremulous.

"Yes! Isn't it wonderful?"

"Why didst thou not say earlier?" Jem exclaimed, the full meaning of Sir Aubrey's words only now beginning to sink in. "Let's go!" he shouted as his heart leapt skyward like an arrow released from its bow.

The relief Jem felt could not be measured in time, money or years. Coral was alive. Every part of him exploded with joy. He set off across the bell-heather, fuelled by burgeoning hope.

"At first I thought that Coral was a ghost like me," Sir Aubrey explained, shooting through the air like a rocket, his coat-tails emitting sparks of white and yellow light. "Then Coral complained of being unable to lift her arm through the clay. So I placed my ear next to her right ventricle and to my utter shock I could hear her heart pumping away loud and clear! But when I placed my ear to her left ventricle, her heart-beat was much weaker. I fear that if we don't get Coral out soon, she may lapse into a coma. The trouble is the cold! The heart is a pump, you know, and Coral's heart seems to be struggling to function at such low temperatures."

Jem raced across the moor. He reached St George's Chapel and tumbled through the kissing-gate, sweat streaming down his forehead. Then the droplets of sweat combined with tears of joy as he neared Coral's grave and he flung himself down on the ground beside her.

"Coral, canst thy hear me?" Jem said eagerly, kneeling down in the long wet grass and casting the bouquets of flowers aside so that he could get closer to her. "It's me Jem! I've come to get thee out!"

There was no answer. Jem pressed his cheeks against the earth praying that he would be able to hear the sound of her heart-beat.

Meanwhile Sir Aubrey performed a victory circuit of the churchyard, cock-a-hoop that Coral would imminently be freed from her prison-tomb. Then he puffed up his chest, feeling mighty pleased with himself at having played such an important role in facilitating her rescue.

"Coral don't leave me! Thou canst leave me now!" Jem pleaded fearfully, shifting sideways and crushing the spray of chrysanthemums flat in his urgency to free Coral from her frozen grave.

"Jem, whatever is the matter with you?" Sir Aubrey exclaimed, totally ignorant of the alarm that gripped Jem like a bush-fire.

Jem did not answer. Sir Aubrey cut short his victory parade and floated down to see what all the fuss was about.

"Dear me, Jem, the poor flowers! Spare a thought for the poor vicar! He will be most put out when he discovers that you have trampled roughshod all over his churchyard."

"I've good reason to Sir Aubrey!" Jem shouted, scooping up huge handfuls of red clay with his bare hands.

Jem launched himself at the top layers of earth and tunnelled away like a madman, barely pausing to draw breath. At length his hands hit a layer of solid red clay. He slammed his fists down hard on the clay blocks. Trickles of blood oozed from his knuckles. He pounded the clay barrier again and again, desperate to break through.

"What on earth do you think you're doing Jem?" Sir Aubrey said sternly. "And why the devil don't you fetch a spade from the vicarage potting shed? It would make your job considerably easier."

But Sir Aubrey's sensible suggestion fell on death ears and the wise old ghost was obliged to watch helplessly as Jem's excavation expanded to include an area ten feet square. The heaps of earth and grassy bank surrounding Coral's grave now took on the form of a major archaeological dig.

"This is ludicrous! Whatever is the matter with you?" Sir Aubrey demanded as Jem's digging motions became more and more erratic.

"She's not answering me. That's what the matter is!" Jem snapped tersely, his eyes bloodshot.

"Not answering you? Why the devil didn't you say so in the first place?" Sir Aubrey exclaimed, his frockcoat draining of all colour. "I'll go down and investigate straightaway."

Jem watched as Sir Aubrey pointed his toes and descended feet-first, passing seamlessly through the layers of sun-scorched clay without difficulty. Then one last twist of white hair and the elderly ghost disappeared totally beneath the earth's crust.

Sir Aubrey alighted on the edge of Coral's rosebay willow-herb pillow. A twinge of sadness infected his kind heart. Coral looked so cold, still and lifeless! Had he arrived too late? A sense of trepidation chilled him.

"Wake up Coral dearest," Sir Aubrey whispered softly in her ear.

Coral did not answer. The colour drained totally from Sir Aubrey's entire body so that for once in his life he actually looked like a ghost, his whole visage a wheat-sheaf white.

Sir Aubrey froze with fear. Then he espied Hazel's fire-coral necklace clasped in Coral's right hand and he perked up. Coral had **not** been holding the necklace when he had left her. It was a promising sign. He jettisoned his cowardice and pressed his ear against Coral's ribcage and listened for the sound of her heart-beat.

His frockcoat flashed a vivid emerald green. Coral's heart was still beating! The beat was faint but regular. However her cheeks were tinged with blue and she looked so terribly cold.

"Hold on Coral. Jem will get you out," Sir Aubrey whispered in her ear, then he ascended back up to the surface, determined to extol Jem to work faster.

"Is her heart still beating?" Jem demanded anxiously.

"Yes. But she's most terribly cold. What you need is a spade. I'll go and look inside the chapel. It's quicker than going back to the vicarage."

Jem nodded and redoubled his efforts, angry with himself for having got embroiled in an argument with Sir Aubrey earlier about the merits of being a ghost. It had been so incredibly selfish and self-centred of him and it had lost them valuable time! If they hadn't got side-tracked, Sir Aubrey would have got to the point earlier about Coral.

"We're in luck Jem!" Sir Aubrey shouted, cannoning back across the churchyard, his tailcoat sprouting plumes of techno-colour. "There's a trowel in the vestry alongside a tray of Michaelmas daisy seedlings waiting to be planted out! Thank goodness for the good ladies in charge of the flower-arranging!" Sir Aubrey exclaimed enthusiastically. "But you'll have to break into the church. It shouldn't be too difficult. The exterior door into the bell-tower is pretty weak. One shove of the shoulder should do it."

Jem stopped digging and bounded across the churchyard to the bell-tower. It took more than a few shoves to break open the door but finally the central panel gave way, enabling him to put his arm through and unlock the door.

In a few minutes Jem had returned to Coral's grave and was attacking the hard ground with the sharp edge of the diamond-shaped trowel.

Sir Aubrey perched himself on the wing of a beautiful angel headstone and watched on tenterhooks as Jem used the edge of the spade to piece through the stubborn clay soil. The marble angel marked the grave of a little girl called Mercy Evans who had died in 1760 aged just six years old.

"You're nearly through Jem!" Sir Aubrey extolled brightly, trying to encourage Jem.

Sir Aubrey's frock-coat changed to brilliant silver, streaked with white, in honour of the little girl. The spirit of little Mercy and all the other children buried in the graveyard combined to cheer Jem on, all praying for a happy ending.

At long last the metal blade sliced through the final layer of clay. Jem threw the trowel aside and set to work with his bare hands, levering up whole clods of baked earth with his thick fingers. Then he carefully scraped away the residue of red dust with his nails to reveal the willow casket beneath.

He held his breath and stared down at the beautiful craftsmanship. Then he set about separating the willow leaves with the delicacy of a small boy who has woven fishing-nets for a living since the tender age of eight. The willow leaves parted. He gazed down at Coral's white cotton dress, Antonia's leather heart resting lightly on the embroidered lace bodice. Then his eyes travelled along to Coral's right hand, clasped tightly about Hazel's fire-coral neck-lace.

Jem carefully removed the soft white willow bark encasing Coral's chilled marble-like face. His heart trembled. He stared down at Coral's pale blue lips and owl-shaped lids as if in a trance. He dared not touch her. He could barely look at her! And yet he **must**.

Emboldened, he scooped her up in his arms and rapidly began to rub the life back into her arms and hands at the same time as showering her neck and throat in cherry-blossom kisses.

Sir Aubrey politely averted his eyes. But as the minutes ticked past and Coral still did not open her eyes, Sir Aubrey could contain himself no longer and he cried out:

"Don't just kiss her neck Jem. Kiss her lips as well!"

Jem blushed, checked himself, and then planted a rosebud kiss on Coral's ice-cold lips.

Coral stirred in her meadow sleep. Hazel and John sipped iced lemon tea on the verandah of La Boheme. But instead of smelling the familiar fields of French lavender, she smelt fields of English heather. Her lips tingled as something warm touched them. She parted her lips expecting to drink iced tea but instead she imbibed a mouthful of heather breath.

Then ever so cautiously and only half-believing, Coral opened her eyes and looked up into Jem's stolid gaze.

"Jem!" Coral said sweetly, staring up at those concerned topaz eyes, beads of sweat shimmering on his forehead like dewdrops. "Am I day-dreaming or did you kiss me just now?"

"I kissed you," Jem replied shyly, his muddy palm cupping her left cheek.

Coral's lips curled into a fire-coral smile.

"Did you just say you?" Coral asked softly.

"I did," Jem replied stolidly. "I think Sir Aubrey has a point when he says that it's time I learnt to speak Modern English. I've been stuck in the past for far too long."

"Oh I don't know about that. Charging into the burning wreckage of Sudbury Court and saving all those lives took quite a few steps forward, especially when most people were running the other way," Coral replied cheerfully. "You didn't get badly burnt did you?"

"Yes. But the wounds have magically healed if that makes any sense…"

"No that doesn't make any sense at all!" Coral replied, still finding it hard to believe that he had just kissed her. Then she paused and added slyly: "But kissing me made a good deal of sense and is definitely a step in the right direction."

Jem blushed, wondering whether he could ever be a thoroughly modern twenty-first century man. He could cope with the modern vernacular but he drew the line at flowery board-shorts! And when it came to midnight swimming, it was either canvas trousers or nothing.

"Penny for your thoughts?" Coral asked, pressing his palm with her leaf-like hand, her blue eyes sparkling with love.

"I was just wondering whether you would consider coming swimming with me this evening. We won't be alone. The harp seals and grey seals can be our chaperones."

A polite cough echoed through the still air.

"May I join you?" Sir Aubrey asked tentatively. "I've always been partial to a midnight dip. One can't beat floating on ones back looking up at the stars!"

Jem smiled wryly.

"It looks like Sir Aubrey has decided to be our chaperone," Jem remarked light-heartedly, scooping Coral up in his arms and walking slowly towards the cliff-top.

The sun blazed, its gilded rays bathing every blade of grass with live-giving energy. The sea waxed a deep crystal-blue then liquid-gold.

Coral and Jem sat down on the grassy plateau and stared out across the vastness of the Atlantic Ocean with its secret world of wonders hidden beneath the rippling ocean waves.

"What do you think Coral? Should we allow Sir Aubrey to come skinny-dipping with us tonight?"

"Of course! There's enough room in the sea for everybody provided we look after it. Enough room for you, me, Sir Aubrey, the harp seals, Kim, Tom, James, Antonia, the whole lot of us!"

"Especially James and Antonia," Jem replied wisely. "The coral reefs can't survive without all our help."

Then the staccato call of a harp seal pup calling to its mother as the sunlight clipped the serrated edge of Old Man's Elbow. All was still.

The End

APPENDIX 1

Miscellaneous 'bits and bobs'

All Hallow's Eve. All Hallow's Eve is the date of Jem's death, more commonly known as Halloween. There are two notable occasions in the calendar when the spirit world and the actual world are alleged to mysteriously intermingle.

The first date in the year is Walpurgisnacht, the night before May Day. According to Bavarian folklore, witches are said to gather in places such as the Brocken in the Harz Mountains of Germany.

The second date is October 31st, All Hallow's Eve. Legends vary but in some stories the souls of the dead are said to rise from the bowels of the earth. I chose this date for Jem's transformation into a sentient corporal entity in memory of my mother Anne-Marie Mazuc who died on All Hallow's Eve in 1975, aged only forty.

Bluebeard or Le Barbe Blue. This scary fairytale was written in 1697 by Charles Perrault as a moral warning instructing children to be wary of being over-curious. The wealthy aristocrat

Bluebeard persuades a naïve young peasant girl to marry him. Shortly afterwards, Bluebeard announces that he has to go away on business. He entrusts the keys of his chateau to his young wife with strict instructions not to enter one specific room. Being of a curious disposition, the young girl opens the forbidden room and is confronted with the corpses of her husband's former three wives in various states of decay! The language is bloody, brutal and sparse. Surprisingly, perhaps, Perrault elects to write a happy ending - the young girl is rescued from certain death by her brothers - but Perrault leaves the reader in no doubt as to what might have happened to the wayward strong-willed girl. Life and death is finely balanced: circumstance, luck and wise judgement all have a part to play in survival.

Bull-baiting. Bull-baiting is most commonly associated with Spain as Bull Fighting. However, it is a little known fact that bull-baiting was practised throughout Europe in various guises throughout the Middle-Ages. In Axbridge, Somerset, villagers gathered outside the church every spring to engage in the yearly 'bull-run' which involved chasing the animal across Axbridge Square into the meadows where it was summarily clubbed to death by men and women with sticks, stones and all manner of implements. At the John's Hunting Lodge in Axbridge there is an exhibit of a 'bull-stake and collar.' The latter was used to tether the animal once it was 'caught,' thus enabling the final brutal ritual to take place.

Coral reefs. Coral reefs are one of the oldest eco-systems on the planet. They rival rainforests in the amount of diversity they support. Thousands of creatures rely on coral reefs for their survival. Although individual coral polyps are tiny, they create the largest living structures on earth. The Great Australian Barrier Reef is visible from space. However humans are actively destroying the reefs. The corals are over-fished, smothered by sediment and choked by algae growing on nutrient rich sewage and fertilizer run-off.

Dumbledore. The character Albus Dumbledore needs no explaining. The wizard is the creation of J.K. Rowling, the magical mind behind the wonderful Harry Potter series of books.

Fairy Godmother. In modern cinematic history there is an endless conveyor-belt of Godmothers of various guises whose function is to save the down-trodden heroine. However in traditional fairy-tales authors routinely delivered valuable warnings about the violent aspects of adult life and the sexual underpinnings that define and motivate human behaviour. The stories were written to educate and inform, not purely to entertain. (See Bluebeard entry)

Gig/trap/carriage. A **gig** is a light-weight two-wheeled **one-horse** carriage. **A trap** is a two-wheeled carriage with springs. I have deliberately used both words to describe the **two-horse vehicle** pulled by Delilah and Flaxen because I got bored repeating the words trap and carriage. Gig sounded much more fun at the time! Sorry! (I hope you will forgive me).

Harp Seals. Throughout the book there are frequent references to harp seals. I confess that they do not live around the British Isles so you will be disappointed if you go looking for them! I have used 'poetic licence' and transported the seals from their native home in the frozen north to the North Devon coast. However, I have done this for two main reasons. Firstly, harp seal pups were hunted for centuries for their prized white coats and I wanted to draw attention to this fact. Secondly, in the back of my mind lurked a darker image - that cast by Hermann Melville (1819-91) in his two masterpieces - 'Moby Dick' and 'Billy Budd, Sailor' - wherein the killing of both **man** and **beast** was the ruthless routine order of the day. I wanted to explore in 'Jem and Coral' to what degree 'nature is red in tooth and claw' and to what degree 'human nature' is equally bloody and brutal.

On a lighter note, **the harp seal -** *paguphilus groenlandicus* **-** spends little time on land and is distributed throughout the North Atlantic and Arctic Oceans. Harp seals can remain submerged for up to fifteen minutes. The young pups are born on the ice in breeding grounds in Newfoundland, the Greenland Sea and the White Sea. They have soft white fluffy fur that historically has made them a target for hunters.

Joni Mitchell. Canadian folk singer/song-writer, active from the early 1970s to this day. It would be unusual for a kid of Coral's generation to know the words of Big Yellow Taxi: "They paved paradise and put up a parking lot." However Coral, with a hippy-chick like Hazel as a mother, is bound to have heard the track and taken its message to heart.

King Crab. Jem uses the term to describe any large edible crab. However, there is a crab known as *Paralithodes camtschicus* meaning **King crab** which is commercially fished off Greenland and in the Arctic Circle.

King James Bible. In 1604, King James I of England authorised a translation of the bible from Latin into English. It was completed in 1611 and is widely considered to be one of the most beautiful translations of all time.

King James I of England. Sir Aubrey is quite correct in asserting that the king took an active interest in the spirit world. He attended several prominent witch trials and wrote a seminal book on witchcraft which was widely read at the time.

Lundy Island. Lundy lies off the North Devon coast in the Bristol Channel. The seas are home to an impressive range of wildlife, such as grey seals, lobsters and eight species of coral, including pink sea fans, red sea-fingers and dead-man's fingers. Lundy is the only place in the UK where five 'cup corals' co-exist. The five kilometre island is a Site of Special Scientific Interest, designated for its plants and sea-birds. The waters around Lundy became the UK's first Marine Conservation Zone in January 2010 as a direct result of the 2009 Marine and Coastal Access Act.

Metric or imperial measurement. I have deliberately mixed the two in the text. Jem thinks in imperial, judging distant by inches, yards, miles and fathoms. Coral and Antonia think in metric when it comes to judging short distances like the height of Old Man's elbow and the distance between the fourth floor landing and the plaster-block in Sudbury Court. But both girls think in miles when it comes to the distant between villages. (English road signs are all shown in miles such is the higgledy-piggledy nature of our heritage). The narrative sections reflect my mind and use imperial.

Peter Pan. Peter Pan written by J.M. Barrie was published in 1904. It is one of my favourite children's books of all time. I've seen it staged as both a play and a musical on numerous occasions and regularly use it in workshops of my own at the Merlin Theatre. In 'Jem and Coral' I deliberately chose to take a look at the genre of children's books with reference to Peter Pan. On a wider issue, I have sympathy with John's view when it comes to the role of fairy-tales. What's your view?

NB. Today polemic in a book of fiction is considered 'bad form.' However in the past many authors used their works of fiction as a means to provoke thought and promote debate amongst their readers on a variety of topics. Jane Austen slips in the odd reference to the government policy on 'enclosures' whilst in the middle of describing ribbons and poking fun at social etiquette. Dickens subtly comments on the Victorian penal system, legal system and the many social ills of his era. George Elliot does it all the time with a magician's 'sleight of hand'.

Quadrille. The quadrille is an historic dance performed by four couples in a formation that is vaguely 'quadratic' in shape. Think square coffee-table, rather than arithmetic, and you can't go far wrong. The dance was a precursor to traditional square dancing, now more popularly associated with the American folk tradition. In 1760 the quadrille was introduced to the French Court. England took a little while to catch up (1808). However by 1813 the quadrille was all the rage in London. (if we are to believe Wikipedia…let's be daring and believe).

Regency dress. The Regency Period is one of the most elegant periods in English history. In relation to English architecture, it is generally used to refer to the period spanning the reign of the four King Georges, namely 1714 to 1830. During the Regency period, female fashion was especially elegant. Gowns were made of transparent lightweight material with no complicated bustles or layers and a refreshing lack of ornamentation. For the brief period of 1795 to 1820, women could actually move unencumbered! Sir Aubrey's dancing girls wore high-waisted sleeveless gowns. They tied a band of ribbon around the top of their rib-cages.

However during the day women wore 'morning dress,' a very different arrangement. Morning dress had long sleeves and a high neck-line. Women donned bonnets when they went outside. Think of Beatrix Potter's illustrations of Jemima Puddle-duck wearing a bonnet and you can't go far wrong.

Sarabande. The Sarabande is a dance in triple metre, popular in Spain in the sixteenth century until it was banned in 1583 for being too 'provocative.' However the Sarabande that Sir Aubrey likes to dance is the Sarabande that appears in the fourth movement of Handel's keyboard suite in D minor for the harpsichord. Jem likewise would have hummed to Bach's Sarabande whilst untangling his father's fishing-net.

Sea-sponges. Sea-sponges come in all shapes and sizes. They are found in marine habitats ranging from the inter-tidal zone to the greatest ocean depths, and also fresh-water lakes and rivers. Some form flat, brightly coloured incrustations; others form a variety of single or multiple structures in the shape of vases, chimneys or purses. Some sponges are only one centimetre long but some in the Tropics and the Antarctic gargantuan sponges can reach more than one metre in height and breadth!

Adult sponges are *sessile* meaning that they spend their lives attached to rocks or other hard surfaces. They feed by extracting small particles from the surrounding water. A typical sponge has a honeycomb-like structure of canals separated by cells and a hard skeleton. Water is drawn in through pores in the external surface by beating the flagella of special cells lining the chambers that open off the canals. These flagellated cells are responsible for removing food particles from the water. Filtered water, along with any waste products, is passed through a single opening at the top of the sponge and expelled. The loose structure of sponges makes them an ideal shelter for many other species and a single sponge may have thousands of other animals living within it.

On the ablutions front, sponges have been used for centuries for washing and bathing purposes. No film about Ancient Rome or the French Court should be without one. Mary Queen of Scots (brought up in France and married at the age of fifteen to the Dauphin Francis) most certainly would have been familiar with tube sponges as would have Philip II of Spain. The Spanish Armada might have lost repeatedly in their skirmishes against Sir Francis Drake but they would have been well-scrubbed when they did.

Scallop-dredging. Large-scale scallop-dredging disturbs the sea-bed, resulting in a reduction of flat-worms, anemones and other species. Of course scallops are great to eat and can be harvested in more traditional ways but the process is labour intensive.

Spider Crab. Coral makes several references to the Spider Crab, *Maia Squinado*. These can be found in Spanish, French and British waters, notably to the south-west of the UK from Cardigan Bay down to Cornwall and the Scilly Isles.

Triumph Thunderbird. The 6T Thunderbird was produced between 1949 and 1966 by the Triumph Motorcycle Company. It shot to fame following the premier of the 1953 film, The Wild One, starring Marlon Brando. The iconic image of a gorgeous Brando astride his Triumph can still be seen on the walls of cafe-bars and bijou restaurants the world over (and also in my husband's shed!)

APPENDIX 2

Historical 'bits and bobs' that might interest you

Throughout the book there are references to social, military and political history; not to mention historical fashion and the ever evolving minefield that is English grammar. These are my sources, enjoy.

Bony's Folly. My French great-grandmother used to refer to sunflowers as Bony's Folly - quite why, I really can't imagine - but I couldn't resist weaving her colourful vocabulary into the story of Jem and Coral.

The Crusades. I hesitate before attempting to define the word 'crusade'. The Crusades and Crusader Knights mean so many different things to different people. I would recommend reading Chronicles of The Crusades (ISBN number: 1-85833-589-2) for the simple reason that is jam-packed full of original documents and primary sources thereby leaving you free to make up your own mind about the 'whys and wherefores' of the 'Crusading

Period.' However, I will say this: the theatre of war was wide, and definitely not confined to the Holy Land. Christian crusaders also fought the Muslim Amoravids in Spain. The conflict then spread - as conflict invariably does - to the Baltic, Italy, Greece and North Africa. After the fall of Acre in 1291, crusades continued for another three hundred years. Some might argue that they are still going on to this day. I think I'll stop there and let you do your own research.

Napoleon Bonaparte. The British love to hate Napoleon but I have to confess to having a soft spot for him. Born in Corsica on August 15th, 1769, Napoleon was one of the most successful military leaders of his generation. Following the traumatic and protracted machinations of the French Revolution in which a goodly section of the French Aristocracy including Marie-Antoinette had their heads chopped off, (1789-1799), Napoleon staged a coup d'etat and became First Consul. Five years later the Senate proclaimed him Emperor of France and he embarked upon the modernisation of the French legal and education systems. The former is still in use today and is known as 'the code Napoleon'. It is also little known that most of his campaigns were essentially to defend France from invasions from Austria, Prussia and Russia, (usually orchestrated by Britain) who intended to re-instate the French Bourbon monarchy.

Battle of Waterloo. The battle took place at Waterloo, in central Belgium, on June 18th, 1815. Historians are divided on the effectiveness of the stratagems of the individual Commanders-in-the-Field. What can be said with certainty is that it ended Napoleon's rule of France once-and-for all!

Hartland Abbey. Built in the twelfth century, the Abbey was a monastery for four hundred years prior to becoming the family home of the Stucley family. It is built in a long narrow sheltered valley in an area of outstanding natural beauty, one mile from Hartland Quay. I have taken numerous liberties in my description of the building, preferring to write from memory rather than re-visiting with a note-book. The building truly is magical and the contents so inspiring that I decided to recall the essence of the place rather than some pedantic listing of every detail.

Saladin. Born in 1138 into a Kurdish family at Takrit in present-day Iraq, Saladin entered the service of Nur-ad-Din at Damascus in circa 1155 and accompanied his uncle on three campaigns in Egypt between 1164 and 1168. By 1171 Saladin had seized power in Egypt on behalf of the powerful Sultan, Nur-ad-Din, and abolished the Fatimid Caliphate. After the Sultan died from natural causes in 1174, Saladin married Nur-ad-Din's widow and rose to become the uncontested ruler of a united Muslim Levant.

Wellington hats, boots and bonnets. Following Wellington's triumph at the Battle of Waterloo, Wellington-mania swept the nation. All the ladies wanted to be seen wearing a Wellington bonnet and all the men took to wearing items of clothing associated with the great man. The Duke of Wellington himself was born plain Arthur Wesley in Dublin in May 1769 albeit to an Anglo-Irish aristocratic family. In 1798, the family changed their name to Wellesley. He joined the army in 1789. He fought against the French in Flanders and in 1796 was sent to India where he took part in the Mysore War against the Tipu

Sultan. He was knighted for the role he played in the successful subjugation of the Mahrattas at the Battle of Assaye in 1803. Following his victory at Waterloo his parliamentary career took off and he became Prime Minister in 1828. He died in 1852 and was given a state funeral. However, he had considerable respect for Napoleon and was heard to utter the following words after the carnage of Waterloo *'the saddest thing next to a battle lost, is a battle won'*

APPENDIX 3

Herbal 'bits and bobs'

Arrowroot. I remember being given numerous bowls of arrowroot as a child whenever I got a chest cough which was far too frequent for my liking. Fortunately, there was always a window to climb out of and friendly neighbours who never breathed a word to my mother if they spotted me on the garage roof. Dishes made from milk were a common remedy until recently for common ailments such as coughs and colds. In the seventeenth, eighteenth and nineteenth centuries, dishes like junket, semolina and rice pudding were also popular. The common theme was a creamy dish made from milk with some starch or other ingredient used to thicken it.

Bloodwort, (achillea millafolium/ Indian name Rojmari). It is hard to date the medicinal use of a herb! Gladiators are alleged to have applied bloodwort to their wounds. Roman soldiers used preparations containing bloodwort to combat blisters whilst they marched on campaign. The herb grows to about sixty centimetres in height. If you want to see some growing, visit the Medicinal Herb Garden at Glastonbury Abbey in Somerset and ask a Living History presenter to explain its properties to you. If you live too far away to visit, try a Botanical Garden near you.

Florida Swamps. I made this reference to alligators in the Florida Swamps as one of the primary causes of the Wall Street Crash in order to provoke debate. (I studied politics, economics & philosophy at college for my sins). John Galbraith's seminal book: The Great Crash (first published in 1954) is one of those rare academic books that is short, snappy and readable. The bit that really interested me was the section about 'Selling on the Margin' in which Galbraith goes into great detail about the crazy real estate speculation which resulted in useless Florida swampland being sold as an investment on the assumption that holiday homes could be built there.

Soapwort. Visit Glastonbury Abbey to see the herb in flower. The washing-up liquid that can be made from the plant is a pale pink colour and really works. If you put some in a bottle and shake hard you'll get bubbles: the definitive monastic washing-up liquid over one thousand years old!

APPENDIX 4

Jem's language and some of the mysteries of the English language

Jem's language is unique to him. Initially I researched traditional North Devon and Somerset accents but in the end I decided not to use either and to create a language for Jem that reflected all the periods of history he had lived through.

The English language has spread all over the world and evolved into the concurrent forms in use today. It is still changing daily with the advent of new scientific terms, youth culture, text-speak and job related jargon.

English owes much of its richness and variety to the multiplicity of peoples whose separate languages have been stirred into its melting pot. The indigenous Celts poured Gaelic and Welsh words into the pot, the Romans added Latin words, the Angles, Saxons and Jutes contributed Germanic languages to create Old English vocabulary and syntax, the Vikings gave us a smattering of Old Norse and the Normans from 1066 added swathes of French vocabulary to the English Language recipe.

Jem's influences are no less diverse. He would have been born into a household where everyone spoke with a broad Devonian accent but as the centuries passed he would have adapted to the language he heard spoken in public places. He would have acquired a working knowledge of 'Received Pronunciation' via exposure to Sir Hugh **Stucley's** aristocratic forebears at Hartland Abbey. He would also have heard the more familiar Devonian accent spoken by the maids and kitchen staff.

However, the local Devonian accent would have changed subtly as the decades passed until such point as Jem's own dialect ceased to exist. This would have had a great impact upon him. Hence his brave decision to improve himself by reading widely in the Abbey Library. Jem is not just seeking knowledge in books. He is also seeking safety and permanence. The language of the literature in the library books provide him with a bed-rock of permanence. He becomes familiar with the lexis, grammar and semantics of the books that he reads. He likewise becomes acquainted with the differences between Chaucer's fifteenth century English, Shakespeare's late sixteenth and early seventeenth century English and Dickens's nineteenth century English.

The books give him consistency and a sense of belonging that he lacks in real life. In the twenty-first century new inventions are brought to the market-place on a yearly basis. However when Jem was born, there were no cars, no trains, no electricity, no telephones, no central heating, no hot running water, no flushing toilets, no telephones, no mobile-phones, no lap-tops, and certainly no 'Blackberries.' As far as Jem is concerned a blackberry is a fruiting berry that flowers in late September and is best cooked in a crumble or a pie.

Another rich source of vocabulary for Jem would have been the BBC news service. He would have kept abreast with the evolution of the English accent via the radio broadcasts on his wind-up radio.

In the 1920s, whilst watching the raucous Hartland Abbey Beach Parties, Jem would have picked up phrases like 'Cheerio' for 'Good-bye, 'scent' for 'perfume' and 'good egg' for a 'laid-back guy.' However, I'm probably out-of-date already using the words 'cool' and 'guy.' You probably know the latest fashionable vocabulary far better than me.

Jem's other great source of knowledge is the King's James Bible. Faced with the onslaught of modernity, Jem speaks more and more to himself in a hybrid language composed of the English written in his mother's English prayer-books, the local hymn books at Saint Merriam's Church and the King James Bible. Thus Jem uses 'couldst' instead of 'could,' 'hadst' instead of 'had' and 'shouldst' for 'should.' He uses 'thou' for 'you' and 'thine' and 'thy' for 'yours.' He uses 'doth,' 'durst' and 'dost' for 'does' and 'do.'

Jem does not always use these terms correctly or consistently as his mind is constantly at war with itself, grappling with the old and the new. Only when Coral arrives in his life does his language acquire a new coherence and his existence greater meaning. The modern twenty first century world loses it sharp teeth and he begins to feel more at ease with himself and those around him. He is at last free to embrace the language that you and I both speak.

"On ne voit bien qu'avec le coeur,
l'essentiel est invisible aux les yeux."

"One sees best with the heart,
the essential is invisible to the eye."

(Antoine de Saint Exupery)

One third of the royalties from the sale of this book shall be donated to
the following charities: The Woodland Trust and Marine Conservation.

Jem and Coral is the sole work of C.A. Heaven.
Copyright: August 31st, 2011.

Made in the USA
Charleston, SC
11 April 2012